Lucy couldn't possibly be *that* bad a kisser

Well, that's that, Lucy thought, settling back in front of the fireplace. Zack kissed her once and then he ran up the stairs to get away from her. Maybe she wasn't his type. He probably went for women who wore black lace and had long, thick blond hair.

As opposed to, say, dry, fuzzy green hair. Could hair as bad as hers send a man running?

"It's not the hair," she said out loud. "It's me. I'm dull and unemotional. I should have jumped him when he kissed me, but did I? No. I was too polite."

She considered the advice her sister had given her. *Be spontaneous. Be impulsive.* She should just go right up those stairs and climb into bed with Zack and seduce him.

Except she wasn't sure how. She tried to figure out how black lace nightgowns and champagne would go over with Zack. He would probably prefer somebody who just crawled into his bed naked.

She couldn't do that. And then there *was* her hair. . . .

Jennifer Crusie lives in a small Ohio town with four cats, three dogs, two mortgages and a teenager. She began reading romances for a university research project—and enjoyed them so much, she decided to try writing one. She not only tried but has succeeded extremely well. Her first Temptation novel, *Manhunting,* was published last October, and coming next month is *Sizzle,* a short novel in Worldwide Library's Stolen Moments program.

Books by Jennifer Crusie

HARLEQUIN TEMPTATION
463—MANHUNTING

GETTING RID OF BRADLEY
JENNIFER CRUSIE

Harlequin Books

TORONTO • NEW YORK • LONDON
AMSTERDAM • PARIS • SYDNEY • HAMBURG
STOCKHOLM • ATHENS • TOKYO • MILAN
MADRID • WARSAW • BUDAPEST • AUCKLAND

For Betsy Struckman, the perfect friend;
And for Steve Struckman, the perfect man;
And for Murph and Cassie, and Mollie, and
Maggie, and Rose, and Bernie, and Lucy, and
Liz, and Annie, and Chuck, and Ed, and Jasper,
and Max, and Mose, and Sam.

ISBN 0-373-25580-2

GETTING RID OF BRADLEY

Copyright © 1994 by Jennifer Crusie.

1

"I'VE NEVER KNOWN anyone who was stood up for her own divorce before," Tina Savage told her sister. "What's it feel like?"

"Not good." Lucy Savage Porter tried to smooth her flowered skirt with a damp hand. "Can we go? I'm not enjoying this." She gave up on the skirt and clutched her lumpy tapestry bag to her as she glanced around the marble hallway of the Riverbend courthouse. "Bradley signed the divorce papers. We don't even need to be here."

Tina shook her head. "Psychologically, we need to be here. You had a ceremony when you got married, you need one when you get divorced. I want you to feel divorced. I want you to feel free. Now sit over there on that bench while I find Benton to tell me why this is taking so long."

I'd feel a lot freer if you'd stop ordering me around, Lucy started to say, and then blinked instead. She'd been having rebellious moments like that a lot lately, but they were hard to hold on to, especially since the only time she'd actually followed through on one, it had been a disaster. Right now she was sitting under a brassy head of curls because she'd decided to go blond as a symbol of her freedom. Some symbol. She looked like Golden Barbie with crow's-feet.

Maybe the problem was that she wasn't an independent kind of person. Other than the hair fiasco, every time she'd decided to be more independent, logic stopped her cold. After all, Tina was right. She did need the closure of hearing the divorce decree. And the bench was the best place to sit. It would be illogical to disagree just for the sake of disagreeing.

No matter how good it would have felt.

She went over and sat down on the bench.

Tina was gone already, trying to find her hapless attorney in the flood of suits that washed around her. Poor Benton. He'd gone beyond the call of lawyerhood in ramming Lucy's divorce through the courts in two weeks, but that wasn't enough for Tina. Tina wouldn't be satisfied until Benton brought her Bradley's head on a platter. Lucy had a momentary image of Tina, dark and svelte and dressed in her white linen suit, standing in front of a flustered Benton who was offering her Bradley's handsome head on a turkey plate.

She liked it. Tina always did have the best ideas.

Tina suddenly appeared before her, parting the suits before her like the Red Sea. "There's some kind of delay. It'll be another hour, but then we'll go have lunch."

Another hour. "All right. At Harvey's Diner?"

Tina shrugged. "Whatever you want."

"Thank you." Lucy dug her physics textbook out of her bag.

"What are you doing?"

"I have to teach Planck's constant tomorrow." Lucy paged through the book. "It's a tough one to get across. I'm reviewing."

"You know, the next thing I'm getting you is a new job," Tina said, and disappeared back into the suits.

A new job?

"I like my job," Lucy said, but Tina was already gone.

Okay, that's it, Lucy decided and closed her book with a thump. *That's the last straw. Nobody's ordering me around anymore. From now on, I'm going to be independent even if it is illogical. I'm going to be a whole new me.*

That's it.

I'm changing.

"OKAY, THAT'S IT. I'M quitting," Zack Warren said to his partner. His shaggy dark hair fell across his forehead, almost into his eyes, but he was too mad to brush it back.

"Don't tell me, tell Jerry." Tall, cool, and controlled, Anthony Taylor nodded toward the man who had just pulled a gun on them.

Zack turned back to the gun, wavering now in the hands of the balding, middle-aged embezzler who stood quivering in his bad suit behind his empty desk. Jerry watched them warily, as warily as a cautious man might regard two big guys he was holding a gun on.

"I'm quitting, Jerry," Zack said. "You can let me go because I'm not going to be a cop anymore. You can have the badge."

He started to reach into his worn black leather jacket, and Jerry squeaked, "No!"

Zack froze. "Okay. Fine. No problem." He gauged the possibilities of taking Jerry there in his office. They weren't good. Jerry was very nervous and the office was very small, leaving them no room to maneuver and nothing to take cover behind. It was furnished only with a metal desk, two plastic chairs, and Jerry. The furniture was marginally more interesting than Jerry, or had been until he'd reached into his desk drawer and pulled out the gun.

They deserved this. Just because the guy was pathetic, they'd gotten careless. Zack looked at the gun wobbling in Jerry's hand with respect. A .45. The office currently had no windows, but Zack knew it could have a couple at any minute, a .45 being the kind of gun that left large holes in walls.

And people.

"Why do we do this?" Zack asked Anthony, scowling at the gun. "Life isn't depressing enough, we have to do this, too? I'm not kidding, I'm quitting."

"Stop complaining." Anthony carefully picked a speck of nonexistent lint off his tailored tweed sleeve, keeping his eyes steadily on Jerry the whole time. "You're the probable cause of this anyway. You walked in here in that black leather jacket, looking like you hadn't shaved in a week, and Jerry probably thought you were some lowlife." He smiled at Jerry, an oasis of perfect calm in a very sweaty situation. "I'd have pulled a gun on him, too, Jerry. I understand. Why don't we talk about this?"

Jerry shook his head, but he kept his eyes on Anthony, listening to his even, relaxed voice. Zack moved very slowly a few inches to his right, taking care to seem as if he were only shifting on his feet.

Jerry suddenly shifted his eyes to Zack, so Zack picked up the conversation. "Oh, and if we'd both been dressed in pimp suits like you, he wouldn't have pulled the gun. I ask you, Jerry, was it the jacket that made you pull the gun? Or the badge?"

Jerry narrowed his eyes at Zack, and Anthony moved slightly to the left.

"Just don't move," Jerry said as he swayed back and forth. "Keep your hands up."

"We're not moving, Jerry," Anthony said soothingly. "You are. Relax. You'll feel better."

"Don't get smart," Jerry said, and the gun wavered between them again. "I'll shoot."

"You don't want to shoot us, Jerry." Zack spread his hands apart. "The hassle from shooting a cop is enormous. You wouldn't believe it."

"Oh, yeah." Jerry looked at Zack as he talked, distracted by the movement, and Anthony eased another couple of inches to the left. "And the hassle from stealing thirty thousand from your boss is nothin'."

"Well, it's not like shooting a cop," Anthony said, and Jerry's eyes darted over to him. Zack moved a little more to the right. "Shooting a cop?" Anthony shook his head slowly. "They throw the key away. We don't want that. Put the gun down, Jerry."

"I don't think so." Jerry breathed a little faster and shifted his eyes to Zack. "I don't think so. And you guys are *moving*." He closed his eyes as he aimed the gun at Zack and slowly squeezed the trigger.

Zack dove for the floor as he fired, and Anthony yelled, "*Jerry!*" and Jerry swung the gun toward where he'd been. Zack threw himself over the desk and tackled Jerry as Anthony flattened himself on the floor, and Jerry put a bullet neatly through the center of the door.

Then Zack slammed him down on the floor on his stomach with his hands twisted behind him.

Anthony rolled to his feet to help. "You all right?"

"Me? Oh, I'm as good as I get," Zack said, breathing a little heavily as he reached for his handcuffs. "Which is a hell of a lot better than Jerry is right now. How about you?"

"There were people in that hall." Anthony went out the door to see what Jerry had hit on the other side while Zack cuffed him.

"You have the right to remain silent, you jerk," Zack said and finished reciting Miranda sitting on top of him. Anthony came back and lounged in the doorway.

"Congratulations," Anthony said to Jerry when Zack was finished. "You shot a water fountain."

"Up yours," Jerry said, but it came out more embarrassed than defiant.

Zack stood and glared down at him. "We've got to start hanging out with a better class of criminals."

"Actually, this is the cream," Anthony said, checking his jacket for damage. It was, as always, spotless. "You want to work Vice or Homicide?"

"No," Zack said. "I want to arrest polite people who don't point guns at me. In fact, I don't want to arrest anybody anymore. I want to hang out with good people. Is that possible? Are there any good people anymore?"

"Well, there's you and me," Anthony said patiently. "We're supposed to be the good guys. Are you sure you're all right? You've been acting strangely lately."

"Could you guys hurry this up?" Jerry whined from the floor. "I'm not *real* comfortable down here."

"You know, Jerry—" Zack was suddenly soft-spoken as he looked down at him "—I could kick your brains out very easily right now." He gently nudged Jerry's head with his foot. "Resisting arrest. Don't push your luck."

Jerry shut up.

"Here's some advice, Jerry." Anthony reached down and hauled him to his feet with one hand. "Don't get smart with a guy you just pointed a gun at. He's likely to be feeling hostile. And frankly, Jerry, we didn't like you much before you pulled the gun."

Jerry closed his eyes.

"I was kind of hoping he'd resist arrest," Zack said.

"No, you were not," Anthony said. "You have plans for lunch. You're arresting a master embezzler at Harvey's Diner. What's wrong with you?"

"Nothing." Zack pushed Jerry into the hall. "The weather. I hate February. And I hate office buildings." He looked around at the smooth gray walls. "Maybe I will quit. Get a nice job out in the open someplace. No guns. You think I'd make a good forest ranger?"

"You know, you worry me," Anthony said.

"That's your problem." Zack moved down the hall, prodding Jerry in front of him. "So, Jerry, what'd you do with the money?"

LUCY SAT SLUMPED across from her sister in a battered turquoise booth in Harvey's shabby diner and tortured a salad.

Tina scowled down at her salad. "Are you sure it's safe to eat here? I think turquoise Formica is bad for you, and I'm positive this lettuce is. It's white." She tapped a cigarette from the pack on the table and lit it smoothly, like a forties' movie star.

Lucy leaned forward to put her chin in her hand so she could pretend to listen to Tina, and her brassy hair fell into her face again. Tina smoothed a dark, silky strand of her own precisely cut hair, and Lucy looked at her with envy. Maybe they weren't sisters. Maybe Mother had lied to them. No, they had the same cat face: wide forehead, big eyes, little mouth, pointed chin. It was just that Tina looked like a purebred, and she looked like something condemned at the pound.

Stop it, Lucy told herself. *Stop feeling sorry for yourself. You're just having a bad hair day.*

Well, okay, a bad hair week. And then there was the divorce.

You're just having a bad month. Pull yourself together. Spring is coming.

"You are going to get rid of his name, aren't you?" Tina asked. "Lucy Savage Porter always sounded like you'd married a rabid bellboy."

Shut up, Tina. Lucy blinked. "Could we talk about something else?" She squashed her hair back to peer around the dim restaurant, hoping no one else had heard. Since the place was not only dim but small, it was a real fear, but it was also almost empty. There was only a bored waitress leaning on a chipped plastic counter beside a fly-specked case of doughnuts, and two men in a booth identical to theirs on the opposite side of the room.

Lucy was having a hard time ignoring one of the men.

One was tall, slender, and elegant, leaning calmly back in the booth, not a crease in his beautifully cut tweed suit.

The other man was his antithesis. Shorter, thicker, tense as a coiled spring, in a creased black leather jacket, he leaned across the table and stabbed his index finger into the Formica. His unshaven face looked like it was made of slabs, his hair was dark and shaggy, and his smile came and went like a broken neon sign. He was so intense, he was practically bending the table with the force of his personality. Lucy had been reluctantly aware of him ever since they'd entered the diner, kicking herself for stealing glances at him but stealing them just the same.

This was the kind of man who could leave a woman scarred for life. She wasn't so dumb after all. She could have ended up married to somebody like him instead of Bradley.

But think how much excitement she would have had before the end.

"No, that would have been dumb," she said aloud.

"What would be?" Tina asked.

"Nothing." Lucy turned back to her. "That's a beautiful suit you're wearing."

"It should be. It cost a fortune. You couldn't afford it. If you had to make a bad marriage, and I suppose you did since it runs in the family, couldn't you at least have chosen somebody with money?"

"No." Lucy picked up her fork and jabbed at her salad, spearing a cucumber slice because it was there. "Money isn't important."

"Oh? And what is important? And, whatever it is, why did you think that loser Bradley Porter had it? In fact, why did you marry him at all?"

Lucy thought of several cutting things to say about her sister's second and third husbands and then blinked instead. "I married him because of the second law of thermonuclear dynamics."

"You married him because of a physics theory?" Tina put her cigarette out in one of her salad tomatoes, pushed the bowl away, and lit up another. "Well, at least you didn't say 'for lo-o-ove.'" She blew her smoke away from Lucy. "So what's the second law of thermodynamics?"

"It says that isolated systems move toward disorder until they reach their most probable form, and then they remain constant."

"I don't get it. And what does that have to do with Bradley?"

"Nothing. But it has everything to do with me." Lucy pushed her bowl away with one hand and shoved her hair out of her eyes with the other. "I was an isolated system. I mean, there I was, living alone in that little apartment with Einstein for company, and Einstein is great company, but he's also a dog."

"I wondered if you'd noticed that."

"Well, of course, I noticed. And I'd been teaching science for twelve years. Lecturing to kids all day and then going home alone to grade papers at night. The only real social contacts I had were at your weddings."

Tina stuck her tongue out at her and pulled a pepper strip from Lucy's salad bowl.

"And then one day in class, we got to the second law, and I thought, 'That's me. I'm an isolated system, and I'm just going to get more isolated until I reach my most probable form which is probably where I am now, living in an apartment with Einstein.' So I decided to get un-isolated. And that's when Bradley picked me up in the library and I thought, 'This must be it. Physics has brought us together.' I mean, his timing was so perfect. It was so logical."

Tina shook her head. "No wonder you're so screwed up. Life is not logical, and marriage certainly isn't. Stop analyzing things so much. Try impulse for a change."

"I was impulsive once. I married Bradley after I'd only known him two months." Lucy felt a twinge of shame even as she said the words. She'd been stupid. Really stupid. "So I'm not a fan of impulse anymore. And, no offense, but I don't see impulse doing much for you."

Tina smiled. "I've got twelve and a half million dollars, darling. And what have you got? A moth-eaten house and custody of three dogs. Impulse has done more for me than logic has for you. Just look at you. Do you ever have any fun?"

"Fun?" Lucy's eyes went to the dark-haired man across the room. "Fun." She shifted her gaze back to Tina and picked up her fork to attack her salad again. "I don't think I'm the fun type."

"Well, I think you're taking life too seriously. It's time you cut loose. Do something wild. Something spontaneous."

Lucy frowned at her. "I told you. I did something spontaneous once. I married Bradley. Face it, Tina, I'm not the spontaneous type."

Tina shook her head. "Marrying Bradley was not spontaneous. You just gave me a very sensible reason why you married him. Spontaneous is when it's not sensible but you do it anyway because you want to."

"That's not spontaneous, that's irresponsible."

"Fine, then do something irresponsible. In fact, do something spontaneous *and* irresponsible. Do something just because you have the urge to do it, because it feels good. Do something selfish, just for you."

Lucy's eyes went back to the dark-haired man across the room. "I don't think so." She stabbed her salad again.

"How do you know unless you've tried it? You've never done anything selfish in your life."

"Well, you know, I did," Lucy said slowly, her fork frozen in her hand. "Once. In fact, I think that's the real reason why I married Bradley. I dated Bradley because of the second law, but I think I married Bradley to get my house."

Tina looked interested. "Really? That's so unlike you."

Lucy nodded. "I think I just convinced myself I loved him because it was so sensible that I should, and then when he offered me the house, it was just too much." She poked at her salad again, averting her eyes from Tina. "I love the house more than I ever loved Bradley. I think he knew it finally, and that's why he cheated on me."

"Well, I'll be damned." Tina put her cigarette out and leaned back in the booth. "This explains a lot. Is this what that fight you had last October was about?"

"How did you know . . . ?"

"That's when you moved upstairs to the attic bedroom. I never bought that story about Bradley snoring. I knew there had been a fight."

"No." Lucy frowned. "There wasn't. We never fought. We just had a . . . disagreement. Over one of the dogs."

Tina winced. "For anyone else that would be a minor disagreement. For you . . . if Bradley did something to one of those dogs, he couldn't have known you very well. And this explains why you're not brokenhearted over the divorce. You're upset, but it's not because you miss Bradley. You're glad he's gone, aren't you?"

"Yes," Lucy whispered. "That's awful, but I am."

"No, it's not. That's healthy. What I don't understand is what you're so upset about. You're free. You can do anything you want. What's wrong with you?"

"I feel stupid," Lucy said.

"What?" Tina leaned forward. "You? You've got more brains than . . ."

"Not real-life brains. I have science brains. But real life?" Lucy shook her head. "I don't even know what happened in my marriage. I know it was awful for me, but I would have sworn to you that Bradley was happy and he loved me, and then out of the blue, I come home and find him with a blonde. In my house. And she says they've been having an affair in my bedroom, and he flusters around, obviously guilty, and when I get upset, he leaves." She sat back. "He just leaves."

"Men," Tina said.

"So I don't have a clue where I went wrong. The only thing I've ever known for sure in my whole life is that I'm smart. And now I'm not even sure about that. It's upsetting."

"Well, if you think he was angry about the house . . ."

"It's not just that he cheated on me. It's that he won't talk to me now. In the lawyer's office, all he said was, 'Is this what you want?' And I said yes, because it was, but . . ." Lucy bit her lip. "He hasn't even come by to pick up the rest of his papers and things. It's like a chunk of my life just dropped out of sight."

"Oh." Tina shifted uncomfortably. "Well, I may have had something to do with that."

Lucy froze. "What did you do?"

"Well. You know how upset you were when you called me that day and told me that Bradley and the blonde had just been there?"

"What did you do?"

"Well, I had the new locks put on...."

"Yes, I know." Lucy nodded. "And you threw all his clothes out on the front lawn. I know all that. What else did you do?"

"Well, when he came to the door to talk to you..."

"He came to the door to talk to me?"

"You were upstairs in your bedroom crying." Tina paused. "I was... angry."

"Oh, no."

"I know, I know. I lose it when I get angry." Tina lit another cigarette, inhaled, and blew out another stream of smoke before she went on, faster now to get it over with. "Anyway, I told him that if he ever tried to talk to you again, I would have private detectives digging up every slimy thing he'd ever done, and that I would personally see that they all made the front page of the *Inquirer*, and that I would also find every asset he possessed and take it from him."

Lucy looked at her, stunned.

"I think I might also have mentioned bodily harm. I was really upset. You never cry."

"So that's why he hasn't called? You are something else, Tina."

"I'm sorry," Tina said. "But I could just see him talking you back into that damn marriage. I couldn't stand seeing you unhappy anymore."

"I wouldn't have gone back. But I would have liked to have talked to him." Lucy took a deep breath. "I love you, Tine, and I appreciate everything you've done for me, but you've got to get out of my life. It's my life."

"I know, honey." Tina fiddled with her cigarette. "But you need help. I mean, I let you pick the restaurant and look where we ended up." She glanced around at the plastic walls and the chipped Formica. "This place is a dump."

"I had a reason for wanting to come here," Lucy said. "Bradley wrote to me. He said if I'd have lunch here with him, he could explain everything." Lucy looked around the cheap diner again, perplexed. "It doesn't seem like his kind of place."

"Do you want him back?" Tina asked. "I'll get him back if that's what you want."

"No." Lucy pressed her lips together and stabbed her salad again. "That's not what I want."

"Well, what do you want? Just tell me what you want. I'll make it happen."

Lucy smacked her fork down. "You can't. Or you won't. I want to live my own life. I want to make my own mistakes. I want you to be my sister, not my keeper. You don't have to take care of me."

"I know I don't have to." Tina frowned. "But I want to. I want you to be happy. You never have any fun."

"I don't want to have fun." Lucy took a deep breath. "Do you know what I want?"

Tina shook her head, her eyes on Lucy.

"I want to be independent. I want to take care of myself, without you racing to the rescue with money and lawyers. You always tell me what to do, and you're always right, and most of the time I don't mind it, but then I married Bradley, and he was worse than you are. Between you and Bradley, I haven't made a decision on my own in almost a year because everything you told me to do was the sensible thing, and it would have been stupid for me to argue. Only I did all the sensible things, and now look at my life. It's a mess." Lucy stuck her chin out. "So, I'm changing. I want to make my own mistakes and mop up after them myself. I want to talk to my ex-husband without you threatening him with death. And if I want to dye my hair purple or adopt another ten dogs or . . . or . . . ." Her eyes twitched to the man across the room.

"Or go out with inappropriate men. I want you to stay out. It's my life. I want it back."

"Oh."

"I appreciate everything you've done for me. Just stop doing it."

"All right." Tina picked a cucumber slice out of Lucy's salad. "Inappropriate men, huh?"

Lucy slid down a little in her seat. "Probably not. That was just big talk."

"What about that guy across the room you keep looking at?"

"Oh, no." Lucy closed her eyes. "I'm that transparent?"

"Well, he doesn't seem to have noticed." Tina glanced across the room. "He really is attractive, though. Your instincts aren't so bad."

Lucy looked at the two men across the room again out of the corner of her eye. The one in the black was talking, his fingers slashing the air while he spoke.

"He's gorgeous," Lucy said.

"Actually, he looks a little dull. But if that's what you want, let me see what I can do." Tina started to get up.

"Dull?" Lucy said. "He looks insane."

Tina stopped. "You're talking about the one in the tweed, not the one in the black.leather, right? You can't be serious about the black leather."

"It's my fantasy," Lucy said. "And sit down. You're not going over there and embarrass me."

Tina sat down. "The black leather would not be good for you."

"I can't tell you how tired I am of things that are good for me," Lucy said.

"I know." Tina nodded sympathetically. "But that doesn't mean you should commit emotional hari-kari. That guy is unstable."

Lucy's eyes went back to the black leather. "Actually, you know, he's just what you ordered. What I'm feeling for him is definitely spontaneous and irresponsible."

Tina looked at him and frowned. "Maybe if you just used him for the cheap thrill and then discarded him."

"I couldn't do that." Lucy tore her eyes away from him. "I could never do that. I'd better just concentrate on being independent without the inappropriate-man part."

But she looked back at the man in black leather one more time and sighed.

"I CAN FEEL IT." In the booth across the room, Zack tapped his fingers on the scarred table. "Bradley's here. Or he's been here. Or somebody he knows is here. Or . . ."

Anthony leaned back. "All right. He's here. So are we. But it's been an hour and I'm getting bored, so just point him out to me, and we'll arrest him and go. He's disguised as one of those two women, right?"

"Fine." Zack glared at him. "Don't help. I'll do this without you. Fine." He drummed his fingers on the table.

"Zack, I want to get him as much as you do," Anthony said patiently. "He's thumbed his nose at every cop who's tried to nail him in the last nine months. And the million and a half he's traveling on is not chicken feed. But I need more than just one of your instincts to keep me in this dive any longer."

Zack slapped the table and then drummed his fingers again. "Look, we got an honest-to-God phone tip that he'd be here, and it's the best thing we've got so far. It's not like we have anything else on this thing. It's not like—"

"Zack," Anthony interrupted him. "You're driving me crazy."

"What? Oh. The fingers?" Zack stopped drumming on the table. "Sorry."

"No, not the fingers. Although that's got to stop, too. No, it's the way you've been acting lately." Anthony shook his head slowly. "That was a bad moment today with Jerry. I thought you were really going to kick him."

"Me? Naw." Zack paused. "Probably not."

"Exactly." Anthony nailed him with a frown. "That's what I'm talking about. The 'probably' part. And all this rambling about quitting. I don't like it. You've always been nuts. That's fine. I can deal with nuts. But lately, you've been depressed nuts. I can't deal with that."

"I'm not depressed." Zack picked up a package of sugar, tore it savagely across the middle, and dumped it in his coffee. "I'm not *elated* right now, but I'm not depressed."

"You just decapitated a sugar packet. That should tell you something."

Zack stared at the mutilated packet and then tossed it on the table. "I'll tell you something. I was really disappointed in old Jerry today. I mean, I felt sorry for the poor sap, and then he pulled a gun on us, and I thought, damn, nobody's decent anymore. And then he shot at us, and I was really mad." Zack shook his head. "Sometimes I think there aren't any decent people in the world anymore." He tasted his coffee and frowned. "So maybe the job's getting me down a little, but I'm not depressed."

"You are depressed." Anthony spoke clearly and calmly, as if he were speaking to the mentally ill. "And your depression is affecting our work. I know what's wrong."

Zack glared at him. "I hate this. Have I ever mentioned how much I hate it that you were a psych minor? A minor, for cripes' sake. With a minor, you're not even allowed to psychoanalyze dogs."

"It's because you're worried about getting older. It started when you turned thirty-six."

"I don't want to talk about it." Zack turned his attention back to the restaurant. "Do those two women look guilty to you? There's something strange about the blonde. I think it's her hair. That hair is not real."

"Ever since your birthday, you've been snarling at the younger men on the force. And I have shoes older than the women you've been dating." Anthony shook his head. "You are really transparent on this one."

Zack scowled at him. "It's not age. Hell, you're the same age I am."

"Yes, but I'm not depressed about it."

"Well, you should be." Zack fiddled with his spoon, spattering the scarred tabletop with flecks of coffee. "Remember Falk, the old guy I started out on patrol with? There's a kid on patrol with him right now.... I was in *high school* when he was born. He lived down the block from me."

"Zack, you're thirty-six. These things happen. So there are people who are younger than you are. Deal with it."

"I'm not as fast as I used to be, either." Zack dropped his voice. "When we play one on one? I'm slowing down. A lot."

"This is all in your mind. I haven't noticed you getting any slower."

"That's because you're getting slower, too."

Anthony narrowed his eyes. "Do you mind if we keep this your depression? Personally, I am getting better, not older."

"You're getting older. But you don't care because you've always been the brains. Brains don't age."

"Oh, fine. And that makes you what? The brawn?" Anthony leaned back and folded his arms. "I can take you anytime, turkey."

"No, I'm the instinct. Lightning-fast instinct." Zack sent his eyes around the diner again before he turned back to Anthony. "But lately, I'm losing it. When we were chasing that guy on the fortieth floor yesterday? The one on the roof? For a minute, just for a minute, I thought, 'This is nuts. I'm going to fall off a roof because somebody just boosted somebody else's camcorder. It's not worth it.' And then today with Jerry? I kept looking at that damn desk, thinking, 'That's going to hurt when I have to go over it.' I kept hoping he'd surrender so I wouldn't have to go over that damn desk. I tell you, I'm losing it."

"Look, lightning. You are not getting slower, you are not losing your instincts, and you are not going to die. You are just growing up. And, may I add, not a moment too soon."

"I'm serious—"

"So am I." Anthony pointed his finger at Zack, and Zack shut up. "You have been going ninety miles an hour ever since I met you eighteen years ago. I used to watch you and think, 'How does he do that?' and marvel. Then I grew up, and now I watch you and think, '*Why* does he do that?' You have nothing to prove to anybody, and you're still acting like some hotshot TV cop." Anthony leaned forward. "Not chasing the camcorder off the roof was good. It was a sign of maturity."

"Don't say that word," Zack said. "Maturity means death."

"It does not. What's wrong with you?"

Zack started drumming his fingers again. "I don't know. Sometimes... You know, my brothers are all married. They've got wives, they've got kids, they've got big houses, they've got responsibilities." He scowled at Anthony. "It's like they're living death."

"I've met your family. They're happy. What are you talking about?"

"Responsibility," Zack said. "Maturity. The minute I stopped chasing that camcorder, death said hello."

Anthony started to laugh. "I don't believe this. You've always been a flake, but this. This is new. You know what you need?"

"Nothing. I need nothing. I'll be fine."

"You need to settle down. Look, you used to live for this job, but it's not enough anymore. That's good. But you look at your brothers, and you want what they've got, and it scares you, so you become depressed instead. That's bad. Face it. Maturity is not death. It's just the next step in life. Most people encounter it sooner than you did, but you'll do fine." Anthony sipped his coffee. "You will have to change the kind of women you date, though."

"What's wrong with the kind of women I date?"

"They're younger than your car, they carry knives, and they ride motorcycles naked on I-75."

"Well, they beat those plastic Yuppies you hang out with. What's the latest one's name? Cheryl? Please." Zack rolled his eyes.

"Cheryl has many fine qualities," Anthony said without much enthusiasm.

"Name one."

"She can read. Have you ever dated anyone literate?"

"Look, I don't want to date anybody right now."

"You're not dating?" Anthony frowned at him. "There are no women in your life?"

"I'm resting." Zack leaned back in the booth and tapped his fingers on the cracked upholstery. "I'm concentrating on my career."

"Oh, good for you. So how long has it been since you . . . dated?"

"Since New Year's Eve."

Anthony shook his head. "That's two months. That alone could make you depressed."

"I'm not that depressed." Zack's tapping picked up speed. "Could we get off this please?"

"All right, you're not ready for a wife. Start small. Get a dog."

"A dog? A dog?" Zack slapped the table. "A dog. That's all I need is some dopey dog with big sad eyes telepathically telling me he never sees me and where have I been?"

"Zack . . ."

"Besides, I had a dog once. I got him when I was three. He died."

"Zack . . ."

"I went away to college and he died. Dogs are a responsibility. You can't leave them."

"You went away to college." Anthony cast an imploring look at the ceiling. "I don't believe this. Zack, if you got him when you were three, he was fifteen by the time you went to college. That's 105 in dog years. He died because he was old, not because you went to college."

Zack wasn't listening. "You start taking responsibility for things, they worry you. I don't need that. Worry slows you down. You start to second-guess everything. And then, pretty soon, the instincts go. That's why I hang out with you. Nothing ever happens to you."

"Thank you," Anthony said. "I think. All right, a dog is not a good idea, but maybe—"

"Look, could we get back to work here? This conversation is really depressing me."

"Fine. But think about what I said." Zack scowled at him and Anthony held up his hand. "All right, back to work. Now, which one of those two women over there does your sixth sense tell you is John Bradley, embezzler?" He studied them. "The hot brunette has a mean look to her, but I suppose the blonde's a possible, too."

"You don't think the blonde's hot?" Zack shook his head. "You have no taste in women. The hair's a little weird, but the face is good, and the body is excellent."

"How do you know? They're sitting down."

"She went to the counter to get another fork. I may be getting older, but I'm not dead yet. The blonde would definitely be worth some time." Zack squinted over at her. "You know, I think she's been looking at me."

"Right."

"Hey. Women look at me. It happens."

"Well, at least you're not depressed anymore." Anthony checked his watch. "We've wasted an hour here for nothing. Would you like to arrest the blonde so you can pat her down, or shall we just leave?"

"Fine. Make fun." Zack shoved his coffee away and tossed some coins on the table as a tip. "But I'm telling you right now, there's something here that would have helped us break this Bradley case. And now we'll never know."

"I can live with that," Anthony said.

"That's because you have no instincts," Zack said.

"Okay," Tina said as Lucy finished her salad. "Let's concentrate on the basics—getting your new life started."

"Let's not," Lucy said.

"First of all, you've got to get rid of anything of Bradley's that's left. Then we've got to change your hair. And then I'll fix you up with some presentable men I know. Everyone I know has money, so at least you'll be eating in decent restaurants. Not like this dump."

"Wait a minute."

"The first thing you do when you get home—"

"Tina," Lucy said. "No dating. I will fix my hair because it looks awful, but no dating."

"What about Bradley's things? I think you should throw whatever he left out on the lawn. Or better yet, burn it and dance around the flames."

"Tina, that's ridiculous. You're blowing this out of proportion."

"No, I'm not. Psychologically, this is a very big deal. Get rid of his things and you'll get rid of him."

"I am rid of him," Lucy protested. "I just want to talk to him so I know what happened. I don't want him back."

"Good. Remember that." Tina stood and took her black silk trench coat from the rack at the end of the booth. Then she handed Lucy her bright blue quilted-cotton jacket and bag. "What have you got in that bag? It weighs a ton."

"My physics book, remember? I brought it so if the divorce got boring, I could review. And sure enough . . ."

Tina closed her eyes. "I have to save you. This is too painful." She jabbed her finger at Lucy. "You go home and start throwing Bradley out. I'll make an appointment for your hair tomorrow."

"Tina. No. If I want my hair done, I will do it."

"I know this wonderful woman on Court Street. . . ."

"*No.*"

Tina stopped. "All right. But at least get rid of Bradley."

"Maybe." Lucy took a deep breath, full of independence. "Maybe."

"Damn it. I was sure there'd be something about Bradley here." Zack stood.

"Your blonde's leaving," Anthony said and they both turned to watch.

They were splitting up, the brunette heading for the back door to the parking lot, the blonde to the street door. Just before she got to the door, the brunette turned.

"Lucy," she called, and it sounded like an order. "I mean it. As soon as you get home."

"All right, all right," the blonde said. "As soon as I get home, I will get rid of Bradley." Then she turned and walked out the door.

"Instinct," Zack said and took off after her.

"I hate it when you do this," Anthony said, and moved toward the parking-lot door to stop the brunette.

2

THE FEBRUARY WIND CUT at Lucy's face as she set off at a dead run to find her car, her purse banging heavily into her hip. She'd almost reached the alley next to the lot when somebody grabbed her arm, and she swung around and fell against the brick wall of the building behind her.

It was the black leather from the restaurant. "Excuse me?" he said. "We need to talk." He blocked her against the wall and reached inside his beat-up leather jacket. "I'm—"

"No." Lucy shook her head until the street blurred. "I'm very busy. Really. You probably noticed me staring at you? That was a mistake. I'm sorry. I have to go." She tried to slip away, but he caught at her arm again.

"I have to ask you about Bradley," he said, and Lucy stopped pulling away.

"Bradley?" She blinked. "Oh, you mean with my sister back there? Getting rid of him? That was a joke. Sort of."

He smiled down at her, and Lucy lost her breath. He was too intense to be handsome and too electric to be ignored. "I love jokes," he said. "Tell me about it."

I'd tell you anything, Lucy thought, and then she heard a sound like a car backfiring. There was a pinging sound and a chip of the brick wall behind them struck her on the cheek and the man swore and yanked her into the alley. He shoved her behind a trash bin and pinned her to the metal with his body, so close to her that her heart thudded against his chest. He was solid and a lot stronger than she was, and she tried to push him away, but he didn't budge.

"What are you doing?" Lucy tried to push him off. "Let go."

"Quiet."

He eased himself off her slightly, reached inside his jacket, pulled out a gun, and aimed it carefully at the street.

Lucy froze. A part of her mind marvelling at actually seeing a real gun in the hand of a real felon, the rest of her mind was in meltdown. *Move,* she told her feet, but she stayed frozen against him. She shoved her chin up his chest to get a better look at him, trying to decide whether he was just run-of-the-mill violent or totally deranged.

He looked big and tense and concentrated. His anvil-like jaw was clenched and his crazy blue eyes swept up and down the street.

Totally deranged.

She shifted again, and he whispered without looking at her, "Would you hold still, please?"

Please? At least he was polite.

She tried to shove him off her, but he weighed a ton, so she decided to fall back on her former strong suit: brains. "You're squashing me," she said, trying to breath around his jacket, and he eased off her a little more, just enough to give her room to lunge for the street. He caught her by the coat before she could take another step, yanking her back and yelling, "Are you crazy?"

"Me?" Lucy yelled back, trying to jerk her coat away. "What about you? Grabbing women? Let me go."

"Listen, lady," He tried to push her back behind the Dumpster. "I'm . . ."

"I don't care who you are. *Let go!*" She swung her purse filled with five pounds of physics book and connected with his solar plexus.

His gasp was an inverted scream, and his grip tightened on her convulsively. She jerked away again, and her shoulder bag swung up hard into his face, catching him solidly on the mouth and neatly splitting his lip. His head jerked up, and then Lucy slugged him along the temple, this time on purpose, not even wincing as his head made a *thock* sound when

her book-filled bag connected. After the last blow, he let go
of her and lurched back a step, and she ran down the alley in
the opposite direction, propelled by so much adrenaline that
when she finally rushed out into the next street, she almost
ran into the patrol car that was cruising by.

"Some horrible man just grabbed me and dragged me into
an alley," she said to the two patrolmen who piled out of the
car. She jabbed her finger behind her. "He's big, and he's got
dark hair and a big jaw, and he's wearing a horrible old black
leather jacket, and he needs a shave, and he's probably a drug
dealer or something!"

The two men exploded into action, the taller, younger one
pounding down the alley while the older, stockier one yelled
at her to wait and then followed him. Lucy paced back and
forth beside the patrol car, vibrating with energy.

Wow, *this* was what Tina was talking about. Spontaneity.
This was great. This was wonderful. She felt *good*. Of course,
she couldn't go around beating up every man she met,
but . . . oh, she felt good. She felt really good.

Lucy checked her watch. The police had been gone forty-
five seconds. Einstein's theory of relativity. Of course. Time
passed slower when you were moving. Here she'd been
standing still, watching her life rush past her, and all she had
to do was *do something* and it slowed down and became this
wonderful, rich . . .

Oh, she felt good.

Sort of.

She slumped suddenly against the side of the patrol car, her
adrenaline spent. Maybe she'd killed him. He deserved it, but
maybe she really had hurt him. That physics book was heavy.
What had she done? What was she doing? She looked at her
watch again. A minute gone now. She couldn't stay there. She
had to go. She couldn't . . .

Lucy put her hand up to her face in confusion and when
she brought it down again, there was blood on it. Her cheek.
She was bleeding.

She tore a piece of paper out of her address book, wrote her name, address and phone number on it, and left it under the windshield wiper of the cruiser. Then she went back to her car and drove home, still vibrating with the aftereffects of the adrenaline, stopping only once along the way, at a drugstore.

"SHE SAID YOU WERE A horrible drug dealer." The young patrolman grinned at Zack.

"Arrest her." Zack tried to breathe normally. He leaned on the wall by the alley, his gaze still searching the street. "Lock her in the back of the car until I can breathe again. She knows something about the Bradley job."

The young cop snorted. "She didn't look like she knew her own name."

Zack looked at him with distaste. He was tall, blond, and reasonably good-looking if you liked the movie-star type, but mostly he was just young. "Look, Junior," Zack said. "When you've been around as long as I have, you'll find out that it isn't what they look like, it's what they do." He touched his lip, and his fingers came away bloody. "Ouch."

"And I heard you were a tough guy." The younger cop grinned again.

Zack stared him down until his grin faded. "You know who you remind me of? The kid cop in *Lethal Weapon 3*. You know, the one who says, 'It's my twenty-first birthday today,' and right away you know he's dead meat? You knew the bad guys were going to drill him." Zack squinted at him. "Of course, in your case, it'll be friendly fire."

"Ha," the young cop said.

"So where's my suspect?" Zack said. "Do *not* tell me you've lost her. She's the only link we've got to an embezzler."

"My partner Falk went to get her." He grinned again. "He said he knew you, and that I shouldn't shoot you even though you were obviously a dangerous drug dealer. They're gonna love this back at the station."

Zack glared at him, and he swallowed and said, "Really, he'll be back any minute." He looked over Zack's shoulder, suddenly relieved. "See? Here he comes now."

Zack eased himself off the wall with great care. Then he looked in the patrol car as it pulled up and straightened quickly. "Where is she?"

"Wait." Falk held up his hand as he got out. He slammed the car door and waved a piece of paper at Zack. "The good news is, she left her address." He handed it over to Zack, who had slumped back against the wall. "You want Matthews and me to go pick her up?"

"'Lucy Savage,'" Zack read. "Well, the last name's right. That woman's damn near feral. No, I don't want you to pick her up. The reason I have to go pick her up now is because the two of you couldn't hold on to her. I'll handle it."

"You want us for backup? She must have been all of five-seven, maybe one thirty-five. You probably only got six inches and sixty pounds on her."

"Very, very funny" Zack pushed himself gingerly away from the wall. "Call Forensics and get some lab people down here. There's a bullet in this wall."

"Your instincts tell you that?"

"No," Zack said with obvious patience. "The chunk of wall that sliced that hellcat's cheek told me that. Somebody was shooting at her."

Matthews went over to the wall. "He's right."

"Well, of course, I'm right. Just what I need—infant cops checking my work. Will you call that in? Please?" Zack glared at the younger man, who stomped back to the car, grumbling.

"Was I ever that obnoxious?" Zack asked Falk.

"What do you mean, 'was'? You still are. You sure they weren't shooting at you? I'm serious," Falk added hastily when Zack turned his glare on him. "Not everybody loves you like we do back at the station."

"No," Zack said. "It was her." Zack looked back at the wall. "Helluva sloppy job, though. Broad daylight, not a chance of hitting her unless he was a lot closer. This guy is either a real amateur, or he was just trying to scare her and didn't care if he picked off an innocent bystander. Like me."

"You sure you don't need backup on this?"

"Yeah." Zack turned back to him. "I think I may just possibly be able to handle one medium-size woman by myself."

"I don't know. She did a nice job on you. I think you need us."

"Oh, yeah, I need you and Junior here." Zack jerked his head at the other cop who'd joined them again. "What was it, Falk? Nobody would work with you, so you stopped by the junior high for help?"

"Hey," Matthews said. "I'm twenty. I got two years of college."

"So do I," Zack said, touching his lip again gingerly. "Fat lot of good it's doing me here. Get on that bullet." He turned and walked toward the parking lot and his own car.

"Hey, Warren," Falk called after him. "Did you have one of those famous instincts of yours right before she nailed you? Or right after?"

"All great men are persecuted," Zack said and kept on walking. He knew he was right about this Bradley thing. And Lucy Savage was very shortly going to be very sorry that she and John Bradley had ever messed with him.

As soon as he took some aspirin and got some ice on his damn lip.

LUCY UNLOCKED HER massive front door with its jewel-colored leaded glass and then crossed the vestibule to unlock the beveled-glass inner door. It immediately burst open under the pressure of the three dog bodies that were pressed against it.

"Easy," Lucy said, still worn-out from her adrenaline surge. She dropped down onto the tiled floor to pet them, and they piled around her in the warm glow of the colored sunlight that streamed through the stained glass.

Einstein, the big sheepdog, flopped down beside her, but Heisenburg, the walking mop, and Maxwell, the little miscellaneous dog, both climbed into her lap to lick her face and burrow under her hands. She gathered them all to her, loving them and the warmth and color of her beautiful old house and, for once, herself.

"I beat up a mugger today," she told the dogs. "He attacked me and I beat him up. I *won*." The dogs looked suitably impressed. That was one of the many great things about dogs. They were easy to impress. Not like Tina.

But even Tina would be impressed with this. Carefully tipping the little dogs off her lap, Lucy stood and went inside the house.

Her house. Every time she walked into it, she felt safe. The living room was papered in huge flowers in shades of rose and edged with wide oak woodwork, and the floors gleamed in the soft sunlight that filtered through her lace curtains. The fat, worn, upholstered furniture was splashed with flowers, too, in roses and blues and golds, and the mantel and tables were crammed with pictures, and flowers in vases, and books. She sank into the big blue overstuffed chair by the wobbly piecrust phone table and looked through the archway into her dining room, warm with the glow of the stained-glass windows there.

Her house. She felt all the tension ease out of her. Her home.

Einstein barked at her for attention, and she remembered Tina. She dropped her purse and the bag from the drugstore on the floor and dialed her sister's number, absentmindedly scratching behind Einstein's ears while she listened to the ring.

"Tina?" she said when the ringing stopped, but it was Tina's machine, so she left a message. "This is Lucy. I wanted you to know, I just beat up a mugger. I really did, and it was *wonderful.* And don't worry, I'm okay. In fact, I'm great. You were right. I love you!"

And then she hung up and relaxed into the threadbare softness of her chair, hugging herself.

She really did feel wonderful. Sort of tired, but wonderful. Good tired.

Her gaze fell on the drugstore bag where she'd dropped it, and she stood, swooping it up as she straightened.

"Look at this," she told the dogs. "I went to the store to get disinfectant for my cheek, and right there, in the checkout line, was a big display that said 'On Sale! Discontinued! 1/2 Off!' and it was this!" With a flourish, she pulled a box out of the bag. "So I bought it."

Einstein squinted at the box, decided it wasn't biscuits, and collapsed with disappointment. Maxwell contemplated the air. Heisenburg rolled over onto his back.

Lucy ignored them to study the photo on the box: the model's hair was a rich cloud of midnight curls and she looked sultry and provocative. "This is the new me," she told the dogs. "It's time I changed. I just made a mistake with this blond mess because I didn't think it through. I'm not the blond type, you know?"

Maxwell and Einstein looked at each other. Heisenburg stayed on his back.

"Oh, you may laugh. But I'm changing my hair and I'm changing my life. No more mousy, timid brown or brassy, tacky blond. I'm going to change into a whole new Lucy. I'm going to be a brunette. Dark, fascinating, dangerous. Independent. All men will desire me. All men will fear me."

Einstein sighed, Maxwell scratched, and Heisenburg stayed on his back.

Lucy looked back at the picture on the box. "Well, maybe not. But they won't ignore me or stare at my hair in disbelief. And I'll *feel* tougher with this hair. I'll take chances. I'll date exciting men." She remembered the last exciting man she'd been attracted to, the one who had mugged her in an alley.

"Well, maybe not. You know, I don't have very good taste in men. Maybe I'll hold off on the dating for a while."

Like maybe forever.

She looked down at the dogs who were staring at her now with adoration. Even Maxwell's usually glazed eyes were shining with puppy love, and Heisenburg had let his head fall back so he could worship her upside down. "I should just stick with you guys. You're the best."

Okay. No men for a while, no matter how lonely she felt. But she could still change. She could still be independent and control her life. She could do it.

"I'll tell you something else," she told the dogs. "I'm really being independent. I'm even taking back my maiden name. In fact, I already did. I just signed a note with it. And not only that, later, when I'm done, we've got *real* fun. Do you know what we're going to do?"

Einstein and Maxwell cocked an ear at the lilt in her voice. Heisenburg lay doggedly on his back.

"All right, all right," Lucy said to him, giving in to canine blackmail. "Dead dog?" Heisenburg jumped up, delirious at finally being noticed.

"You are spoiled rotten," Lucy told him. "Now as I was saying, do you know what we're going to do?"

The dogs waited.

"We're going to get rid of Bradley!" Lucy said, flinging her arms wide.

The dogs went wild with joy.

"My sentiments, exactly," she told them and went upstairs to start transforming herself.

AN HOUR AND A HALF later, Zack pulled up in front of the address Lucy Savage had left on the patrol-car windshield.

It was in an older neighborhood, close to the university and in the throes of gentrification. Some of the big old Victorians were completely restored, some hadn't been touched, and some were in transition. The Savage house was one that someone had begun to make an effort with.

Zack sat in his car and checked the place out. The three-story cream brick house, like all the others around it, was on a hill bisected by the cracked concrete driveways that consumed the narrow side yards that separated the houses. A small blue Civic, its windows rolled up tightly in the February cold, sat in the driveway to the left. The drive to the right was empty.

There was no one in sight.

Great. This is why he needed a partner with him so he could say, "It's quiet . . . too quiet." So where was Anthony? Chasing brunettes. You couldn't trust anybody these days.

He got out of the car and climbed the concrete steps to the house.

He twisted the knob on the antique doorbell, and its hellish scream echoed through the big rooms of the house, followed by the barking of what seemed like a thousand dogs.

His grandmother had once had a doorbell like this one, and he remembered how wonderfully godawful it had sounded, the kind of ring that went right up your spine and out the top of your head. Then one day, his grandmother had had enough and put chimes in instead, and he hadn't felt the same way about his grandmother's house since.

Or his grandmother, for that matter.

And now Lucy Savage had the same godawful doorbell. It figured. Savage woman, savage doorbell.

He twisted it again. A thousand dogs barked again.

The door opened.

She was a brunette, sort of. Actually, she had the blackest hair he'd ever seen in his life on anyone. Or anything. It was the kind of dead, dull black that seemed to absorb light and air, and her face was surrounded and overwhelmed by it. For a moment, he wasn't even sure it was the same woman, and then he recognized the pointed chin and the big eyes, now widening in startled recognition. She started to slam the massive wood door, but he put his foot in it to block her.

He'd forgotten he was wearing canvas shoes, not leather. She slammed the heavy door into his foot and yelled, "Go away. I have vicious dogs. I'm calling the police!"

"I *am* the police!" Zack clenched his teeth against the pain. He shoved his badge in against the shoe-width crack in the door. "Do you know the penalty for assaulting a police officer?"

"What?" She stared at his badge and then slumped against the doorframe, letting the door fall open. "I don't believe this. I just don't believe this."

"Believe it, lady. Can I come in, or do you want to beat on me some more?"

She stood back so he could go in, her eyes wide in her woebegone face, and Zack would have felt sorry for her if he hadn't been in so much pain.

"Thank you." He limped past her into the vestibule. She closed the door behind him and then opened the vesitbule door, and the dogs attacked.

The big sheep dog was the first to reach him. It immediately leaned heavily against his leg, shedding all over his jeans and drooling into his shoe. The little skinny brown one draped itself harmlessly over Zack's uninjured foot and stared off into space at nothing in particular. And the one that looked like a floor mop barked at him once and then rolled over onto its back with all four short legs in the air and lay there, motionless.

"These are vicious attack dogs?"

"I thought you were a mugger." She shoved her impossible hair out of her face. "And they sound vicious." They both looked down at the dogs. "Sort of."

"What's wrong with the mop?" Zack asked.

"He's not a mop. That's Heisenburg and . . . Never mind. Am I under arrest for beating you up?"

"You did not beat me up, lady. The only reason you hit me at all is that I wasn't defending myself because I didn't want to hurt you." Zack looked down at Heisenburg. "Is he sick?"

"No," she said. "It's a dog joke. It's the only one he knows."

"A dog joke."

"Yes. You feed him the setup, and then he does the punch line. Like a knock-knock joke."

"You taught this dog a joke?"

"No." She looked down at the mop with pride. "He thought it up on his own."

Zack looked around the spotless vestibule and through the open door. The next room was spacious, with high ceilings and hardwood floors covered with worn Oriental rugs. It was full of sunlight and comfortable, threadbare, overstuffed furniture, and he could hear a fire crackling cheerfully somewhere close. He looked at the woebegone brunette gazing down at her three dogs, and at the two dogs gazing back adoringly. And finally he looked at the third dog, Heisenburg, waiting patiently on his back for his setup line.

If this woman was a crook, he was the Queen of the May. He grinned at her so suddenly that she blinked. "You're not a criminal, are you?" he asked, and she shook her head, relieved at the change in his tone.

"Not unless you arrest me for mugging you. I deserve it. I know I deserve it. But you scared me." She frowned. "Why did you drag me into that alley?"

"We need to talk." Zack held out his hand. "I'm Detective Zachery Warren."

She took his hand and shook it. "I'm Lucy Savage, and I'm really sorry I beat you up. Your lip looks awful."

"You didn't beat me up. Would you feed this dog his line so we can go sit down?"

"Oh, no!" Lucy said, with so much enthusiasm that Zack looked to see what was wrong. "Dead dog?"

Heisenburg rolled over and jumped to his feet and barked. Zack looked at Lucy. "That's a dog joke?"

"What did you expect? 'That was no lady, that was my wife'?"

"I don't know," Zack said, confused. "Can we go sit down? My foot is killing me."

"IF YOU DON'T MIND, I'd like to ask you a few questions before I explain about the alley," Zack began when he was finally sitting on the rose-colored love seat across from the blazing fireplace in the living room. So far, he'd turned down coffee, tea, soft drinks, aspirin, and ice for his foot from Lucy, and affectionate approaches from Heisenberg, who wanted to sit in his lap. Now he was anxious to cut to the chase and get some answers before one of the other dogs began a soft shoe or tried to sell him magazines.

"Sure," Lucy said. "Whatever."

She was sitting next to him in a big, ugly olive-green chair that didn't seem to go with the rest of the house, and she looked swallowed up by it somehow, her knees higher than her waist, her shoulders bowing in a little like folded angel wings.

"Are you all right?" Zack said. "You seem . . . depressed."

"I went to court to get divorced today, and my ex-husband stood me up. Then my sister decided to change my life. Then a drug dealer tried to mug me, so I beat him up, and I thought, at last, I'm doing something right, and then he turned out to be a cop. You." She blinked. "I'm having a bad day. I'll get over it."

"You didn't beat me up. I wasn't even trying to defend myself."

"Sure. Whatever."

Zack gave up. "Tell me about Bradley. Everything you know."

"Bradley?" Lucy sat back, confused. "That's what you said on the street. Why do you want to know about my ex-husband?"

Zack frowned at her, equally confused. "I thought your name was Savage."

"That's my maiden name. Bradley did something criminal? I don't believe it." Lucy wrinkled her nose at him. "Are you sure?"

"If he's the man we're looking for, he embezzled a million and a half in government bonds from the bank where he worked."

Lucy's mouth dropped open and she sat up straight. "Bradley? Embezzled from his bank?"

"Banks are the best places to embezzle from," Zack said. "They usually have the most money."

"Right. I'm sorry, I don't mean to be thick about this. It's just that . . . *Bradley?*"

Zack nodded. "I know. It's a shock. Now, when and where did you meet him?"

"He picked me up at the library," Lucy said, still dazed from his announcement. "I was working on some lesson plans, and I looked up, and there he was, and he asked if he could sit down, and he talked to me and bought me a juice from the vending machines, and then he walked me to my car, and two months later we were married."

"That fast?" Zack said, writing everything down.

"Well, I had my reasons." Lucy sank back in her chair and closed her eyes. "They were the wrong reasons, but I didn't know that then."

Zack wasn't listening. This could be it. The dates matched. He looked over at Lucy, sitting lost in an ugly green chair, and he felt a sudden protectiveness for her that was totally out of character for him. The poor helpless kid was just an innocent bystander. That rat Bradley . . .

Bradley.

Zack started to tap his notebook again. "And exactly when did you meet him?"

"And besides," Lucy went on, still lost in her own train of thought, "there was the second law of thermonuclear dynamics."

"I'm sure there was. When did you meet him?"

Lucy came back to earth. "Sorry. We got married June first. We met in the middle of March."

"And you got divorced in February." Zack looked up from his notebook. "Any particular reason? Did he begin acting suspiciously? Did you find more money in your checking account than you could account for? Any..."

"It was the blonde," Lucy said.

"Oh." Zack winced for her. "Another woman? Sorry."

"Girl, really. Very young. Maybe twenty."

"That could be his wife," Zack said.

"His wife?" Lucy said faintly.

"Uh, yeah. Sorry to drop it on you like that. He was married."

"Oh," Lucy said.

"Bianca Bradley. Also blond and young, twenty-four. He must have a thing for blondes." Zack looked at Lucy's impossible black hair and looked back as his notebook. "So..."

"That's funny," Lucy said. "Her maiden name was the same as his Christian name."

"No, her maiden name is Bergman. She..."

"Where did the Bradley come from?"

"What Bradley?" Zack said.

"Her last name."

"When she married John Bradley," Zack said, his patience wearing thin. "The same John Bradley you married."

"I didn't marry John Bradley." Lucy sat up straight. "I married Bradley Porter. I don't believe this. You've been asking me questions about the wrong Bradley. What's going on?"

3

"THIS IS THE DUMBEST thing I've ever heard," Lucy said.

Zack ignored her and tapped on the cover of his notebook while he reviewed the possibilities, trying to think of anything that might point him in a new direction.

Any direction.

"I mean, first you grab me in an alley—"

"Listen." Zack fixed his eyes her. "John Talbot Bradley is six-five and weighs about two hundred pounds. He has brown hair and brown eyes, and he's in very good physical condition. He used to be a high-school phys-ed teacher. Does he sound like your ex-husband?"

Lucy opened her mouth and Zack held up his hand. "Think about it before you answer. I know it sounds dumb, but think about it."

Lucy shook her head. "No. Bradley's blond and good-looking and a little out of shape. I bought him sweats once so he could run with me, and he told me that physical exertion was for people who didn't use their minds. The height is close. But his eyes are gray."

Zack went back to slapping his notebook with his pencil. "He still might be able to pull it off. You met him in March and that's when John Bradley went missing in California."

Lucy shook her head again. "Then definitely not. I met him in March, but he'd already been branch manager of his bank for a year."

"Branch manager of a bank?" Zack stopped frowning. "Two Bradleys, two banks. And then the phone tip and the diner. There's got to be a connection here. All my instincts tell me there's a connection."

"All my logic tells me there isn't," Lucy said.

"Your logic is wrong," Zack said absently.

"I beg your pardon?"

"Why were you in that diner today?"

"I told you, I was at the courthouse...."

"Were you supposed to meet Bradley at the diner?"

"Not exactly. I was supposed to meet Bradley at the courthouse. But he'd sent me a note, asking me to have lunch with him at the diner after the hearing, and then when he didn't show up at the courthouse and my sister Tina wanted to talk, I suggested the diner, just in case he'd be there."

"So you went to the diner to meet Bradley."

"No," Lucy said patiently. "I wasn't even sure he'd be there. But Tina insisted on lunch so she could convince me to become spontaneous and irresponsible, and I picked the diner just in case he might be there. And then thanks to her, I beat up a cop."

"You did not beat up a cop. I told you, I wasn't fighting back." Zack leaned forward until he was almost touching her, his blue eyes blazing into hers. "Now, listen. *Concentrate.*"

Lucy blinked at the heat in his gaze. "Okay," she said, trying to remember what they'd been talking about. He was doing something to her brain, scrambling her thoughts. *I bet he's murder on cellular phones,* she thought, and then dragged her attention back to what he was saying.

"My partner and I were there because a woman called and told us that Bradley was going to be there," Zack said, speaking very clearly as if he thought she was slightly backward. "That is all she said. 'Bradley's going to be at Harvey's Diner on Second at one.' Now, could that have been your sister?"

Lucy pulled back a little so she could think. "My sister would love to see Bradley arrested and shot, but even she wouldn't call and tell you he was going to be there if there wasn't any reason for you to arrest him. Trust me, Tina does not think that Bradley is involved in a crime. And neither do I. And neither do you. You're just annoyed because your instincts failed you."

"No," Zack said. "Somebody shot at you this afternoon."

He watched her while she blinked again. Any lingering suspicions he might have harbored that she was leading him on died at that moment. She looked totally clueless. Really cute, but totally clueless.

"Remember when I grabbed you by the alley?"

"Vividly."

He leaned forward suddenly and touched the cut on her cheek, and she jerked back. "How did you get that?"

"A car hit a stone. . . ."

Zack shook his head. "Somebody shot at you and missed and the bullet kicked back a piece of the brick wall. I saw it hit you. That's why I dragged you into the alley."

"Oh." He watched while Lucy digested the information. "So you thought you were saving my life while I thought you were mugging me."

"I didn't *think* I was saving your life, I . . ."

"And then I beat you up. I'm really sorry."

Zack closed his eyes. He was in the Twilight Zone with three deranged dogs and a woman who thought she was the Terminator. And Bradley—his Bradley—was nowhere to be seen. Either he was losing his touch or he was missing something.

He must be missing something.

He opened his eyes and looked at Lucy again. "Listen to me carefully. Somebody is trying to kill you."

She glared at him. "Listen to *me* carefully. Nobody is trying to kill me, and if you looked at this logically, you would see that."

"Wait a minute."

"There are two people standing against the wall. One of these people is a mild-mannered high-school teacher whose students all adore her. The other is a condescending police officer who grabs innocent women and drags them into alleys and who has probably alienated everyone in the greater Riverbend area. Now, which of these two people is most likely to be shot at?"

"You," Zack said. "My instincts tell me you."

"Your instincts stink," Lucy said and blinked. "I'm sorry. I'm usually not rude. I've had a bad day."

"That's all right," Zack said. "People are rude to me all the time."

He shoved his notebook back in his jacket and stood. "Listen, we'll argue about this later. Right now, I'm going to look around the outside of your house. You stay inside."

Lucy stood, too. "I beg your pardon?"

"Inside. You. And the dogs." Zack looked down at Heisenberg. "Stay. All of you."

Lucy put her hands on her hips and glared at him. "Who do you think you are?"

"Me?" Zack said on his way out. "I'm the guy who saved your life, so you owe me. Stay put."

He glanced back and saw her face creased in fury, and he grinned at her as he went out the door. The last thing he heard as he closed the door behind him was Lucy saying, "Listen, you, you didn't . . ."

Lucy worked at controlling her temper while the dogs watched her. "Who does he think he is?" she asked them. "He just comes in here, out of the blue, and tells me somebody's been shooting at me, and orders me around. Just what I needed. Somebody else ordering me around."

Only she hadn't let him. She'd fought back.

And it really felt good.

"I think I'm on to something with this independence thing," she told the dogs. "I really enjoyed arguing with him."

Of course, it hadn't had much effect on him. He'd just glared at her and charged on ahead. And he hadn't been all that mad, anyway. A minute after the glare, he'd been grinning at her again. She pictured him again, those bright blue eyes heating her and that crazy grin scrambling her thoughts, and she had to remind herself that she was mad at him. "This is my problem," she told the dogs. "I'm too easygoing. I should be mad at him. I should want to *kill* him." She stopped on the last thought.

He'd said somebody was trying to kill her.

Who would want to kill her? That was ridiculous. That was something that happened on TV. A car backfired and kicked up a stone. People did not go around shooting guns in downtown Riverbend.

He must be wrong.

Wrong, but gorgeous.

She pictured him again, much against her better judgment. That grin, that swagger, those blue, blue eyes that connected with hers with such impact on her breathing. "The thing is," she told the dogs, "even though I know he's a policeman, he doesn't look like a policeman. He looks like a very, very sexy bad guy."

She heard a noise in the vestibule and looked up to see Zack leaning in the doorway, and she blushed so hard she almost passed out.

"You talk to the dogs," he said.

"Well, of course I talk to the dogs." Lucy prayed he hadn't heard what she'd said. "It's not like I talk to plants or anything non-sentient."

"What I was going to ask was why you have such expensive locks on this place. You must have dropped a small fortune on the front doors alone, and from what I can see from the front, the windows are locked, too."

"Oh, they are," Lucy said, eager for a change of subject. "Even the attic windows. Did they really cost a lot?"

"So they weren't your idea." Zack looked satisfied. Smug, even. "Bradley ordered them, right?"

"No. It was my sister."

His satisfaction disappeared. "Your sister was afraid you'd be robbed?"

"No, my sister hates my ex-husband. She did it to annoy him. She said it was to keep him from taking anything out of the house that I might possibly be able to strip him of in the divorce. My sister plays hardball in divorce court."

"I bet she does," Zack said, taking out his notebook again. "And when was this?"

"Oh, she had them put on as soon as I told her about...the blonde. I mean, within the hour, the locksmith was here with a crew. That was about two weeks ago." Lucy thought back. "The end of January."

Zack went out to the vestibule. "Do you have burglar alarms?" he called back to her.

"No." Lucy followed him. "Look at this place. Does it look like it needs a burglar alarm?"

Zack glanced around the high-ceilinged hall. "It's not bad. It'll be nice when it's fixed up. So, for protection, you've got the locks and the dogs." He looked down at the three dogs who had followed them to the vestibule and were now sitting in a row, watching him.

"Don't make fun of my dogs," Lucy said.

"I'm not making fun of your dogs. Dogs are a good deterrent for thieves. They make noise. Thieves hate noise. Killers aren't crazy about it, but they'll cope."

Lucy folded her arms. "Nobody is trying to kill me."

Zack spread his arms wide. "Look. Humor me, okay? Just in case somebody really is trying to get you?"

"Who would want to get me?"

He cocked his head at her. "Well, ex-husbands have been known to go after the wives who locked them out of their houses."

"Bradley didn't want this house. He signed the divorce papers without a fight. He didn't want the house or me." Lucy stopped. "Sorry about that last part. I'm not really that pathetic, it's just that—"

"You're not pathetic at all." Zack flashed his grin at her. "Bradley, however, must be an idiot."

"Thank you," Lucy said.

"You're welcome," Zack said. "Now stay inside."

ZACK WALKED AROUND the house, checking the windows and the back door. The basement door was in the back near the neighbor's alley on the right, an old-fashioned, sloping wood door that had two metal bars across it, both with locks. The locks, like every other one he'd seen on the house, were very new, very efficient, and very expensive. Sister Tina either hated Bradley a whole lot or really worried about Lucy.

And possibly she had a reason to be worried. Zack frowned at the scratches on the basement-door lock. He was peering into the lock with his penlight when someone screamed at him, startling him so much that he dropped the light as he spun around.

"I've called the police so you might as well run off like all those other young punks," she screeched. "Go on. Go on!"

"Damn it, lady, you scared the hell out of me!"

The gray and wizened woman on the back porch of the next house was hunched over the rail in a nothing-colored coat three sizes too big for her. Her clawlike hands waved at him while the pleats of skin on her face worked soundlessly for the moment in indignation. Then her voice came back.

"Get out," she screeched. "Smart-mouthed good-for-nothing!"

"Excuse me, ma'am," Zack said, gritting his teeth. "I was startled. I'm a police officer."

"Well, if you are, the world's in worse trouble than I thought, and I thought it was in the toilet." She stared at him viciously, and Zack wondered briefly about the evil eye. If such a thing was possible, this hag could deliver.

"Hello, Mrs. Dover," Lucy called out from the back door. "It's all right. He's with the police."

"I knew this neighborhood was finished when you moved in," Mrs. Dover shouted back. "Torturing my cat. Bringing those vicious dogs in. Coming and going at all hours."

"Lovely day, isn't it?" Lucy came out onto the porch and looked down at Zack.

"Torturing her cat?" Zack asked and Lucy shook her head.

"Phoebe hasn't been the same since the Porters moved in," Mrs. Dover said. "I've called the humane society, but they won't do anything. Oh, no."

"Usually the sun doesn't come out much in February," Lucy said brightly to no one in particular. "We're very lucky to-day."

"And now this trash." She gestured at Zack. "Does your husband know you're entertaining hoodlums?"

"Actually, I'm divorced now, Mrs. Dover. And Detective Warren really isn't a hoodlum. I made the same mistake, too, but he's really very nice." She looked at Zack. "I think it's your jaw and the five o'clock shadow. I know you can't do anything about your jaw, but you would look much more reassuring if you'd shave. And get a haircut. Really."

"Thank you," Zack said.

A patrol car pulled up in front.

"Maybe he's the police." Mrs. Dover climbed down her back porch steps while she kept an eye cocked on Zack. "Maybe. But I bet he's on the Most Wanted list. Ha! We'll know soon." She nodded and hobbled down her driveway to the street to meet the uniforms.

"Great," Zack said. "This makes the second time today somebody's called the cops on me."

"Well, as I was saying, I think your image needs work. I realize you're probably undercover—"

"No, I'm not."

"Oh. Sorry."

"Forget it." Zack started for the street. Then he screamed in pain.

A large dirty yellow cat had leaped on his leg, burying her claws deeply into his calf through his jeans. Zack kicked out, and the cat dropped away while Mrs. Dover screeched at him from the street.

"Meet Phoebe," Lucy said.

"Damn!" Zack nursed his shin. "What's wrong with that animal?"

"I think she's psychotic. I hate her because she uses my car for a litter box so I have to keep the windows rolled up all the time, even in the summer. And because all three of my dogs are terrified of her."

"Her, who?" Zack glared at Mrs. Dover's back as she gestured wildly to the police in the street. "The woman or the cat?"

"Both," Lucy said. "Do you want some iodine?"

"No," Zack said, as a young patrolman approached him. "I want to shoot that damn cat."

"Sir?" the patrolman began. "This lady has a complaint."

Zack looked at him closely. "How old are you? Twelve?"

The young patrolman stiffened. "Sir . . ."

Zack got out his badge again. "I'm sorry. I'm having a bad day. I'm investigating an attempt on this woman's life." He nodded toward Lucy.

"You are not," Lucy said. "They shot at you, not me."

"Shut up." Zack looked at the patrolman. "Do you ever get tired of defending the public?"

"All the time," the patrolman said. "I'll just have to call this in, sir . . ." he began, looking at Zack's ID, and then he, too, screamed.

"Shoot the cat," Zack said. "It's assaulted two officers and resisted arrest. Do it."

Mrs. Dover hissed at him, scooped up Phoebe, and disappeared into her house.

"Is this some kind of a joke?" the patrolman asked, nursing his shin.

"No. Tragically, no. Go ahead and call that in." Zack looked up at Lucy as the patrolman made his way back to the car. "What does it mean when everyone you see is younger than you are?"

"It means you're getting old. There's a new teacher at my school. She asked me yesterday what it was like in the old days when I first started teaching."

"Did you deck her?"

"No." Lucy stuck out her chin. "But I may when I go back in to school tomorrow. I've gotten a lot meaner today."

Zack laughed. She looked so funny, neat and round with all that crazy dead black hair haloing her face, calmly announcing that she was a lot meaner today. What a sweetheart.

Dumb as a rock, but sweet.

"You're not going back to school tomorrow," he told her. "You're moving in with your sister until I figure out what's going on."

Lucy frowned. "How long will that take? Especially if you're going to figure it out by instinct. I don't have that much sick leave. I don't think anybody does."

She wasn't that sweet. Zack glared at her, and she blinked.

"Sorry," Lucy said. "I don't know what's gotten into me today."

"Forget sick leave," Zack said. "How much dead leave do you have? I'm not kidding here. You could be in danger."

"I think—"

"Don't. Trust me on this one. I know what I'm doing. Somebody's been trying to pick your locks."

"What?"

Zack pointed his finger to the back door behind her. "There are scratches on your back-door lock, and there's a piece of metal broken off inside this basement-door lock. Somebody's been trying to get in here."

Lucy swallowed. "Bradley?"

"Well, that would be my best guess. He may just be trying to get his golf clubs back. But then again . . ." He shrugged. "Somebody shot at you on the street today."

"At *you*," Lucy said, but her voice held a lot less conviction.

"Just stay with your sister for a while. She's got room, right?"

"Oh, she's got room. But I'm not going. She can't take the dogs, and I'm not leaving them." Lucy stuck her chin in the air. "Besides, I don't believe this."

Zack lost his temper and stomped up the back porch steps. He grabbed her arm and pulled her around to face the door as he pointed at the lock. "See those scratches?" His face was so close to hers they were almost nose-to-nose. "Those were made by a pointed metal tool. Somebody was trying to break in."

Lucy blinked at his closeness. "Well, they didn't get in, did they? So I must be pretty safe."

"Only because they're trying to be subtle for some reason. Sooner or later, they're just going to smash a window and climb in. Lord knows why they haven't already. I advise you to move to your sister's."

"No," Lucy said.

Zack let go of her arm and closed his eyes and counted to ten. Then he looked down at her with all the patience he could muster.

She looked up at him, wide-eyed and trusting.

Oh, hell. If somebody did hit her, it'd be his fault for not taking care of her.

He forced himself to speak calmly. "Look, just do me one favor. Stay inside tonight. I'll call you when I find out more tomorrow, okay? And I'll have the patrol car keep an eye on you. Just until we can get a handle on your Bradley and see what he's up to."

Lucy opened her mouth to speak, and he overrode her again. "Just for tonight and tomorrow. That's not much to ask. Please."

"I'd have to leave, anyway," Lucy said. "I'm a teacher. Even if I wasn't going in to school tomorrow, I'd have to take in lesson plans."

Zack looked again into Lucy's huge brown eyes and thought again about how much she needed a keeper.

Not him, of course.

Still . . .

"I will take them in. Now, about this sick-leave thing. How long have you been teaching?"

"Twelve years."

"And how many sick days have you taken?"

"None."

"That's what I figured. So how many do you have saved up?"

"One hundred and thirty-eight," Lucy said.

"So if you use a couple, you could still develop a major disease and have everything covered, right?"

"Right," Lucy said, "but that's not the point. The point is, I'm not sick."

Why was it he finally found an honest citizen only when it worked against him? "Look. Think of this guy who's trying to kill you as a life-threatening illness. I do."

"I really think—"

"I told you, don't think. Just do what I tell you. If it will help, I'll shave and put on a suit and come back and tell you to stay inside. I'll do whatever it takes. Because I really do think you're in danger." He gestured to the basement door. "These are all good locks. Take advantage of them. Stay inside and I'll call you tomorrow."

"Well . . ." Her pointed face was so confused under all that dead black hair that suddenly Zack's annoyance faded and he felt protective again. She seemed so helpless, so soft and round and absolutely clueless about reality.

"Please," he said. "Just for tonight."

"All right." Lucy swallowed at his earnestness. "But I still think you're wrong. Anyway, if you give me a couple of minutes, I'll print out the lesson plans. This is very nice of you. Thank you, Detective Warren."

"Zack." He grinned at her in relief. "Detective Warren is for people who haven't hit me with a purse."

Lucy smiled back uncertainly. "Zack." She hesitated. "I'm Lucy." Then she turned and went back inside.

Cute. A little snippy but very cute. Even with the hair. Very, very cute. And she thought he was sexy.

Maybe he could convince her that he really had saved her life, and she'd be grateful.

He tried to picture Lucy, naked and grateful, but all he could see was Lucy, blinking at him, surrounded by dogs.

That could be a bad sign. He was losing his ability to fantasize.

Maturity.

Death.

"Sir?"

Zack turned back to the patrolman who had joined him again.

"You're cleared," the patrolman said. "What's going on here, anyway?"

"I'm not sure," Zack said. "I need you to question the neighbor."

"The old lady?"

"Yeah. I don't think she's going to talk to me."

"I don't think so, either. She wanted me to shoot you. So what do you want me to ask her?"

"She said she'd seen somebody hanging around here, possibly trying to break in. And the locks have been tampered with." Zack frowned back at the house. "Find out what she saw, and when she saw it, and get it to me as fast as you can, okay?"

"You got it. Anything else?"

"Yeah. Keep a close eye on this place for the next couple of days. I think she might really have trouble."

"With neighbors like she's got, that's no big deduction," the patrolman said.

"You should see her sister," Zack said.

"I ALMOST INVITED HIM back in," Lucy told the dogs when Zack had driven away with the lesson plans. "That would have been stupid." She pulled back the lace curtain at the front window and looked out at the empty street. "He was just so different, you know? I just didn't want him to go. So much for my new life. I make these big plans to be independent, and then I cling to the first man I meet an hour after my divorce. Still, you should have been there when he told the other policeman to shoot Phoebe. You would have loved it."

She dropped the curtain and turned to the living room.

Her room.

Her house.

She remembered the first time she'd seen it. She'd passed it one day when she'd taken a wrong turn near the university. A big old cream brick house on a hill with a porch and a cracked old driveway and big beautiful beveled-glass windows.

And a For Sale sign in front.

And she'd wanted that house with a passion that she'd never in her life felt for a man. A big, safe, *warm* house she could fill with dogs and books and comfortable things. Beautiful things. A house with a big kitchen where she could make cookies and bread and soup. A house with a huge fenced-in backyard where Einstein could run. And maybe another dog. Or two. She didn't want Einstein to be an only child.

A house. A house instead of her cold, tiny little apartment where Einstein took up half the floor space, and the oven didn't work right, and she never felt safe. A house.

Her house.

After that, for three months, even after she started seeing Bradley, she'd drive by the house and long for it hopelessly, the way some women long for movie stars. She knew it would never be hers but it was the dream of her heart. And then one day she'd been with Bradley and they'd driven by, and she'd said, "Slow down so I can see my house," and he'd asked her what she meant, and she'd told him. And he'd said, "If we were married, we could buy that house. Will you marry me?"

And she'd said, "Yes."

What she hadn't realized at the time was that she was saying "Yes" to the house, not to Bradley.

"Maybe it wasn't a mistake," she told the dogs as she moved back into the room. "At least we have the house."

It sounded cynical. And selfish. Tina would be pleased.

Einstein barked at her.

"I know," Lucy told him. "I should pull myself together and stop talking to dogs. Well, you're the only ones who listen to me without telling me what to do. Especially Tina, lately..."

Tina. Telling her to get rid of Bradley. Actually, packing up all his stuff in a box might be another small step toward independence. She wouldn't throw it out on the lawn, of course, but she could store it neatly in the basement. That would make the house seem more like it was hers alone.

Alone.

With Zack gone, she suddenly felt alone, as if something warm was missing.

She wasn't sure she wanted to be alone. Especially if Zack was right about the shooting and the scratches . . . Except of course, he wasn't right because it was ridiculous that anyone would be threatening her, and besides there was probably a perfectly good explanation for those scratches.... And if there wasn't, what was he doing leaving her alone? He should be there, protecting her. Obviously he didn't think she was in danger, or he wouldn't have left her alone.

Alone.

Of course, she wasn't alone. She had the dogs.

And besides, there were some kinds of alone that were good. In fact, wonderful. For example, the without-Bradley kind of alone was heaven. No more chill in the air, no more one-right-way-to-do-things, no more long silences and emptiness. Just her and the dogs and the fireplace. Warm.

And alone.

"Enough of this daydreaming stuff," Lucy told the dogs, suddenly straightening. "We have work to do. Let's get rid of Bradley."

Lucy packed up everything of Bradley's that she could find in the house, surprised to find it filled three boxes, not one. "There was more to Bradley than I thought," she told the dogs. Most of the stuff was papers and books. His clothes were already gone; Tina had thrown them all out the front door while the locksmiths were changing the locks. By the time Bradley had come back that night, his entire wardrobe was on the front lawn.

Mrs. Dover had enjoyed it immensely.

He hadn't argued much. He'd knocked on the door and called her name, and then Tina had opened it and threatened him, and he'd gone away.

Not much of a fighter, Bradley.

Not much of a lover, either.

Or maybe that was just with her. Maybe he was better with the blonde.

The blonde. Lucy tensed as she remembered the shock she'd felt when she'd come home to find the blonde standing in the middle of the living room. Her living room. Saying that she and Bradley had been together in the house. Her house. Her bedroom. How could she have been so stupid, not to even have had a clue? How could Bradley do that to her?

He had just stood there with his mouth working like a fish, saying he could explain.

Except he never had.

He was a creep. Bringing that woman into her house. Her house. What a creep.

At least she was free of him now.

Her eyes fell on the boxes.

Or she soon would be.

She stood, gently displacing Einstein's head from her knee, and carried Bradley's boxes to the basement door. She set them down, opened the door, picked them up again, and threw them down the stairs, watching them turn and smash against the steps as they fell.

"Too bad there wasn't anything breakable," she told the dogs, and shut the door.

Then she went back into the living room and studied it. Beautiful. Bradley-less. Un-Bradleyed.

Almost.

His chair still sat in the middle of the room beside the love seat. It was ugly—a recliner upholstered in synthetic olive-green flecked with red. If Bradley had been born a piece of furniture, he would have looked like that chair. Practical, boring, and irritating. The fact that he'd loved it and wouldn't let the dogs on it only made it more Bradley-like. The dogs had been napping on it regularly since he'd gone, but it was still an annoyance.

"What do you think?" Lucy asked the dogs. "Getting rid of a perfectly good chair would be totally irresponsible, right?"

The dogs cocked their heads at her.

"Right. Just think how proud of us Tina will be." Lucy opened the basement door. Then she pushed the chair to the doorway, shooing Maxwell away just in time, and shoved the chair down the stairs. Halfway down, it hit the stair rail and broke through it, tumbling over the side of the steps to smash on the concrete below in a small cloud of dust.

"Independence Day," Lucy said, and slammed the door.

4

"So then she said, 'You mean that hood is following my sister?' and tried to take off after you," Anthony told Zack an hour later. They were back in the squad room, their feet propped up on their desks in the thin warmth of the dusty late-afternoon sunlight that filtered through the dirty windows. "I almost let her have you. I was hoping she'd rip that damn jacket off you and shred it. But then I remembered you were my partner, and I saved you."

"Thank you." Zack was stretched out in his desk chair, feeling every bruise that Lucy had given him that afternoon. "I gather she did finally talk to you?"

"Of course."

"There's no 'Of course' about it," Zack said. "Lucy told me about her sister. You're lucky you're still in one piece."

"We had coffee in the diner." Anthony stretched and put his hands behind his head. "She was no problem at all."

"You get the mean one, and she drinks coffee from your hand. I get the nice one, and she tries to beat the tar out of me. God, to have your luck."

"It's not luck. It's charm," Anthony said. "You don't have any."

Zack gave up. "So what does Tina Savage know about Bradley Porter?"

"That he's a womanizing, weak-kneed, slime-covered scum who made her sister cry, so he should be shot, strangled, drawn, quartered, and castrated. I don't think she likes him at all."

Zack scowled. "He made Lucy cry? I'm with her, then."

"But the problem is . . ."

"He's not our Bradley." Zack nodded. "I know. Lucy explained that. I'd hoped for a while there was a chance he might be, but she says it's no-go."

"I know," Anthony said. "But I floated the possibility by the sister anyway, just to see what she'd say."

"And?"

Anthony grinned. "Oh, she's in favor of it. The thought of Bradley in jail for bigamy, embezzlement and tax fraud perked her right up. She was completely cordial by the time she'd thought it through." Anthony shook his head. "This is a waste of time, Zack. Granted somebody shot at you today, that still doesn't necessarily tie Lucy Savage's Bradley Porter with our John Bradley."

Zack scowled. "He's not Lucy's Bradley. He's nobody's Bradley, the rat. And there's got to be a tie. Come on, Tony. We get a tip that John Bradley's going to be at the diner, and Bradley Porter asks Lucy to meet him there on the same day? That's too much of a coincidence."

"Maybe." Anthony leaned back. "I'm not convinced."

Zack stared at the ceiling while he thought. "So what have we got? We've got John Bradley somewhere in the city with a million and a half in embezzled government bonds. We've got Bradley Porter somewhere in the city with an unidentified blonde. We've got an unidentified female caller who tips us that John Bradley will be at the diner. We've got Bradley Porter's letter to Lucy telling her to meet him at the diner, or we will have as soon as she remembers what she did with it. And we've got somebody shooting at Lucy."

"Or you," Anthony put in. "Don't underestimate your unpopularity."

"Or me," Zack amended. "Hell of a coincidence, though, to get shot at when Lucy's right beside me. So what have we got?"

"We have nothing."

"The two Bradleys have got to be in it together," Zack said.

"I suppose it's remotely possible," Anthony said. "If Bradley Porter is keeping a blonde on the side, he could probably use a couple of government bonds. But it's hard to believe that John Bradley would steal the bonds in California and then come clear out here to share with Bradley Porter out of the goodness of his heart."

"Blackmail?"

"Let's not make this any more complicated than it already is. Here's a good question. Why would somebody try to shoot Lucy?"

"Bradley's mad at her about the divorce," Zack said.

"So he shoots at her on the street? I don't think so."

"Here's a better one. Why is somebody trying to break into Lucy's house?"

Anthony jerked his head up, suddenly interested. "Somebody's trying to break into her house?"

"There are scratches on her locks, and the next-door neighbor saw somebody sneaking around the house. Granted, the next-door neighbor is not totally wired, but even so, if she says she saw somebody, I bet she did."

"You interviewed the next-door neighbor?"

"No." Zack looked pained. "She won't talk to me. She thinks I'm a punk. I had the patrolman ask her."

"A punk. That's not so bad." Anthony grinned at him. "At least punks are young."

"Thank you."

"So you think somebody's trying to break in to get Lucy?" Anthony shook his head. "That doesn't make sense. There are a hundred easier ways to grab somebody than breaking into a house. Hell, you grabbed her on the street today." Anthony looked at Zack's lip. "Well, it might not be that easy. She does seem to have a fairly healthy sense of self-preservation."

Zack gave him a dirty look. "I was trying not to hurt her. If I'd wanted her, I'd have had her. Hell, anybody could have grabbed her."

"So they're breaking in for something else." Anthony leaned back in his chair. "Like to get a million and a half in government bonds that John Bradley gave to Bradley Porter who put them in the silverware drawer and then forgot to take with him when Lucy kicked him out? I don't think so."

"Wait a minute." Zack swung his chair around and planted his feet back on the floor. "He couldn't get in. Tina put locks on. She wouldn't let him in."

"So he just went meekly away and left a million and a half there? No," Anthony said. "I bow to no one in my respect for Tina Savage's temper, but I'd walk over her in a minute if it meant a million and a half. Particularly a million and a half that could put me away if somebody else found it. Like my ex-wife. No."

"Something's in that house, and the two Bradleys are involved." Zack drummed his fingers on the desk. "I've got to get her out of that house until we find it. Only the dummy won't go."

"Can't she stay with her sister for a while?"

"No. She won't go without Einstein and Heisenburg and Whosis. She won't budge at all." His scowl changed suddenly. "At least I hope she hasn't budged."

"Einstein?" Anthony said, but Zack ignored him to flip through his notebook until he found the page he wanted and then dialed the number he'd found.

"Lucy? This is Zack Warren." He listened for a moment. "I'm fine, thanks. I was just checking to make sure you hadn't gone out." He listened again, looking exasperated. "No, I don't trust you. Because you're a flake, that's why. Now, listen, did Bradley leave any papers behind? He did? Have you looked at them? Great. Did you find any official-looking certificates? No, I'm not patronizing you. Did you find any government bonds? A lot of them. About a hundred of fifty, to be exact. Oh."

He covered the receiver and spoke to Anthony. "She packed up all his stuff. No bonds."

"I gathered that," Anthony said. "Maybe he hid them. Did she check the cookie jar?"

Zack ignored him. "Lucy, do you have a safe anyplace in the house? Any place where you keep your valuables? No?" Zack sighed and tapped his fingers on the desk. "Listen. We're going to have to come over tomorrow and search your place. Yeah, sometime tomorrow. Now, listen to me. *Stay in that house and don't answer the door tonight.* And stay away from the doors and windows. Those lace curtains are a joke. When the lights are on, anybody can see in. Why? *Because I said so.* What do you mean, who do I think I am? I'm the guy who saved your life today. Yes, I did, damn it. What?" He listened to her again, frowning. "I told you, you did not beat me up. Thank you. *Now stay inside that house.* Good night."

He hung up and glared at the phone. "I don't know why I worry about that woman. She could *argue* any attacker to death."

"I thought you were never going to worry about anybody," Anthony said, trying to suppress his grin. "I thought responsibility meant death. And what's with you calling her 'Lucy'? The two of you are on a first-name basis already? What's going on?"

"She has a dog that does a dog joke." Zack rolled his eyes in disgust. "It's the most pathetic thing I've ever seen. She's all alone in that big house with three of the most un-vicious dogs that ever barked. She was married to a rat, and now somebody's taking potshots at her. *Somebody* has to look out for her."

Anthony began to laugh. "Zack, she split your lip and gave you what the doctor calls a minor concussion. He said you should be home in bed. You're talking about a woman who beat you up in an alley."

"She did not . . ."

"All right, all right. So what's the plan? To search the house tomorrow?" Anthony shook his head. "I hate to tell you this, but we've still got paperwork from Jerry this morning to finish. I can put it off for a little while, but not the whole morning. Isn't there some way we can short-circuit this search thing?"

"Yeah," Zack said. "We can go to interview Bradley Porter first and see if we can get him to spill everything he knows. Lucy told me he's a branch manager of a bank out in Gamble Hills. Nobody knows where he's staying right now, but he'll be at work tomorrow. We can start with him first." He stared at the ceiling again. "Actually, I'm really looking forward to meeting him."

Anthony narrowed his eyes. "Why?"

"I want to see what a rat like that looks like. You wouldn't believe what a sweetheart Lucy is."

"A sweetheart?" Anthony grinned. "She beat you up."

"She did not . . ." Zack closed his eyes and gave up. "Forget it. I'm sore. My head hurts. I need a hot bath and a beer. I cannot argue with you anymore. You win. She beat me up."

"When you can't fight, we're definitely finished for the day." Anthony stood. "Want some help getting down to your car, old man?"

"Drop dead," Zack said, and got up carefully, trying not to groan from his bruises.

BEFORE LUCY WENT UP to bed, she found the phone table on its side and the receiver thrown off its hook.

"Did you do this?" she said to Einstein as she righted the table, and he immediately turned and walked away. "Most nights I wouldn't care," she said to his swaying rear end. "But tonight I thought maybe I might actually get another call from him."

Einstein turned his head and looked at her over his shoulder.

"Right," Lucy said. "That is pathetic."

Then she put the phone back on the table and went up to bed.

LUCY GOT UP TO RUN at eight on Friday morning, but she stopped at the front door.

She wasn't supposed to go out. Every muscle in her body wanted to run, but she wasn't supposed to go out.

Zack Warren had forbidden it.

"I don't believe this," she told the dogs. "He just says 'Stay put,' and I stay put. And today was supposed to be the first day of the rest of my independence. If I had any backbone at all . . ."

On the other hand, he said he was coming by to search the house. She had to be home for that. It was her civic duty. Sort of.

Also, she didn't want to miss seeing him again.

She sighed and started to run up the stairs. Three steep flights. About a thousand trips up and down should do it.

But just for today. Tomorrow, she was going out to run like a rational human being, no matter what Zack Warren said.

"HE TOOK TWO WEEKS OFF?" Zack glared at the immaculate matron behind the mahogany manager's desk at Gamble Hills First National. She wore her dark hair styled like a helmet, and she glared back at him militarily through horn-rimmed glasses.

Zack scowled at her. "How can a bank manager take two weeks off?"

"He was getting a divorce." She jerked on the cuffs of her navy polyester suit jacket for emphasis. "He was very disturbed about it. The past two weeks, he couldn't concentrate at all. Mr. Porter was always very efficient, so it wasn't like him. Not at all. We all understood that he needed a little time off."

"We appreciate your help, Mrs. Elmore," Anthony said, trying to reduce the fallout from Zack's scowl. He was rewarded with a slight smile and a nod. "We have just a few more questions and we'll go. We know how busy you must be with Mr. Porter gone. Now, his last day was yesterday?"

"Day before yesterday." Mrs. Elmore lowered her voice. "Yesterday was the Divorce."

"Ah." Anthony smiled at her in sympathy. "This must make a lot of extra work for you."

The woman smoothed her jacket and smiled complacently. "I don't mind. It's the least I can do for the poor man."

"The poor man?" Zack said, thinking of Lucy.

Mrs. Elmore glared at him.

"Zack, why don't you go over there and interview somebody?" Anthony jerked his thumb toward the tellers.

"Fine." As Zack wandered off, he could hear Anthony saying, "That's terrible. Mr. Porter must have been very upset for the past couple of weeks. Did he say anything . . ."

"Hi."

Zack turned around to see a very young, very blond teller smiling at him.

"Can I help you with anything?" Her smile deepened.

"Full service banking?" Zack said and grinned.

"Well, we try to please," she said, dimpling at him. "I'm Deborah."

"So tell me, Deborah." Zack leaned on the ledge across from her and smiled into her eyes. "What's it like to work for Mr. Porter?"

"It's boring," Deborah said. "And I don't talk about my employers."

Zack showed her his badge. "I'm one of the good guys, Deborah. Tell me about Mr. Porter."

"You don't look like a good guy." She smiled at him again.

"Mr. Porter, Deborah. Concentrate. Other than boring, what was he?"

She shrugged. "Nothing. He came in, worked hard, and went home."

"Ever make a pass at you?"

Deborah chortled. "Mr. Porter? Not a chance. He was so crazy about his wife, he didn't even know there were other women on earth."

Zack stopped smiling. "But he just got divorced."

"Oh, that was her idea." Deborah looked around and dropped her voice. "Long overdue, if you ask me. I mean, he would have bored me to death. I met her at the Christmas party. She was really nice. Quiet, but nice. Mr. Porter showed her off like she was something he owned, but he was crazy about her. You could see it. I mean, Evan Hatch just asked her to dance, and he was furious about it. He hasn't spoken to Evan since."

"Evan Hatch?"

Deborah jerked her head to her right and Zack stepped back to look at the teller two windows down. He was about five foot four, a hundred and twenty pounds, and bald.

Zack frowned at Deborah. "Porter was jealous of him?"

"He was jealous of everybody. I told you. He was crazy about her."

Zack tried again. "I thought I heard the divorce was because he'd had an affair."

"No way," Deborah said. "It was his wife and nobody else. And listen, he had his chances. I mean, have you ever seen him?"

Zack shook his head.

"Check out his picture. It's over there." Deborah nodded her head in the direction of the big glass doors. "He's really great looking. Believe me, a lot of women were interested." She cocked her head. "Not me. I like my men a little rougher, not as handsome, if you know what I mean." She smiled at Zack again.

"And I even shaved," Zack said.

"What?"

"Nothing. So aside from being boring, he was the perfect boss?"

"Well, he was a nitpicker." Deborah made a face. "But we got used to it. And then about two weeks ago, he really let up and stopped watching us all the time. It would have been really nice, except he was so grumpy. That's when Mrs. Elmore came around and told us about the divorce. She said we should be understanding."

Zack squinted back at Mrs. Elmore. "She doesn't look like the understanding type."

"She's not," Deborah said. "Unless it's Mr. Porter."

"Oh."

"The divorce may have depressed Mr. Porter, but it cheered Mrs. Elmore right up. When he comes back, he's not going to have a chance."

"Maybe I won't arrest him then." Zack gazed over his shoulder at Mrs. Elmore. "That could be punishment enough."

Deborah's mouth dropped open. "You're going to arrest him?"

"No." Zack turned back hastily. "That's a little police humor. Very little. Did you notice anything else different about Mr. Porter lately? Besides the grumpiness?"

"Nope. The grumpiness was it."

"Okay, listen. Here's my card." Zack handed it over. "If you think of anything else, call me, please."

"Anything?" Deborah batted her eyelashes at him.

"Anything about Mr. Porter. You should be ashamed of yourself, trying to pick up a cop on duty."

"Don't you ever get off duty?"

"No. I live for my work." Zack turned to see Anthony waiting patiently by the door. "Well, I've got to go, my driver is waiting. Thanks, Deborah. You were a great help."

"Anytime," Deborah said. "Really."

On his way out the door, Zack stopped by the gallery of employee portraits that Gamble Hills First National had assembled to give the customers a nice feeling of family as they parted from their money. Among the dozen or so faces, Deborah dimpled, and Mrs. Elmore grimaced and, at the very top like the Big Daddy of banking, Bradley Porter stared down and was not amused.

He was classically handsome—thick wavy blond hair, a straight Roman nose, a chiseled chin with a hint of a cleft, and the coldest grey eyes Zack had ever seen.

What the hell had Lucy been thinking of to marry this . . . this . . . *fish?*

"Zack?" Anthony called from just inside the door. "You ready?"

She needed a keeper. Not him, of course, but still . . .

"Zack?"

"Yeah." Zack followed him out to the car.

"Another blonde?" Anthony said when Zack got in the car beside him. "Is this a trend for you?"

"Blonde?"

"The teller."

"Deborah? No. Blondes are too dangerous. I'm only interested in brunettes. Like Mrs. Elmore. Drive and tell me all about her undying passion for Bradley Porter. And then tell me what motel she's been meeting him at so we can go get him."

Anthony put the car into gear and pulled out of the parking lot. "We can't go get him. He's in Kentucky."

"Kentucky?" Zack scowled at him as if it were his fault. "What the hell is he doing in Kentucky when we want him here?"

"Communing with nature to heal his tortured soul. Or something like that. He's brokenhearted. His wife, who is cold and unfeeling, did not understand him."

"He said that? The rat. Drive to Kentucky."

"I don't think so. We have reports to fill out. And we do not have any conclusive link between our Bradley and Lucy's Bradley."

"He's not Lucy's Bradley." Zack tapped his fingers on the window edge. "I tell you what. Let's search the house. We'll find the link. Trust me on this one. I've got . . ."

"Reports to fill out," Anthony said.

"Oh, hell," Zack said.

THE SHOWER FELT wonderful.

The hot water stung Lucy's body and made her skin tingle, which made her think of Zack, which made her tingle more.

It was ridiculous. He'd mugged her in an alley, then he'd argued with her in her living room, and now she couldn't stop thinking about him. It was particularly ridiculous to be looking forward to seeing him again. Of course, that was mostly because he was coming to search her house, and when he didn't find anything, then he'd have to admit that he was wrong and she was right, and that the only criminal thing Bradley had ever done was bring that blonde into her house.

Lucy tested herself for pain on the last thought. Did that hurt anymore? Maybe it never had. Maybe the emotion she'd felt was more repressed rage that Bradley had brought that woman into her house. She was going to have stop repressing her rage.

She definitely wasn't feeling any pain over Bradley's blonde anymore.

And she'd lost the feeling she'd had that the house had been contaminated. That really went when she threw Bradley's chair down the stairs. That had been a wonderful moment. For just a moment, she'd felt totally out of control.

Like Zack.

Zack. What did she see in him? The man was a patronizing maniac who thought he had a hot line to the universe. Trust his instincts. Ha, as Mrs. Dover would say.

Well, sort of ha.

Actually, she was willing to bet that he had great instincts for some things. In fact, she was willing to bet that he had better instincts than she'd ever had. She was willing to bet...

Lucy stuck her head directly under the water from the showerhead, trying to wash Zack out of her mind.

Think about something else. Think about anything else.

Well, there was exercise. Like running the stairs instead of the road because some maniac with incredible instincts . . .

Try again.

Running the stairs was terrific for your heart, but murder on your quadriceps. Lucy glanced down to look at hers only to stop, horrified, all thoughts of Zack gone, as she stared at the water as it swirled into the drain.

It was black. The blackest water she'd ever seen.

Which meant her hair wasn't anymore.

"Oh, no," she moaned and leaned her head against the shower wall.

It left a big black smudge when she stood straight again.

Five minutes later, her body wrapped in a full-length white terry-cloth robe and her head in a terry-cloth towel, Lucy stood in front of her bedroom mirror and prayed. Then she took a deep breath, pulled the towel off her head, and stared at her hair in the mirror.

It was a strange color, like very bad moss; a sort of intensely dull, dark grey-green that absorbed all the light and energy around it.

"My hair has turned into a black hole," she said to the mirror. "Complete absence of light." She looked down at the towel. It was covered with black smudges. "How long before this washes out of my hair? How long before I'm a horrible blonde again?"

As she stared at herself, a new and even more horrible possibility hit her.

How long before it *falls* out?

Einstein waddled into the bedroom and stopped to stare.

"Independence is not working out for me," Lucy told him.

"THE LAB REPORT IS IN," Zack said when he joined Anthony back in the squad room. "The brick wall did not help the bullet at all." He tossed the report to Anthony who was typing a report of his own. "As always, Patricia will be glad to hazard an unofficial guess if we ever find another .38 to match, but she says no way will we ever have anything to take to court based on the bullet from the wall."

Anthony shoved the report out of the way so he could go back to typing. "So we have nothing."

"Not exactly. We have Lucy." Zack sat on the edge of his desk. "And Lucy's house, which we're going to have to search now that we can't find Bradley the rat. I need to talk to Lucy again anyway."

"Is this an instinct?" Anthony hit the return carriage.

"Oh, yeah. Definitely. I have a real instinct about Lucy Savage."

"So now the only question is, What kind of instinct?" Anthony grinned while he typed.

"What?" Zack looked confused and then caught his drift. "Oh, no. Not a chance. I can't even imagine her naked."

"What?" Anthony stopped typing and started to laugh. "I don't believe it. You were the one who once described Queen Elizabeth naked."

"That was in college."

"Yeah, but I've never forgotten it." Anthony shook his head to clear it of the image. "So now you've lost the ability to imagine women naked? That's a bad sign, Zack." He turned back to find his place in his report.

"I haven't lost anything," Zack snapped. "And it's just with Lucy. It's her fault. She's just not that kind of woman."

"And Queen Elizabeth is? I don't think so. I think you're attracted to her. You respect her. This could be it. Love. Marriage." Anthony paused. "Maturity."

"Don't be juvenile. Did you try those phone numbers that Elmore gave you for Porter? The motel in Kentucky and the one for the place where he's been staying here in town?"

"Just a couple of minutes ago. He has a room in Kentucky, but he's not answering. The one here is a hotel in Overlook. The room is rented to a guy named John Beulah. And the phone is busy."

Zack frowned. "What would Bradley Porter be doing registered under an assumed name in a hotel in Overlook?"

"Saving money? It's definitely the lowest of the low-rent districts."

"Well, then, that's our next move." Zack stood. "Let's check out the hotel right away before whoever it is gets off the phone. I love Overlook. It always makes me feel like a real cop—paranoid."

"I have to finish this first." Anthony frowned as he typed. "It's almost done. Patience."

"And after the hotel, we can hit Lucy's place," Zack said. "I think we're making progress." He started to pace. "Could you hurry up? We've got things to do here. I want to get to Lucy's before lunch."

"Just a minute. Just one minute. Amuse yourself." Anthony's phone rang and he answered, "Taylor, Property Crimes." Then he looked grim, and said, "Right away," and hung up. "We have a gunshot victim. Female."

Zack's heart stopped for a moment. "Not Lucy. Tell me I didn't leave her alone for some creep to—"

"Not Lucy. Not unless she went blond again and checked into a hotel in Overlook."

Zack shook his head, relieved. "No. Not a chance. The dogs wouldn't like Overlook." Then he stopped. "Overlook? It can't be."

Anthony nodded. "Same room number as our rat Bradley. After I called, the desk clerk went up to check and found her unconscious, still clutching the phone. He called the rescue squad, and she's on her way to Emergency now."

"I'll be damned. He's shacked up with the blonde in the slums, and then he shoots her and leaves for Kentucky? This makes no sense. Wait. How did they know this was our problem?"

"Because they found your name and phone number on a paper in her purse. Detective Warren. Property Crimes. And you'll love this part . . ." Anthony paused for suspense.

"Come on, come on."

"Shot with a .38."

Zack smacked his hand on the desk. "She's our phone tip. John Bradley found out, shot at us on the street, and then went back and shot her. So where is Bradley Porter in this? This makes no sense, but at least it's a connection between Bradley Porter and crime. Let's go."

"What about Lucy? Aren't you going to call her?"

"And tell her what?" Zack grabbed his jacket. "She'll keep. Let's go."

"What did you do, hypnotize this woman?" Anthony said, but he picked up his jacket and followed him out the door.

IT WAS EARLY AFTERNOON when Lucy's phone finally rang.

"Hello?" she answered, trying to sound nonchalant.

"You didn't call me last night," Tina said. "I got your message on the machine and called you back, but all I got was a busy signal. What happened?"

"I forgot," Lucy said, trying not to feel disappointed. She curled up in her blue overstuffed chair. "And the busy signal was Einstein. He knocked the phone table over."

"Why you don't have everything bolted to the floor in that place is beyond me. If you must live with a herd of animals, you should be prepared. Anyway, tell me about the mugger. You really beat one up? That's terrific!"

"Well, sort of."

"You only 'sort of' beat him up?"

"No, it's only sort of terrific. I really beat him up. His lip looked awful. Of course, he keeps swearing that I didn't beat him up—"

"You talked to this creep? That means the police got him. Good!"

"Well, in a manner of speaking. I sent some policemen after him, but I didn't realize what had happened until he showed up at my door—"

"Who?" Tina asked, confused.

"Zack. He . . ."

"Who's Zack?"

"The guy in the alley," Lucy said, and Tina groaned.

"And now you're on a first-name basis with him and you won't press charges because he's told you about his horrible childhooood in reform school. Lucy, you are too damn nice!"

"Not exactly—"

"Forget it. I'm coming over, and we're going to the police and get this Zack character sent up the river for life. I know a cop now. That suit in the diner yesterday turned out to have a badge. You stay there. I'll call him and Benton."

Lucy sat up straighter and clutched the phone. "No, Tina—"

"Do you think the police will be able to find him?"

"Probably. He works for them."

There was a short silence. "What?" Tina said finally.

"He's a cop," Lucy said.

"You beat up a cop?"

"That depends on who you talk to. From my point of view, yes. From Zack's, no."

"Zack."

"Zack Warren. Detective Zachary Warren." Lucy relaxed into her chair again. "He has blue eyes. You remember. He was the black leather in the restaurant yesterday."

"Don't do this," Tina said.

"What?"

"We've got to talk. Meet me for lunch at the Maisonette."

"I can't. Zack told me not to leave."

"What? He just told you . . ."

"He thinks somebody's trying to kill me."

There was another silence.

"Stay there," Tina said finally. "I'm coming over with Chinese takeout, and you are going to tell me everything."

"All right," Lucy said. "But I better warn you. My hair is . . . different."

"Different," Tina said. "I can't wait."

"SHE'S UNCONSCIOUS." Zack slumped, defeated, in a plastic chair outside the hospital-room door. "Of course, she's unconscious. She's been bleeding into the carpet for hours. No ID. Nothing. This is making me crazy."

"You were already crazy." Anthony checked his watch. "Come on, we have things to do. The desk clerk just identified John Bradley as the man who used the room. We have to get a picture of Bradley Porter to him, too."

Zack stared into space. "Bradley. Rat Bradley. I wonder where he is now?"

"Well, not back at the hotel. Let's go check out the room. Forensics hasn't found anything so far, but maybe . . ."

"I really want to arrest him," Zack said. "Attempted murder is as good a reason as any."

"Better than most," Anthony agreed. "Now move. We need to get started on this. It's looking like it will take us the rest of the day and most of the night, as it is."

"Rat Bradley," Zack said, and Anthony gave up and pulled him to his feet and out the door.

TINA BROUGHT HER A baseball bat.

"Thank you." Lucy looked at it doubtfully. "You haven't signed me up for intramurals or anything, have you?"

"Of course not. It's February. It's for your protection."

Tina marched through the living room and dining room and into the kitchen, while Lucy trailed behind her with the bat. She dumped two bags of Chinese food on the kitchen table, and then took the bat from Lucy and propped it by the back door. "If anybody tries to break in here, you hit him with this. Hard."

"Tina, nobody is trying to kill me. That's Zack's fantasy, not reality."

"Tell me about it." Tina opened the first carton of food.

AN HOUR LATER, SHE WAS still curious. "So he really thinks somebody was shooting at you?" she said as she polished off her Mu Shu pork.

"Yes. Isn't that the dumbest thing you've ever heard?"

Tina thought about it. "No. Not if there were marks on the locks, too. He's right. You stay inside."

Lucy shoved her plate away, exasperated. "What is it with you two? I don't even talk to my dogs the way you two talk to me."

"Well, you should," Tina glared at Einstein who was eyeing the Mu Shu pork carton. "They'd have better manners. So what's Zack like?"

"Erratic. Quick temper. Never still. Gorgeous blue eyes. Very short attention span. Not my type at all." She stopped and then added primly, "Although I have had some inappropritate thoughts about him. Very inappropriate. Not that I'll ever do anything about it. Still, the dogs like him." She pulled her plate back and scooped up some garlic chicken while she contemplated Zack. "He's sort of bossy, but I like him."

Tina grinned. "Imagine my surprise. I've changed my mind. I think you should do something about it."

"About what?"

"About this thing you have for Zack."

Lucy shook her head. "Not a chance. My hair alone would send any sane man screaming into the street."

Tina looked at Lucy's moss-colored hair. It made her look like a wood nymph from the wrong side of the woods. "Maybe if you wear a lot of forest green. Maybe he's a Tolkien fan."

"Maybe I'll kill myself," Lucy said.

"Don't be ridiculous," Tina said. "I brought Häagen-Dazs. Triple Brownie Overload."

"Maybe I'll live," Lucy said.

WHEN TINA FINALLY LEFT Lucy's house at eleven, Zack still hadn't called.

It was for the best, Lucy knew. After all, she'd just gotten divorced. After all, he was too much of a loose screw to ever be good for her.

After all, her hair looked like a bad carpet.

"Tomorrow is another day," she told the dogs. "And it's the first day of the rest of my independence. The heck with Zack Warren. The heck with all men. It's easier to be independent without them anyway."

The dogs looked skeptical.

"Oh, forget it," Lucy said. "Let's go to bed."

"OF COURSE, IT WON'T GO into court," Anthony said at eight the next morning as he hung up the phone. "But Patricia and the lab send you their best wishes and the considered opinion that the bullet from the blonde is a match for the bullet that missed you."

"I think it's time we talked to Lucy." Zack picked up the phone and dialed. "I was going over there later today, anyway."

"That explains why you shaved two days in a row. We're all grateful."

Zack ignored him. "Come on, pick it up," he said into the phone. "I told you not to answer the *door*. It's okay to pick up the phone." But after the twelfth ring, his annoyance faded and turned to cold fear. "She's not answering."

Anthony grabbed his jacket. "Let's go. Looks like she opened the door, after all."

5

LUCY TRIED TO RUN OFF her anger in the cold Saturday-morning light. After all, it was a waste of time to be angry with a man because he didn't call or come over when he said he was going to. Men never did.

Especially men like Zack, who ran around one minute shouting, "Somebody's trying to kill you," and the next minute forgot you existed. If he was so worried about her being killed, why hadn't he called all day yesterday? Him and his instincts. As Mrs. Dover would say, Ha.

She turned to jog back down her street, and when she looked up at her own house, Zack was on the front porch.

Her first thought was that he was even more magnetic than she'd remembered him. He seemed, even from a distance, to be vibrating with energy.

Her second was that her hair was probably even stranger in the daylight than it was in artificial light.

Her third, when she got closer, was that he wasn't vibrating with energy, he was vibrating with anger. Well, the heck with him. So what if he was angry. So was she. He hadn't called. He'd just left her there like a potted plant, and he hadn't called. Who did he think he was? Who the *heck* did he think he was?

Yeah.

He came to meet her as she walked up the steps, and he looked wonderful—tall, dark, and enraged.

"You shaved." She was still breathless from running. "And your lip looks much better. You look much more reliable."

"Reliable? Me? What about you?" Zack stabbed his finger at her. "I told you to stay put!"

"Listen." Lucy tried to keep an edge on her anger. It was hard because she really was glad to see him, and he really was gorgeous. She put her hands on her hips and concentrated. "Listen, you. You told me it was for one night and then you'd call. You didn't call. Which isn't surprising because you're a man, and men never call, but still, in this situation, you would think . . ."

"I've been out of my mind with worry about you," Zack said through his teeth. "I had you pictured dead in a pool of blood in front of the fireplace. And now you show up alive, and I want to kill you myself."

"And anyway, who do you think you are, saying 'Stay put' like I'm some . . . I don't know . . . trained dog, or something."

"I thought you were *dead*." Zack grabbed her arm. "I thought somebody had grabbed you. I thought I was going to have to raise your damn dogs. . . ."

"Why would you have to raise my dogs? I just needed exercise." Lucy tried to tug away from him. "I ran two miles. Big deal. Let go of me."

"My partner is next door right now, calling for help to look for your body." Zack tightened his grip. "I'm so damn mad at you. . . . Just . . . *get in that house.*"

"*Now wait just a minute!*" Lucy began, but then she stopped, distracted by the streak of yellow that blurred past her feet. "Look out, Phoebe's loose again."

In an instant, the cat had raced across the lawn and dived into the window of Lucy's car.

"No!" Lucy jerked free from Zack. "That's it. That's the last straw." She started across the lawn to the car, and Zack grabbed her sweatshirt and yanked her to the cold ground, falling on her as he rolled them both down the hill into Mrs. Dover's driveway.

They landed with a thud, Lucy on the bottom, and all the breath went out of her lungs as Zack fell on top of her. "Hey," she said, but all that came out was a whisper.

He was covering her with his body, one hand braced over her head, listening for something. He looked exactly the same as he had the day he'd flung her into the alley—the same anvil jaw, only clean-shaven now, cocked away from her at the same angle while he tensed against her.

Just like in the alley.

Lucy stopped trying to shove him off and clutched at his arms. "Zack? Was somebody shooting at you again?"

He looked down at her, focused and sharp. "I thought you said you always rolled your car windows up. Because of Phoebe."

"I do . . ." Lucy began and stopped, distracted by the realization of how warm he was on top of her. "Uh, Zack . . ."

"They're down now. Phoebe jumped in."

"Big deal." Lucy tried to shift his weight off her without enjoying it. "Maybe I forgot. You're squashing me. Get off."

"They were up when I left day before yesterday. It's February, for crying out loud. And you haven't been in the car since, right?"

Zack was almost nose-to-nose with her, his electric blue eyes staring down into her brown ones, his hand cradling her face, the weight of his body stretched warmly along the whole length of hers, and she lost the thread of her argument in the heat she was feeling everywhere. It was so unfair. He was gorgeous, he was on top of her, and he was asking her questions about a cat. She might have to kill herself, after all.

"Zack." She pushed gently at him. "Nothing is happening here. There are no gunshots. Get off me."

She stopped when her eyes connected with his. She could feel him relax against her as his attention shifted from the car to her.

"I wouldn't exactly say nothing is happening." Zack smiled down at her.

"Well, nobody's trying to kill me," Lucy said, trying to sound reasonably calm. "Get off."

"So you're telling me I overreacted." The warmth in his eyes went to her bones, and she swallowed hard.

"I know." Lucy tried to keep her tone cool while she melted under him. "You couldn't help yourself. It was an instinct. I forgive you. Now, get off me."

He raised himself up on one elbow and flicked one of her curls with his finger. "You know, in this light, your hair looks sort of ... green."

"*Get off me now!*" she said, and Mrs. Dover came onto her front porch and screamed, "*Perverts!*" at them, and Phoebe raced across Zack's back using every claw she had for traction, and Zack yelled in pain.

And the car blew up.

"Zack!" Lucy threw her arms around him and pulled him down to her, and Mrs. Dover screamed again and fell backward into her house, and Phoebe hit high C and disappeared under the porch.

After a moment of silence, Zack raised his shoulders off Lucy and gazed cautiously over the hill at her burning car.

"Nice little bomb," he said reflectively. "Very neat."

Lucy eased the top of her body up, too, still under him, and watched the flames, horrified. He looked down at her, and when she turned back they were nose-to-nose.

"You okay?"

"Zack," Lucy said. "Somebody's trying to kill me."

"You know," Zack said, "I had an instinct about that."

"OKAY," ZACK SAID HALF an hour later from where he stood in front of the fireplace. "One more time. How long were you gone?"

Lucy leaned back against the love seat. "I told you. I just ran two miles. Fifteen, maybe twenty minutes. I didn't check the clock when I left."

"That's not enough time." Anthony had been sitting between them in an overstuffed armchair for the past half-hour, his head swiveling back and forth like a referee's at a tennis match, and he was tired of it. "In broad daylight, with a delayed fuse? And no one saw him? Face it, Zack. It doesn't matter when she ran. He must have set this up last night." He turned back to Lucy. "Do you remember if the windows were up or down when you left to run?"

"Zack already asked me that. I didn't pay any attention. I didn't even notice the windows when I came back until Phoebe jumped inside the car." She stopped again. "That was such a nice car. It's totaled, right?"

Zack smacked his hand on the mantel from exasperation. "Lucy, you dummy, this was a bomb, not a rear-end collision!"

Lucy looked back at him, just as exasperated. "Well, it's totally destroyed, right? Which means it's totaled, right? What are you so mad at me for? And don't call me a dummy, either, you . . . you . . ." She blinked.

"Listen, lady . . ." Zack began, stabbing his finger at her.

"Okay, children, that's enough," Anthony said. "Fight on your own time. We've got a serious problem here."

"I'm sorry," Lucy said to him. "I'm usually not this rude. It's just Zack. He brings out the worst in me."

"That's good to know," Zack said. "I'd hate to think this was your best."

"I beg your pardon," Lucy said.

"Zack, shut up." Anthony turned to Lucy and smiled. It was a great smile, his sure-you-can-trust-me smile, and Lucy smiled back.

Zack glowered at both of them.

"Now look, Lucy," Anthony went on. "I know Zack didn't call you, and that was wrong." Zack started to say something, and Anthony shot him a warning glance that was pure venom. Zack shut up, and Anthony returned to his persuasion. "That won't happen again. I promise. The important thing is that now that we know for sure that somebody is trying to hurt you, we have to get serious about this. What we'd like to do—with your permission, of course—is put you in a hotel...."

"No," Lucy said.

"I told you so." Zack looked at Lucy. "You're either going to a hotel or to your sister's and that's that. No arguments. Get your stuff."

"No," Lucy said.

"I'll look after the dogs," Zack said. "Get your stuff."

"You won't remember," Lucy said.

"Of course, I'll remember. Get your stuff."

"Like you remembered to call me? No."

"Lucy!" Zack loomed over her.

"Forget it. I'm not leaving my dogs." She turned to Anthony. "How long would I be in this hotel? Two days? A week? A month?"

"I don't know," he said. "I think we can solve this within the week, but I can't promise you."

Lucy shook her head. "I can't leave them. They wouldn't understand. And what if this man decides to get me by burning the house down? They trust me to take care of them. I'm not stupid. I know I'm in danger, and I'm scared, but I'm not leaving them."

"Then we'll have to put somebody here with you," Anthony said.

"No," Zack said.

"Fine," Lucy said.

"We're shorthanded." Anthony stood. "I think I can get Sergeant Eliot—"

"Are you crazy?" Zack said. "Eliot is sixty-four, legally blind, and waiting for retirement. Lucy would have to protect him."

"Your other choice is Matthews," Anthony said. "And we'll have the patrol cars keep an eye—"

"Who's Matthews?" Zack asked.

"The tall blond one you keep calling Junior," Anthony said. "Stop doing that, by the way. It annoys him. Anyway, he's young, strong, and he's got 20/20 vision. Happy?"

"No." Zack searched for a good reason why. "He's young. He's new. He doesn't know . . ."

"Great," Anthony said, a savage edge creeping into his voice. "You want somebody not too old, not too young, who knows. That leaves us with a middle-aged cop with experience. The only one of those available is you. Are you volunteering?"

Zack looked first at Lucy and then at Anthony, and said, "Yes. Watch her while I go get my stuff. And by the way, I am *not* middle-aged."

"What?" Lucy said.

"You're kidding," Anthony said. "I thought you were hot on the trail of Bradley the embezzler."

"I think the trail's here. When I get back, we're going to search this place."

"I thought you needed a warrant for that," Lucy said.

"Not if the home owner gives us permission." Anthony tried to signal Zack to shut up, with no success.

"And you're going to give us permission because I just saved your life," Zack said.

"You did not . . ." Lucy began. "Oh. I guess you did."

"Right. Remember that." Zack turned back to Anthony. "I'll be back in half an hour. Watch her every minute so she doesn't leave again. She has no survival instincts."

And then he was gone.

Lucy bit her lip and looked over at Anthony. "I'm not stupid. I just didn't believe him when he said somebody was trying to kill me."

Anthony smiled down at her. "That's all right. I didn't, either. It's the most annoying thing I know about Zack. He makes these stupid assumptions, and then he turns out to be right. Fortunately, he's also a great guy. You just have to get used to him."

"Oh, I could get used to him," Lucy said, and Anthony heard a note of wistful enthusiasm in her voice. *Well, this is interesting,* he thought, and he sank back down into the big soft chair again as she went on. "I just don't know why he's always grabbing me and yelling at me. I'm a very calm, logical, unemotional person. It really isn't necessary."

Right. That's why you were spitting at him. Calm and unemotional, my eye. But all Anthony said was, "He worries about you."

Lucy blinked.

That is also interesting. I wonder if Zack has noticed that she blinks every time she thinks of something she can't say aloud. I bet he has.

I bet he's noticed just about everything about her.

"He didn't even call yesterday," Lucy went on. "He forgot me. He put me in this house, and then he forgot me."

Anthony shook his head. "No, he didn't. We had some problems yesterday. Big ones. A woman was shot." He watched her closely as she flinched at the news.

"That's awful."

"It was. It's the only time I've ever seen Zack look worried."

"Why?"

"He thought it was you."

"Oh." Lucy blinked again.

Bingo. She was a darling, and she liked Zack. If he moved in with her for a month, he'd be a goner, and Anthony could stop worrying about him. It was perfect, although he might have to start hiding evidence to keep Zack there for that long.

Now all he had to do was convince Lucy.

"You know, Zack really needs to solve this case," Anthony said. "He's been depressed lately, even thinking about quitting the force. If he could just relax a little, it would do him a world of good. Moving in with you for a while may be just the thing he needs. A calm, secure environment to grow up in."

Lucy grinned. "You make him sound like a foster child."

"That's pretty much the way I think of him. And by the way, I know he's obnoxious, but please don't hit him again. He's still got a concussion from the last time."

"He does?" Lucy said, appalled. "He told me he wasn't hurt."

"Well, he thinks he's Superman. Take care of him."

Lucy looked at him suspiciously on his last remark, but he smiled back at her, as artless and open as the sun, and finally, she smiled, too.

"All right," she said.

Anthony's smile widened.

All right.

ZACK DUMPED HIS BAG on the quilt-covered spool bed in the attic bedroom. The ceiling was slung low and canted under the eaves, the wallpaper was scattered with tiny yellow flowers, and the little windows at the end of the room were patterned with diamond panes. "This is a great room," he told Lucy, who'd followed him up the stairs. "If you had any sense, you'd be sleeping up here."

Lucy took an extra blanket from the closet and draped it over the end of the bed. "I know. I wanted to put our bedroom up here, but Bradley said the one downstairs was bigger."

Zack felt the same spurt of annoyance he was beginning to feel every time Lucy mentioned Bradley in the same breath with herself. "Why'd you listen to him?"

"Well, it was going to be his bedroom, too," Lucy said, and Zack felt really annoyed.

He opened a drawer, unzipped his bag, and upended it into the drawer to unpack it. "Bradley is an idiot."

Lucy shrugged. "Not really. It is warmer downstairs. You have to leave the door to the stairs open at night or this place gets really cold."

Zack stopped trying to shove everything into the drawer. "How do you know?"

"I started sleeping up here in October. Bradley and I...had a disagreement."

"Good for you." Zack felt much better, and then he felt like a fool for feeling much better. Aside from that flash of lust he'd given in to in the driveway, he had no interest in this woman besides a passing sense of responsibility. All he had to do was find out what was in her damn house, get rid of it, and possibly arrest her ex-husband for attempted murder. Then he'd never have to see her again.

As long as he remembered to stay out of driveways with her.

Lucy brushed against his arm as she moved beside him to spread his shirts evenly into the drawer. She smelled faintly of flowers and warmth.

Never seeing her again suddenly didn't have much appeal.

He left the drawer open and stepped away from her. "Let's start searching this place. Where's the best place to start?"

"I threw all of Bradley's stuff into the basement," Lucy said, shoving the drawer closed. "You probably want that first."

"Threw? Literally?"

"I stood at the top of the stairs and pitched it. It felt wonderful."

Zack grinned at her suddenly, and Lucy looked startled. "I thought you were mad at me."

"Naw. I just thought you were dead, and it threw me for a minute."

"A minute?" Lucy said. "That's all?"

"Well, then you showed up and the car exploded. I haven't had much time to dwell on things lately." Zack took her shoulders and turned her toward the stairs. "C'mon. Let's go to the basement, so I can solve this case, and you can get rid of me."

Well, let's not hurry, Lucy thought, but she went downstairs with him anyway.

ZACK WHISTLED WHEN HE saw the wreckage at the bottom of the stairs. "Boy, you weren't kidding."

"I'll pick it up." Lucy started past him, and he grabbed her arm.

"Look out. The stair rail's gone."

"I know. The chair fell through it."

"The chair?"

"The chair I shoved down here." Lucy peered cautiously over the broken rail. "See? It sort of rolled to the right, back there."

"You threw a chair down these stairs?"

"I felt like it. Are we going down there or not?"

"Stay close to the wall, behind me." Zack went down the stairs. "Don't fall over the edge, or I'll be picking splinters out of you for a week."

Lucy put her hands on her hips and glared at him. "You know, I'm not helpless."

Zack ignored her. He dragged the smashed cartons into the middle of the basement and shoved the chair upright. "Nice chair."

"No, it's not." Lucy followed him down the stairs cautiously. "It's ugly."

"That's just the upholstery. Cover that up and it's a good chair."

"It's too big."

"It's a man's chair." Zack deepened his voice. "A manly chair for a manly man."

"It was Bradley's."

Zack shrugged. "Okay, so it's not that great. Are these all the boxes?"

"Just those three. And there's nothing in them. I packed them up so I know. Just papers and junk."

"Papers? I love papers. Do these papers have numbers on them?" Zack sat down on the floor next to the first box and pried at the layers of tape that sealed it. "Did you seal these for life? There must be twenty pounds of tape here."

"I was a little enthusiastic." Lucy turned back to the stairs. "Let me get a knife."

"Good. Get me a beer while you're at it."

Lucy stopped halfway up the stairs. "I don't have any beer."

"Yes, you do. It's in your refrigerator. I put it there myself. Can you cook Mexican?"

"I suppose," Lucy said coldly. "Why?"

"I got some stuff when I picked up the beer on the way here. Nachos, olives, cheese, that kind of stuff." Zack continued to poke at the box while he spoke, missing Lucy's frown. "I figured you could cook. You look like the type. Could I have that knife, please?"

Right between your ribs, Lucy thought and blinked. Then she turned and went upstairs to get him his knife and beer.

TWO HOURS LATER, THEY'D looked at every piece of paper and book in Bradley's boxes and hadn't found a clue.

"Half of this stuff is years old," Zack groaned. He sat on the floor by the stairs and stared at the mess. "Doesn't he ever throw anything out?"

"I guess not." Lucy threw the last of the papers back in the box. "It's kind of sad, isn't it? All his personal papers are business papers."

Zack frowned at her. "Don't start feeling sorry for him. He's a rat."

"Well, he wasn't always a rat."

"Oh, yeah. What was he?" Zack leaned back against the stairs and watched her. "What do you know about him? Where did he come from?"

Lucy sat down on one of the boxes. "I don't know much. He's from a little town in Pennsylvania called Beulah Ridge. It's on the high-school yearbook in that box there beside you, remember? His parents are both dead, and he hasn't been back in years. We had a very small wedding, and Bradley didn't invite more than two or three people, and he said none of them would be able to make it. It was just my parents and Tina and some friends from school."

"Who did he send wedding invitations to?"

Lucy frowned, trying to remember. "I think a couple of friends from high school. Not family. And anyway, he was right. Nobody showed up that he invited. It was sad, really, but he didn't seem to mind. Anyway, after the wedding, we just settled in here. He worked at the bank, and I taught school, and Maxwell and Heisenberg moved in. And then the blonde showed up, and he moved out, and we got divorced, and you mugged me in an alley." She shrugged. "It's never going to make a Movie of the Week, but that was my life."

Zack snorted. "Bradley is a rat."

"Oh, not entirely. He was really very nice to me for most of our marriage."

Zack looked at her skeptically. "Then why did you move upstairs in October?"

"He snored."

"Right." Zack turned back to the boxes to pull the year-book out again.

"Why doesn't anybody ever believe that?" Lucy asked.

"Because no man in his right mind would let you out of his bed for just that." Zack flipped through the book. "Is this his high-school yearbook?"

"Yes," Lucy said faintly.

"John Bradley the embezzler taught high school in California," Zack said absently, as he flipped to the senior portrait section. "High-school phys ed. That was his downfall."

"What do you mean, 'downfall'?"

"He seduced a cheerleader." Zack ran his finger down the page. "Knocked her up."

Lucy's head jerked up. "That's awful! He should be in jail."

"I think so, too." His finger stopped on one picture. "Of course, I also want him there for embezzlement. But he paid in his own way."

"He must have lost his job. School administrators can be really good at ignoring anything ugly, but in this case . . ."

"Oh, yeah, he lost his job. But the best part is, the girl's family was really powerful. A bunch of very big guys with very big bank accounts and very big shotguns. They probably could have killed him and gotten away with it, except there was Bianca with a baby on the way, so they did the next best thing. They got him a job in a bank and made him marry her."

Lucy winced. "How awful for her. That's barbaric."

Zack snorted. "More than you know. I've talked to Bianca on the phone, and she is not a pleasant person. I almost felt sorry for John Bradley. I personally would have told Daddy to go ahead and shoot me rather than spend a week with her, let alone six years, but then Bradley and I are different."

"You certainly are." Lucy blushed when Zack looked up. "I mean, I can't imagine you seducing a teenager."

"Well, I tried hard enough when I was a teenager. I just never had much luck. My technique needed work." He turned back to stare at the picture in the yearbook.

It doesn't anymore, Lucy thought. Then she mentally shook herself. The moon must be full or something. Maybe she was ovulating, although she usually didn't get this crazy. As a matter of fact, she'd never been this crazy. Maybe she'd just reached that mid-thirties plateau where a woman's sexual desire was supposed to peak. Just her luck, she was peaking and here came Zack.

Of course, the real problem wasn't that he turned her on. The real problem was that she liked being with him. She felt good around him. Happy. Warm.

Really warm.

Hot.

Okay, the other part of the real problem was that he turned her on.

"He doesn't look like a crook," Zack said suddenly.

"Who?"

"Porter. Your ex."

Zack shoved the yearbook in front of her, his finger pointing to a picture on a senior gallery page. "He looks like an amoeba."

"They all do. They're so young." Lucy looked down at her ex-husband, frozen forever at eighteen. He was as classically good-looking back then as he was now, but he was also as stiff and dull, too. "Poor Bradley."

"Stop feeling sorry for him." Zack took the yearbook back and leafed through it again. "He's implicated in a major crime."

"He is?"

"Yeah. He got a hotel room in Overlook. A woman was found shot there today. We don't have any proof that he did it, but we'd like to talk to him."

"You think Bradley shot somebody?" Lucy shook her head. "No. He's not violent."

"How do you know he's not violent? He's a rat, possibly an embezzler, and definitely a seducer of blondes. You found one in your living room, remember?"

"Not a chance." Lucy's voice was firm. "A rat, maybe, but not a seducer of blondes. The blonde must have seduced him. Bradley just wasn't that interested in sex."

Zack flipped back a page in the yearbook. "Bradley is an idiot."

"Of course, maybe it was just me."

"It wasn't you. Trust me."

Lucy started at the warmth in his voice, but his attention was suddenly riveted to the yearbook. "I'll be damned," he said. "I will be damned."

"What?"

He shoved the book in front of her and pointed to a picture near the bottom of the page. The boy in the picture was good-looking in a sly way.

"I've seen that smile on kids before," Lucy said. "I bet he was a cheat."

"No kidding. Look at the name." He pointed again and Lucy read the legend underneath.

Most Likely To Succeed
John Talbot Bradley

6

"THEY WENT TO HIGH school together." Zack's voice was thick with triumph. "Both of them named Bradley could be a coincidence. Both of them involved with banks could be a coincidence. You in the restaurant yesterday at the same time as the phone tip? Not likely, but could be a coincidence. But now this . . ." He took the book back from her and gazed in satisfaction at the picture. "This is not a coincidence."

"No," Lucy said. "It's not. I don't understand any of this, but it's not."

Zack looked up from the book at the sadness in her voice. "Hey. This doesn't have anything to do with you."

Lucy bit her lip. "I just feel stupid. I never saw any of this in him, and I was married to him for eight months. I feel so stupid."

"You're not stupid." Zack flipped the book closed and stood, holding out his hand. "Come on. Let's shove the rest of this stuff under the stairs and go up and call Tony. Then we can have dinner. What are you making, anyway?"

He grinned down at her, and she forgot Bradley for a minute and just basked in his nearness. Then she took his hand and let him pull her to her feet. "I'm not making dinner." She dusted off the seat of her jeans. "You are." She smiled up at him then, glad to have him so close. It was hard to stay depressed when he was so close.

"I don't know how to cook." He sounded distracted as he stared down at her.

"What's wrong?"

Zack shook his head. "That's some smile you've got there when you let it go all the way. I hadn't seen it before. You should smile like that more often." He turned her around and started her up the stairs, pushing her in front of him, and then stopped after the first step.

"What now?" Lucy looked back over her shoulder.

"Nice jeans," he said, looking at her rear end. "Tight, though."

Lucy felt herself go cold. She went up another step and turned around. "What did you say?"

He let his eyes drift up to meet hers. "I just hadn't thought of you as the tight-jeans type."

"Neither did Bradley." Lucy felt suddenly remote. "Is this a problem?"

Zack frowned at her. "What are you talking about? What problem? I'm leering at your rear end. Slap me if you want to, but don't look at me like that."

"Oh." Lucy blinked.

Zack's frown dissolved. "I get it. Bradley didn't like you in jeans."

"Bradley liked me in suits. He hated jeans."

"Bradley is an idiot. But then we already knew that. As far as I'm concerned, you should be wearing jeans all the time. Enough about you. I'm hungry. Move it." He started up the stairs. "Now, as I was saying, I don't cook."

"You do now." Lucy turned back and speeded up to keep him off her heels, relief making her buoyant. "I'm teaching you."

"Whatever happened to women who like to cook for men every day?" Zack asked as she opened the door to the kitchen at the top of the stairs.

"There were never any women who liked to cook for men every day. There were only women who cooked for survival and pretended to like it. And now there are men who cook for survival. Like you. Think of this as survivalist training. Very macho."

"I don't think so," Zack said, but he followed her through the door into the kitchen.

AN HOUR LATER, ZACK was feeling pretty good.

"I'm really great at this," he announced as they sat on the floor in front of the fireplace, their plates on their laps and their backs against the rose-flowered love seat.

"Zack, they're nachos." Lucy protected hers from Einstein. "They're very good, but they're just nachos."

"Yeah, but I made them. I think I have an instinct for this."

"I'm just grateful you chose Mexican instead of French." Lucy eyed the mound of food on her plate. "We'd be up to our hips in coq au vin."

"We'll do that tomorrow night," Zack said, and Lucy said, "No, we won't. Do you like chili?"

"Yeah, but that comes in a can. I want to chop something." He grinned at her, and she felt her heart lurch sideways.

Oh, boy, she thought, but all she said was, "You can make chili from scratch. And you get to chop the onions. You'll like it."

"Great." Zack scooped up another nacho with pride. "Forget it," he said to Maxwell who was doing his best impression of a starving dog. "It's all mine."

Lucy laughed. "Anthony was right. You are like a little kid. Who's fed you up to now? Your mom?"

"Nope. Mostly, I eat out. Sometimes I open a can or nuke something, but not too often. Canned stuff tastes terrible, and the frozen stuff is worse."

"And you're how old? This is just amazing."

"Hey, I'm alive and healthy. I'm doing okay." Zack scooped another nacho. "What were you discussing me with Tony for anyway?"

"He said you have a concussion." Lucy looked apologetic. "I feel awful about that."

Zack met her eyes. "You still made me cook."

"Well, I didn't feel that awful. Besides, you liked it."

"It's the principle of the thing." Zack ate another nacho. "What else did Tony tell you?"

Lucy blinked. "I don't remember."

"Oh, yes, you do, Blinky. Come on. Give."

"I thought he was very nice," Lucy said primly, her chin in the air.

Zack shook his head. "You stay away from him. You're not his type."

Lucy's chin dropped. "That's not what I meant. And what do you mean, I'm not his type?"

"He's into plastic Yuppies. You know, suits and running shoes and briefcases and car phones." Zack shuddered at the thought and started on another nacho.

"And what's your type?" Lucy asked, and then mentally kicked herself. That's all she needed was for him to start thinking she was interested.

"I don't have a type," Zack said. "I'm an equal-opportunity lover."

"How very broad-minded of you," Lucy said, and fed a nacho to Einstein on the sly.

"Speaking of types, how did you end up with Bradley?"

"Well, I had decided to get married because of the second law of thermonuclear dynamics." Lucy kept her voice brisk to keep herself from getting emotional. "And about that time, he picked me up in the library at the university. I considered it a sign."

"It wasn't." Zack picked up another nacho, gazed at it proudly, and then ate it.

"I thought I was going to end up a crazy old lady living with my dog."

"Dogs," Zack corrected.

"I only had Einstein then. Maxwell and Heisenberg showed up after we moved in. Well, actually, I found Maxwell down on Fourteenth Street across from the Music Hall, but it was the same principle." Lucy looked over at Zack. He was staring into the fire so she slipped Heisenberg a nacho. Maxwell noticed and quietly padded around the love seat to her side.

"So you got married to keep from being a crazy old lady?" Zack shook his head. "It would never have happened, but I guess I can see your point. What I still don't understand is, why Bradley?"

"He was there. It seemed right." She shrugged and slipped Maxwell a nacho.

"It was wrong," Zack said sternly, and then he looked from his empty plate to hers. "Do you want the rest of your nachos?"

Lucy passed her plate over, and the dogs followed silently to sit in front of Zack.

"Listen, I just fed you guys a whole bowl full of dog food, so I know you're not starving. Cut it out." They sat and stared and he said, "Okay, one each. *One.* That's all."

Lucy watched him feeding her dogs nachos and felt a wave of heat roll over her. She was one sick puppy. She'd been having hot flashes ever since she'd first seen him in the restaurant, and now he was turning her on by being nice to her dogs. She'd been divorced two days, and already she was lusting after a hyperkinetic dog feeder.

The phone rang, startling her, but Zack reached over and snagged the receiver off the piecrust table before she could get up and answer it.

"Hello?" He looked puzzled. "They hung up," he said, doing the same. "Who would hang up if a man answered?"

"Well, not Tina," Lucy said. "She'd give you the third degree. Not my parents, they wouldn't notice. Not my friends, they'd want all the dirt about you."

"How about Bradley?"

"Bradley doesn't call here."

"Ever?"

"I've only talked to him once since the blonde. He called the same day, but I was still pretty upset then, so I told him I never wanted to hear from him again. And he asked me to please not tell Tina he'd called, and I was so disgusted, I hung up. Oh, and there was one other time. I saw him at the lawyer's the day we signed the papers. He said hello. And he sent me the note. That's it."

Zack frowned. "That's weird. What's wrong with him?"

"Nothing. He's happy with his blonde."

"When I find Bradley," Zack said, "I hope he resists arrest."

"You can't arrest Bradley. You don't know that he's done anything wrong." Lucy stood, picked up Zack's plate from the floor, and carried it into the kitchen.

"Oh, yes, I do," Zack said. "Even if he didn't shoot the blonde, he's a rat. And I, for one, am going to make sure he's sorry." Then he popped the last of the nachos into his mouth, got up, and followed her out to the kitchen.

Anthony came over to see the yearbook, and they searched the downstairs until eleven that night and found nothing except Bradley's note to Lucy, asking her to lunch.

"He doesn't sound too damn apologetic," Zack said. "Listen to this. 'Please meet me at the diner on Second Street, so that I can explain to you why you've acted hastily.' And you were going to meet him?" He narrowed his gaze at her. "You must still be hung up on him."

"Of course not," Lucy said. "I don't want him back. I just want to understand what happened. And anyway, that's just Bradley's way. He'd never admit that he was wrong. Just the fact that he wrote and asked me to meet him is amazing. Bradley never asked for anything in his life. He always assumed people would do what he wanted, and usually they did. He was very . . . authoritative." Lucy took back the note and read it again. "Poor Bradley. He must have been really upset. He even wrote, 'Please.'"

"I don't like Bradley," Zack said.

"Actually, neither do I," Lucy said.

"Good. Hold that thought," Zack said.

WHEN ANTHONY LEFT AND Lucy went upstairs to take her shower, Zack enjoyed the fire, the dogs, and one last beer. *This is nice*, he thought, stretching his legs in front of the fire. *This is comfortable. This is . . .*

He stopped in the middle of a sip of beer.

This was a lot like what Anthony had been talking about in the diner the other day.

He put the bottle down to consider. Anthony had offered him two impossibilities as protection for Lucy, knowing he'd reject them and volunteer.

He'd been set up.

"I'll kill him," he said to the dogs, and Heisenberg flopped over on his back.

Well, it was no problem. He'd just call Anthony tomorrow and tell him to send over a replacement. Zack picked up his beer to drain it. Not Eliot, of course. He was too old and too slow.

And not Junior, either, because . . .

Zack stopped again, the bottle halfway to his mouth. There was nothing wrong with Junior. He was young and strong and quick, and he would do a terrific job of protecting Lucy.

Right here in her house.

In fact, Junior could be sitting right where Zack was by tomorrow night. All Zack had to do was call Anthony.

Hell.

He got up and stomped to the kitchen to throw his bottle in the recycling box, whistling to the dogs as he went, and two of them went trotting past him as he opened the back door.

Maxwell and Einstein. Zack looked around for Heisenberg, and then remembered. "Oh, for crying out loud, dead dog," he said, and heard the thump as Heisenberg rolled over and the click of his toenails on the hardwood floor.

"Thank you for joining us," Zack said and closed the door behind him.

WHEN HE CLIMBED THE stairs later, he met Lucy at the top, wrapped in a floor-length white terry-cloth robe big enough to cover a couch. Her hair was in loose, damp, greenish ringlets, and she looked vaguely like a cover on a science-fiction book he'd once read.

"I was going down to let the dogs out." She stepped back from the top of the stairs.

"I already did. All present and accounted for."

The three dogs had padded up the stairs by that time and sat watching them quietly. "Bed," Lucy said, and Heisenberg swerved into her bedroom while Einstein and Maxwell went up another flight to Zack's room. "Oh, I forgot." She hesitated. "They sleep on your bed."

"No," Zack said. "Maxwell, maybe, but Einstein, no. There won't be room for me."

"It's a big bed," Lucy said, but she called Einstein back down and held her bedroom door for him. "I did buy beds for all of them. They just didn't like them. They'd rather sleep with me."

They're no dummies, Zack thought.

"I put clean towels out for you," Lucy went on. "In the bathroom. Do you need anything else?"

You, Zack thought. She looked like a bulky mummy in her robe, and her hair was green, and he wanted her. It was crazy. He needed a shower. A cold one. "Thanks," he said. "Good night."

"Good night."

He turned toward the bathroom door, and then decided he'd been too abrupt, but when he turned back, her bedroom door was closing and she was gone.

Good. Because the last thing he needed was to get involved with Lucy Savage and her three dogs.

Even though all his instincts were for it.

He shook his head and went to take a cold shower.

THE NEXT MORNING, Zack took Lucy to the hospital.

"That's her," Lucy whispered, looking at the woman's pale

face under the stringy blond hair. "That's the woman who was with Bradley."

Zack put his arm around her and led her away from the bed, alarmed at how white she was, almost as pale as the woman in the hospital bed.

"Are you okay?"

"Bradley did this? Bradley couldn't have done this." Lucy looked back at the bed. "I know it's the same woman, but he couldn't have . . ." She shook her head, too upset to finish.

"Hey." Zack took her through the door, away from the silence and the whiteness of the room. He found a bench for her in the hall and sat beside her, keeping his arm around her while she bit her lip.

"Somebody violent did that. Bradley's not violent," Lucy said finally. "I don't think Bradley has emotions."

Zack tightened his arm around her. "That's the kind who usually break, honey. The ones who yell all the time blow off steam. The ones who don't, well, when they blow, it's an explosion. And this was a gunshot. It's easy to shoot a gun. Too easy. One bang, and it's over, and you don't even have to get close."

Lucy shook her head. "It's like everything I knew has turned out to be a lie. I can't even trust my own judgment anymore. Look how wrong I've been. And I can't even talk to him to find out why this happened. I've been totally wrong, and I'll never know why. This could all happen to me again because I'll never know why."

Zack watched her bite her lip again, and the sight of her even white teeth cutting into her soft bottom lip disoriented him for a moment. What kind of fool could Bradley have been to risk losing Lucy to be with that blonde? Hell, how could he have wanted to be with anybody but Lucy at all?

Lucy leaned back against the wall suddenly, pulling his arm with her. "How could I be so blind? How could I have been so stupid?"

"Hey." She looked so confused and betrayed that Zack was stung. He pulled her close and cuddled her to him, wrapping his arms around her as if to shield her from Bradley and anyone else who might hurt her. "Look, honey. A lot of people do things that the people who know them say are impossible." He closed his eyes, savoring her soft warmth and feeling slightly guilty about it. "It happens all the time. All we have to do is keep you safe until we catch him. You can talk to him then, if you want. But it won't always feel like this. It'll be okay."

"I feel safer with you after three days than I did with Bradley after eight months," Lucy said into his shoulder. "I'm so dumb."

"Oh, I don't know." Zack tightened his hold on her. "I'd say that's pretty smart of you."

ZACK TOOK LUCY OUT for Sunday brunch so neither of them would have to cook, and by the time they'd finished, she'd relaxed again. She was still quiet, but the terrible tension he'd felt in her while he held her was gone, and for Zack, for a while, that was enough. Anything was better than watching Lucy suffer.

He really wanted to kill Bradley.

"Now we search the upstairs," he told her when they got home. "All your secrets will soon be mine."

"I don't have any secrets," Lucy said.

"Well, then you should get some," Zack said, and they looked at each other for a moment, and then both looked away.

The first room they searched on the second floor was Lucy's—a big sunny room almost filled with a huge Victorian bed covered with an equally huge crazy quilt.

"I made the quilt," Lucy said. "It's just tied, not quilted, which is why it's kind of lumpy, but that's okay because that way I could put more layers of fill in it." She smiled at Zack. "It's really warm. I love it. It's the best thing I've ever done."

Her smile made Zack's mouth go dry. He hadn't seen it often enough to get used to it, and the thought made him both sad and angry. She should be smiling all the time. If she was his, he'd make damn sure she was smiling all the time.

Of course she wasn't his, and he didn't want her to be his because he was too young to settle down, and anyway, he couldn't visualize her naked, which he was pretty sure meant she was like a sister to him, but still . . .

She should be smiling all the time.

"Zack?"

"I really like the quilt. Let's look at your closet."

Her closet had two racks in it. One side was full of soft pastel flowered dresses. The other was full of severe tailored suits in navy and black and dark brown, all with their price tags still attached.

"You schizophrenic?" Zack asked.

"No," Lucy said. "I bought the dresses. Bradley bought the suits."

"Then Bradley should have worn the suits. Why did you stay with this guy?"

"He wasn't a bad person . . ." Lucy began, but she stopped when Zack rolled his eyes. "I know. The blonde. But that isn't the Bradley Porter I knew. He was good to me. He loved me. He just wasn't . . . fun. And he didn't approve of me, really. He wanted to, but he didn't. None of that is enough grounds for divorce. He's not a bad person. He's just . . . lonely. I couldn't leave him. He was so lonely."

"Which would explain the blonde," Zack said and then kicked himself as Lucy winced. "Sorry."

"No, I asked for that one," she said. "What next?"

They tapped the walls, and turned the drawers upside down, and looked under the rug and found nothing. By late afternoon, they'd turned both the second and third floors as upside down as Lucy's drawers and found exactly the same thing—nothing.

"You don't even have any junk," Zack complained as they finished the last room on the third floor. "What's wrong with you?"

"I've only lived here nine months," Lucy protested. "It takes time to accumulate good junk."

"You've had time to accumulate three dogs." Zack stepped over Maxwell, who was staring into space again. "If you could do that, you could accumulate a little junk."

"You don't accumulate dogs." Lucy patted Maxwell, who didn't seem to notice. "You meet them, and you both know that you belong together. And even if you know that that's dumb, and you don't need a dog, and you can't handle the responsibility, and you don't even want a dog anyway, there it is and you have to go with it. It was meant to be."

Zack stopped in his tracks. "Why does this sound like some dumb women's magazine description of the perfect relationship?"

Lucy's head jerked up from Maxwell to him. "Listen, the best relationships of my life have been with dogs. And they aren't dumb at all. Einstein never brought a blonde into my house, and Maxwell never stood me up in a restaurant, and Heisenberg never grabbed me in an alley."

"Hey," Zack said. "How did I get into this?"

"Sorry," Lucy said.

ANTHONY CAME BY THE house late in the afternoon. He stood in the middle of Lucy's soft, flowered living room and said, "This is a wonderful room. It feels good just to be here." He smiled down at Lucy. "It's like you."

Lucy beamed back. "That's the nicest thing you could have said to me." She stood on tiptoe and kissed him on the cheek, and he put his arm around her.

"Hey," Zack said. "Let's be professional here."

"You want to be professional?" Anthony raised an eyebrow. "Get a haircut."

"Very funny. What are you doing here?"

Anthony let go of Lucy and sat down in one of the over-stuffed armchairs. "I went in to catch up on the reports this afternoon and found a message from the lab. You know the bomb that blew up Lucy's car?"

"I'll never forget it." Zack sat on the arm of the loveseat and pulled Lucy down onto the cushions beside him.

Anthony leaned back in the chair and crossed his legs. "It wasn't much of a bomb to begin with, according to the lab, although granted it did a nice job on the car. But the really interesting part is that, besides the extremely long timer that not only gave you time to notice the cat, knock Lucy into the driveway, and then have a long conversation with her—"

"Get to the point."

"It also had a hell of a big alarm clock taped to it with a lot of sinister-looking wires. None of which had anything to do with the mechanism that caused the explosion."

"Oh, hell," Zack said.

"I don't understand," Lucy said.

Anthony turned to her. "If you had looked in your car, you would have seen a big package about the size of a shoe box with a clock taped to it and a lot of wires. What would you have done?"

"I'd have thought it was a bomb and run like crazy," Lucy said. "I still don't get it."

"He's trying to tell you that you were right," Zack said, disgusted. "Nobody's trying to kill you. They're just trying to scare you out of the house. You would have called us, the bomb squad would have confirmed that it was a real bomb. And we would have moved you out of the house for safe-keeping, so the house would have been empty. Except that you wouldn't leave the dogs."

Lucy looked back and forth between them, incredulous. "My car blew up. This guy blew up my car to scare me out of my house?"

"Well, he didn't know about the dogs," Anthony said. "Without the dogs, it would have worked."

"He could have killed me!"

"No," Zack said. "The timer on that sucker was almost five minutes. If the package was as big as Tony says, you'd have been long gone before it went off. This nut was just trying to scare you." He met Anthony's eyes. "Which means . . ."

" . . . there's something in this house," Anthony finished.

"No, there isn't," Lucy said. "We've looked. We've looked everywhere."

Anthony shook his head to stop her. "That's not all. Your report from the patrolman came in. And not only has Mrs. Dover been complaining about prowlers around this house for two weeks, she also phoned in another complaint last night. If she's really seeing somebody, he's still around."

"You know, I wanted to move out of my apartment because I never felt safe there," Lucy said. "I moved here because it felt so safe." She looked around her at the bright, warm room. "I don't feel so safe anymore."

"Are you crazy?" Zack said. "You've got me for a bodyguard and you don't feel safe? What's wrong with you? First no junk, and now this."

"No junk?" Anthony said.

"Cleanest house I've ever searched," Zack said. "No junk."

"That's un-American," Anthony said.

"So what happens when I go back to school tomorrow?" Lucy said.

"We keep somebody in the house," Anthony said.

"You're not going back to school," Zack said.

Lucy and Anthony both frowned at him.

"Don't look at me like that," he told Anthony. "Suppose this guy grabs her and forces her to let him in the house? Suppose he decides to take a hostage? Suppose . . ."

"Suppose you stop scaring Lucy," Anthony said. "He's not going to grab her."

"We don't know that. We've got one attempted-murder charge that could turn into murder at any time. We've got a million and a half that's floating around somewhere. And we've got the guy who's mixed up with both, who also makes bombs and shoots guns. You want to tell me again about how we should dress Lucy up and send her off to the one place where everybody knows she's going to be?"

Anthony considered Zack for a moment. "All right. If it's all right with Lucy."

"All right," Lucy said after a moment and went upstairs to phone her principal.

"What are you doing?" Anthony asked when she was gone, and for once Zack was serious when he answered.

"I'm scared for her. You should have seen her at the hospital. She was absolutely rocked. I just want to keep her safe until we get this guy. We've got to pretty soon. We're close. I just want to keep her safe."

"There's something else," Anthony said. "I spent most of the afternoon on the phone to Beulah Ridge, Pennsylvania, trying to catch people while they were home. I talked to a couple of people who knew both Bradleys."

"And?"

"And John Bradley was the school's golden boy until he got caught one too many times stealing and cheating. The strange thing was, even while people were talking about how bad he was, there was admiration in their voices. And they said, every one of them, that the one person who stuck by John Bradley through thick and thin, no matter what he did, was—"

"Let me guess."

"Right. Lucy's Bradley." He held up a hand when Zack opened his mouth. "Sorry. Bradley Porter. Seems like there wasn't much to Bradley Porter except for straight A's and the cleanest locker in the school. All the excitement he had, he got from hanging around with John Bradley. Hero worship."

"That was twenty years ago."

"Bradley Porter invited him to his wedding."

Zack straightened so quickly that he almost fell off the love seat. "What?"

"Bianca Bergman Bradley found the invitation and set out about two weeks ago to track him here. The Bergmans called this morning. They haven't heard from her since Thursday. Her description matched the shooting victim. We told them about her, and they're on their way now."

Zack sat down on the loveseat, totally confused. "The blonde in the hospital can't be Bianca Bradley. She's Bradley Porter's girlfriend. Lucy ID'd her."

"Maybe she's both."

"How?" Zack almost snarled the question. "How could she be? She was in California until two weeks ago."

Anthony ignored him. "You know, if John Bradley came here to hide with Bradley Porter, a lot of things that didn't fit suddenly make sense. John Bradley embezzles the money in California and escapes from the cops, his homicidal in-laws, and his shrew of a wife. That part I could understand. But then I could never figure out why he'd come here to River-bend. Let's face it, we're not the Paris of the Midwest. But if he's got an old friend here who has always done anything he wanted, that part falls into place, too. He calls Bradley Porter. Bradley gets him a room in Overlook using the name of their old home town as an alias."

"What about the bonds?" Zack said.

"John Bradley hands over the bonds to Bradley Porter for safekeeping. After all, he'd have to be a fool to keep them in Overlook. Those people will kill you for your socks, let alone a million and a half. Then Bianca shows up and calls you to put the pressure on him, and he shoots her."

"Right. How did she get my number?"

"She called the station and asked who was handling the Bradley case. They'd give her either you or me."

Zack leaned back against the loveseat, scowling. "So how did Lucy get involved? Because Bradley Porter hid the bonds in this house?" He shook his head. "We really combed this place. Unless he took up the floorboards, the bonds aren't here."

"Well, something is." Anthony stood to go. "It's possible that Bradley Porter doesn't even know about it. The desk clerk never saw him, so he may still be just an innocent bystander, helping out an old high-school friend."

Zack shook his head. "Bradley Porter is involved. I know it."

Anthony checked his watch and started for the door. "Well, just in case, you take care of Lucy. And don't assume because she sits there and blinks that she's okay."

"Oh, you picked up on the blink, too, did you?" Zack followed him to the door. "You're spending too much time with her. And what's this about telling her about the concussion? What else did you tell her?"

"Nothing important. I'm going home to salvage what's left of my Sunday. Give my love to Lucy."

"No," Zack said, and Anthony laughed as he went out the door.

"THERE'S JUST SOMETHING about it that just doesn't make sense," Lucy told Zack later while she watched him chop onions at the big old porcelain sink in her kitchen. "This whole master-criminal thing. Especially this thing with you and Bradley pitting your wits against each other. Bradley never pitted a wit in his life."

"Maybe he just hid that side of himself from you." Zack picked up the cutting board and moved to the old white stove next to Lucy, where a cast-iron pan full of hamburger was simmering. He dumped the onions into the pan with the hamburger. "Face it, you weren't close."

"We weren't," Lucy agreed. "Bradley's a very...closed person, I guess. I thought he would relax after we were married, but he didn't. And after a while, I didn't try very hard to open him up. I had the house and the dogs, and that was enough." She picked up a wooden spoon and stirred the hamburger to keep it from sticking. "I should have tried harder."

"Why?" Zack took the spoon from her. "He's a rat who possibly tried to murder his girlfriend. That's like Mrs. Bluebeard saying 'I just didn't give enough.'"

"I suppose." Lucy felt herself growing depressed again. She opened a blue enameled cupboard door, took down the chili powder, and handed it to him. Then she changed the subject. "Wait until Anthony hears you can cook."

"Forget Anthony," Zack said.

THEY ATE DINNER IN THE dining room in the soft amber light of the stained-glass lamp over Lucy's big oak dining-room table. They talked about his family and hers and about their jobs, moving in front of the fire to the love seat with their coffee when dinner was done. The hours passed, and they lost all track of time, sitting and laughing in the firelight. The only interruptions were two phone calls, both hang-ups that made Zack uneasy. He didn't discuss them with Lucy, and he made a conscious effort not to talk about either one of the Bradleys or the case, and he watched while all the tension drained out of her, and she smiled and laughed with him.

Maybe when this was all over, maybe then he could call her. Maybe they could go out, or just stay in and laugh.

Maybe when this mess was out of the way, and she was over Bradley, they could make love.

Maybe even fall in love.

It was a terrible thought because it appealed to him so much.

Falling in love meant commitment. Commitment meant marriage. Marriage meant responsibility and adulthood, which led to loss of instincts and old age and death. Or at least children.

Einstein poked his cold, wet nose at Zack's hand.

And dogs.

He looked around him, at the big old warm house, and the three dogs that were draped comfortably over his legs and snuggled next to Lucy, and most of all he looked at Lucy.

He'd be a fool to fall for her. She was a forever kind of woman, and his idea of forever was a three-day weekend.

Lucy looked up and caught him staring at her.

"Zack?" Her eyes were huge in the firelight, and her lips were soft and full, and without thinking, helpless with wanting her, he bent and kissed her.

7

LUCY'S LIPS PARTED A little, and then she kissed him, too, moving gently against his mouth, leaning into him so slightly that he sensed rather than felt her and went dizzy at the sensation.

And he wanted to pull her close more than he'd ever wanted anything. She was soft and warm and the best place he'd ever been, but he had to get away. If he didn't get away, he'd do something stupid like make love to her, and then when he'd leave—and he would because he always left—she'd be unhappy. He'd be worse for her than Bradley had been.

The thought of hurting her cooled him down considerably.

"Sorry." He drew back. "I'm really sorry. Very unprofessional of me. I'm really sorry. Really."

Lucy looked lost.

"Uh, excuse me." He gently tipped Maxwell and Heisenberg off his legs and got up. "I better check in with Tony. I'll use the upstairs phone."

"Oh." Lucy bit her lip. "This late? It must be after ten."

Zack checked his watch as he edged away. "Twelve, actually. But he won't care." Then he escaped to use the phone while Lucy sat with the dogs and hugged herself in front of the fire.

"GET ME OUT OF HERE," Zack said when Anthony answered the phone on the sixth ring. He stood in the hall, stretching the phone cord to peer nervously over the banister into the faint glow cast by the fireplace below.

"Zack?" Anthony mumbled, half asleep. "Are you in trouble? Where are you?"

"Lucy's. Get me a replacement. Now." Zack thought for a moment. "Just not Junior."

"What are you talking about? It's the middle of the night."

"It is not." Zack dropped into a chair on the landing. "It isn't even one yet. Wake up."

"I am awake. But I'm not coming to get you just because you've decided you don't like the company."

"That's not the problem." Zack pressed his hand to his forehead. "I'm crazy about the company. I'm having immoral thoughts about the company. At any moment, I'm going to start making my move on the company, and then I will be in trouble. Get me out of here before I do something to make this permanent."

"Go take a cold shower," Anthony said. "Better yet, grow up. Learn to control your baser instincts."

Zack looked over the banister again to make sure that Lucy hadn't come within earshot. "Listen," he said, lowering his voice. "She runs around in this white thing that's big enough to roof Riverfront Stadium, and she still drives me crazy. A cold shower is not going to do it."

"She has green hair, too," Anthony said. "I meant to ask, did she do that on purpose?"

"Will you please concentrate?" Zack took a deep breath. "I'm serious here. I'm too young to be married. Married is for old guys."

"Married? Zack, you've only been there two days. Get a grip. You're hysterical."

"Listen to me. Lucy is not the kind of woman who plays around. Lucy is the kind of woman who gets married. And I want her, but I don't want to get married. And I don't want to hurt her."

"Good. I don't want you to hurt her, either. I like her."

"Forget it. You'd be worse for her than I am."

"Zack . . ."

"If you really like her, you'll get me out of here. Think what a lousy husband I'd make."

"Zack . . ."

"Tony, get me some backup and get me out of here, or I will end up the stepfather of three dogs."

"Worse things could happen."

"Get me out of here," Zack said.

"No," Anthony said and hung up.

"Hey!" Zack said to the dead phone, so loud that the dogs came up the stairs to see what was wrong, their toenails clicking like castanets.

"Zack?" Lucy called up from the living room.

"Nothing," Zack called back. "It's nothing." He looked down at the dogs. "If you have any loyalty to your mother, you will bite me if I get within two feet of her."

Einstein leaned against his leg, Maxwell stared into space, and Heisenberg rolled over on his back.

"You guys have got to get a new routine." He left them, calling back, "Dead dog," when Heisenberg refused to roll over. "I'm going to take a shower. I'll see you in the morning," he yelled down to Lucy, and then all but ran for the bathroom.

"Zack?" she called after him, but he slammed the bathroom door behind him to shut her out.

And in the morning, I'm gone, he thought. *Because if I don't leave in the morning, I will never leave, and I'll end up remodeling this house, and telling Heisenberg "Dead dog" twenty times a day, and making love with Lucy until I die.*

He stopped, nailed by the thought.

"Cold water," he said, and stripped off his clothes.

WELL, THAT'S THAT, Lucy thought, settling back in front of the fire. He kissed her once and then he ran up the stairs to get away from her.

She couldn't possibly be that bad a kisser.

It must be that she wasn't his type. He probably went for really exciting women. Women who wore black lace and had long, thick, blond hair.

As opposed to, say, dry, fuzzy, curly, green hair.

Could hair as bad as hers send a man running up a flight of stairs?

"It's not the hair," she told the dogs who had padded down to rejoin her when Zack shut them out of the bathroom. "It's me. I'm dull and unemotional. I should have jumped him when he kissed me, but did I? No. I was too polite."

She let her head fall back against the love seat.

"Maybe this is all just fallout from the car blowing up," she told the dogs. "You know, that 'You're never more alive than when you're on the edge of death' thing people are always talking about. Except, even with the car bomb and everything else, I still find it hard to believe somebody's trying to kill me. Which would seem to mean it's not the edge of death that's getting me into trouble here. It's the edge of Zack."

She considered what Tina had said. "Be irresponsible." She should just go right up those stairs and climb into bed with him and seduce him until he was witless.

Except she wasn't sure how.

She thought about it for a while, trying to figure out how black lace nightgowns and champagne and all the other classic stuff would fit with Zack's cheerful eroticism. Zack would probably prefer somebody who just crawled into his bed naked.

She couldn't do that.

And then there was her hair.

Forget it.

She sighed and called the dogs to go upstairs to bed.

AFTER A NIGHT OF frustrating fantasies about a fully-clothed Lucy, Zack came downstairs planning to tell Lucy he was leaving right after breakfast. Then the phone rang, and he answered it, and the caller hung up.

"I don't like that," he told Lucy as she came down the stairs. "That makes me nervous."

"Everything makes you nervous." Lucy moved past him to the kitchen. "You are a walking exposed nerve."

"Hey, I can be calm." Zack followed her to the kitchen, wanting to be with her. "I'm steady."

"Well, I've got to admit I'm amazed you've stayed in one place this long. I thought you'd be out the door by now."

Zack froze in the doorway. "Oh? Why?"

Lucy opened the refrigerator and took out an egg carton and the milk. "I thought you'd get bored. I had no idea you had this much staying power. And I want you to know, I appreciate it." She nudged the refrigerator door shut with her hip and smiled at him. "I'm not really scared. But I appreciate it anyway. What do you want to make for breakfast? Eggs or French toast?"

Zack looked into her calm, open, trusting face. She needed him. "Eggs. We can have leftover chili for lunch."

THE PROBLEM WAS, there wasn't anything for him to do all day but look at Lucy and fantasize. He still couldn't see her naked, but it almost didn't matter.

Anthony was out checking prowler reports for Lucy's neighborhood, calling Pennsylvania again, and running credit-card checks to see if either one of the Bradleys was dumb enough to use his Visa card while he was on the lam. Even Junior was probably arresting jaywalkers. Only he was stuck baby-sitting three dogs and a marrying kind of woman he couldn't imagine naked.

He needed to do something with his hands. Fast. Before he put them all over her.

"You know, this kitchen tile is really ugly," he said, kicking at the gray speckled stuff as Lucy put the breakfast dishes away. "I wonder what's underneath it?"

"I don't know," Lucy said. "It's on my list of things to— Hey!"

As she spoke, the floor had slipped under her feet and she fell against the cupboard. When she turned, Zack was holding the edge of her kitchen floor in one hand, waist high, like a bedsheet.

"I don't believe this. The idiots put tile squares over sheet flooring. What dummies." He looked under it to see what was left on the floor and missed Lucy's glare.

"Zack, put my floor down," she said, but he didn't hear her.

"Come on," he said, dropping it finally. "Water got under here and the whole thing's loose. Let's move the table and chairs out of here and peel this up. There's wood under there!"

"Of course, there's wood under there," Lucy began, but he was already pulling the table toward the door.

"Pick up your end. We're going to have to turn it sideways."

Lucy sighed and obeyed. She was going to have to do the floor anyway sooner or later, and at least it kept him out of trouble.

And with her.

He might even kiss her again, and if he did, she was going to pounce this time. No more shrinking violet.

As long as he made the first move.

"Okay, tilt it to the right," Zack said, and Lucy obediently tilted the table.

Maybe if she wore her old tight jeans. He seemed impressed with them that day on the basement stairs.

Would that be fair?

Did she care?

"Come on," Zack said, and she followed him with the table through the door into the dining room.

"Listen," she said as they put the table down, "if we're going to do messy stuff, I'm changing into my jeans."

ANTHONY CALLED, AND ZACK took it in the living room, sinking into one of the oversoft chairs and moving his arm so Maxwell could climb into his lap.

"Glad you called. I want a phone tap," Zack said. "Somebody is calling and hanging up every time I answer."

"Sounds like a jealous ex-husband. You may want to watch your back. Mrs. Dover reported another prowler. If it's Bradley Porter, and he's the one running around with the .38, he uses it."

"Just so he doesn't use it on Lucy. She insists that he's not violent, by the way." Zack idly scratched Maxwell's ears. "Anything new on the car bomb?"

"I've got the final report here. Very neat. Plastic explosive, timer set on a five-minute delay, controlled damage. Professional job. And our Bradley—John Bradley—was in the Navy. Very tidy."

"If this case is so tidy, why are we still so lost?"

"Speak for yourself," Anthony said. "I'm pursuing the investigation with my usual cold, clean logic. What are you doing?"

"Ripping up Lucy's kitchen floor."

"With your teeth? Well, at least you're calmer than you were last night. What happened, anyway?"

Lucy came down the stairs and walked by wearing her jeans. She smiled at Zack before she went into the kitchen.

He had a sudden vision of her naked.

"Oh, *hell*."

"What?"

"You know that fantasizing problem I was having?"

"Is this the 'Lucy naked' part?"

"Right. Well, I'm not having that problem anymore."

"Oh."

"I'm having other problems."

"Try a cold shower."

"There's not enough water in Riverbend." Zack stood, dumping Maxwell off his lap, and craned his neck to try to see through the dining room into the kitchen. "I'm relying on self-control and maturity."

"I'd be worried," Anthony said, "but I know Lucy can defend herself. How's your lip?"

"Great. I have to go now. You wouldn't believe how tight this woman's jeans are."

"Zack?" Anthony's voice was suddenly serious. "You know, it's not a great idea to seduce a woman you're protecting. All kidding aside, do you want me to send Matthews over?"

"Who?"

"Junior."

"I will shoot him on sight," Zack said and hung up so he could follow Lucy into the kitchen.

BY EIGHT THAT NIGHT, the phone tap was on, the floor had come up with a minimum of effort and a maximum of mess, and Lucy had shown Zack how to make roast beef with dry onion-soup mix for dinner.

"This is amazing," he said, after the floor was in the backyard, and they were in the dining room eating. "All I did was pour some water and that powder stuff on the meat and throw it in the oven, and three hours later, we eat. Do you have any idea what chefs get paid in this town?"

Lucy tried not to grin. "I don't think the Maisonette uses onion-soup mix. I think they chop more than we do."

"Absolutely amazing," Zack said, and Lucy laughed. "What?" he said.

"You just make everything so much fun. Even boring things like cooking and taking out the kitchen floor. You're excited about everything."

"Not everything. Just about some things." Zack watched her for a moment, her face warm and happy in the soft light. She was so calm, there was so much peace wherever Lucy was, that lately, whenever he looked at her, he felt like he was home. It was a dangerous feeling. If she could do that after only three days, where would he be in a week?

"Zack?" she said, and he said, "Tell me about yourself."

Her eyes widened in surprise. "Me? There's nothing to tell."

"Sure, there is. I already know you're a great teacher." He gestured at his plate with his fork. "And I know you're a great cook. And I know you have the sister from hell."

"No, she's not. She's just had bad luck with men."

"Three times? No offense, but that temper of hers must have had something to do with three divorces."

Lucy shook her head. "It wasn't like that. She used to be a lot nicer than me, although she was always really practical. The first time she got married, she thought she was getting married for money. Well, she didn't just think so, she did. Morgan was very rich. And he was a lot older than she was, too."

"A lot?"

"Forty years. She was nineteen."

"That's a lot."

"Yes, but then she fell in love with him. Our parents weren't...well...*warm* people. I mean, they took very good care of us, but there wasn't a lot of hugging. When we were kids, like in grade school, Tina and I used to talk about what it would be like when we got married, and we both swore we were going to marry men who hugged a lot, like the men in the movies. But then when we got older..." Lucy sighed. "Well, I still believed in that, and I think Tina wanted to, but then Morgan proposed. He was crazy about Tina, and Tina was just tired of not having any money, and she wanted to go to art school. Morgan promised to put her through, so she said yes. I tried to talk her out of it, but she said it was stupid to wait for love, and that Morgan was very sweet, and she was going to do it. I cried all the way through the wedding because I thought she'd made a terrible mistake."

"So what happened?"

Lucy's face softened into a smile as she remembered. "He was wonderful to her. It wasn't just the money. He thought all her paintings were beautiful, he thought she was beautiful, and he told her so. He hugged her all the time, praised her all the time..." Lucy's smiled turned rueful. "Six months after they were married, I apologized to her for trying to stop her. By then, she was crazy about him. They were so happy together, people even stopped saying she'd married him for his money."

"So what happened?" Zack repeated.

"Nothing for four years. They were waiting until Tina graduated, and then they were going to go around the world for a year seeing every art museum they could find for Tina, and..." Lucy stopped again. "Tina was so excited. She told me that she was going off the Pill for the trip because they were ready to start a family. She was thrilled."

Zack winced. "Why do I have a bad feeling about this next part?"

"He died," Lucy said. "The week after she graduated, he had a heart attack and died. And Tina was devastated. She was in mourning for almost two years. She wouldn't do anything but paint and listen to music. Morgan had a huge record collection, and she used to listen to it because she said it was like he was there."

Zack shook his head. "That doesn't sound like the Tina I saw in the diner."

"The Tina you saw in the diner has had two husbands since then." Lucy picked up her fork again. "One slept with her best friend and one hit her. Don't criticize Tina. She's a survivor. I should be more like her."

"No, you shouldn't," Zack said, alarmed. "You're fine the way you are."

Lucy looked thoughtful for a moment. "You know, that may be part of the reason I went ahead and married Bradley. I mean, marrying without passion worked for Tina. She got it all anyway. And I didn't seem to be having much luck finding a hugger."

"So you didn't feel passionate about Bradley? What a shame. Pass the potatoes."

"I don't think I'm a passionate person." Lucy carefully avoided looking at Zack as she handed him the vegetable dish.

"Oh, you meet the right guy, and you'll be surprised," Zack said. "You got any plans for dessert?"

THEY SPENT THE REST of the evening scrubbing the old glue off the kitchen floor. At ten, they quit to take a beer-and-pretzel break, and the phone rang. Zack followed Lucy and waited while she picked it up. "It's Tina," she told him, and he took the pretzels and the beer over to build a fire with the dogs.

"So how's life with the cop?" Tina asked.

Lucy curled up in an armchair, draping the phone cord over the arm. "Difficult. But nobody's tried to kill me lately, so I'm not complaining."

"Hell, yes. It's been over twenty-four hours since anything's exploded in your vicinity. By the way, I'm buying you a new car for your birthday. What do you want?"

"Nothing. My insurance will cover it."

"There must be some kind of car that's bomb-proof."

"Forget the car. Get me something that's Zack-proof." Lucy dropped her voice and kept a wary eye on Zack across the room in front of the fire.

"Is he being difficult? Shall I have somebody beat him up?"

"No. If I need that, I'll do it. He's just driving me crazy."

"How?"

"Well, he's ripped up my kitchen floor, for starters."

"Why? He thought Bradley was under there?"

"No. I think he got bored, but he's afraid to leave for fear I'll get killed."

"So he ripped up the kitchen floor."

"Well, it keeps him off the streets. He's also cooking."

"He cooks? He didn't seem the type."

"I'm teaching him. We're starting with the basics. Nachos and chili."

"Lucy, what's going on?"

"I'm crazy about him." Lucy's voice sank to a whisper. "I've had more lustful thoughts in the past three days than in the entire rest of my life. Somebody blew up my car, and all I can think about is ripping off his clothes. I've never had so much fun, and I've never been so turned on, and he doesn't seem to notice."

"Jump him," Tina said.

"I don't know how. Ideas. I need ideas."

"Take off your clothes and crawl into bed with him. I know it's not subtle, but he looked like the elemental type in the restaurant. If you get too subtle, he may not catch on."

Lucy clutched the phone. "I can't do that. What if he says no, and there I am, naked? I'll die."

"He won't say no, but who cares if he does? Do it. Hell, guys go through this every time they make a move on a woman, and none of them has died yet. In many cases, that is, of course, unfortunate, but rejection is definitely not lethal. Go get him."

"I can't." Lucy shot another glance at Zack. "He kissed me last night, but then he stopped. Do you think it was my hair?"

"No. I think you should get your hair fixed, but I definitely do not think it was your hair."

"Maybe I'll make an appointment to get my hair done and then . . ."

"Lucy. You're just using this hair thing to hide behind. When you are ready to be that new independent woman you kept babbling about in the diner, you'll seduce him with your hair the way it is."

"Maybe. But maybe the hair makes a difference. Maybe that's why he kissed me and stopped."

"Maybe he was being a gentleman," Tina said doubtfully.

"Zack?"

"Maybe not. I'll stop by tomorrow night and check him out— No, I won't. I've got theater tickets."

Lucy breathed again. "Good. I don't need you helping. You'll hurt him."

"I'll stop by Wednesday night. If you haven't made your move by then, we'll work something out."

"Tina, really —"

"You have forty-eight hours. Do it. Just don't get hung up on him. I think this lust thing you're developing is very healthy, but Zack is not husband material. Just use him to get over Bradley, and then I'll introduce you to somebody nice and quiet and rich." A doorbell chimed in the background on Tina's end of the line. "Oh, hell. I've got to go. Bye."

"Tina, I don't think so . . ." Lucy began, but Tina had already hung up.

"Lucy?" Zack called from over by the fire. "Is everything all right?"

"Tina says hi," Lucy said and went to join him.

"THIS IS THE LIFE." Zack sat on the floor leaning back against the love seat. "Great food, great fire, great company." He looked over at the three dogs lined up expectantly beside him. "Don't look at me. Your mom's got the pretzels."

"Forget it," Lucy said to them from where she had curled up on the love seat. "Pretzels are bad for your figures."

The dogs lapsed into their favorite activities. Einstein put his head between his paws and watched the food, Maxwell sat and stared into space, and Heisenberg rolled over onto his back.

"Einstein, Heisenberg, and Maxwell," Zack said. "Is there a pattern to these names? Obviously, Einstein even I can figure out. He looks just like the old guy. But why Heisenberg and Maxwell?"

"They're both famous physicists. Heisenberg was because Einstein was suspicious of him, and I thought he was uncertain about whether he wanted to stay. I was wrong about the second part, but the rest of it fit."

"I don't get it."

"Werner Heisenberg said the universe was an uncertain place, with no real rules. He drove Albert Einstein crazy because Einstein wanted to believe that the universe was completely understandable. So when this poor little dog showed up at the front door and Einstein growled, and the next day the dog was gone but he came back again in the evening, I just thought, well, Einstein is suspicious of him and he's uncertain about staying, so ..."

"You named him Heisenberg," Zack finished for her. "What part were you wrong about?"

"Heisenberg wasn't uncertain," Lucy said grimly.

"What?"

"Heisenberg was gone every morning for three days in a row. Bradley would tell me that he'd let him out and he'd just disappear, which I thought was strange because the backyard is fenced, but then Heisenberg is a small dog, so I thought maybe he'd found a hole. So I looked, but I couldn't find one. And then I got up early one morning and glanced out the front window and saw Bradley putting Heisenberg in the car. So I went out on the front porch and asked him what he was doing."

Lucy clenched her jaw, and Zack saw the old anger seep back into her eyes.

"I hate Bradley," he said.

Lucy swallowed and went on. "He didn't say anything, but while he was standing there, Heisenberg jumped out of the car and came trotting back into the house. Bradley just stood there, sort of annoyed. I wanted to *kill* him. I should have known right then that everything was over, but ..."

"But?" Zack prompted.

"Well, we were married. That's serious. You don't go to court and say, 'I want a divorce because my husband tried to lose my dog.' And after all, he could have taken him to the pound, and then Heisenberg would have died."

Zack shook his head, disgusted. "No, he wouldn't have. If Heisenberg hadn't come back one night, what would you have done?"

"Called the pound." Lucy stared into the fire. "Bradley wasn't so dumb."

Her voice was lost, and Zack wanted to hit somebody. Preferably Bradley. "Yes, he was," he said. "He lost you. That was extremely dumb."

"Oh." Lucy blinked. "Thank you."

"You're welcome." Their eyes met for a moment, and then he looked away, searching for a diversion. Any diversion. No matter how lame. "Hey. Stop hogging the pretzels."

She passed him the pretzels, and he tried to remember the part about not getting involved.

"What I need to know," he said finally, dragging his mind back to the investigation, "is the kind of guy Bradley is. You seem really sure he's not a criminal."

Lucy picked up her cue. "It's hard to believe. He has no imagination. He's essentially a good man, but he's boring. If he was a criminal, at least he'd be interesting."

How boring? Zack wondered. *Was he boring in bed?*

"Actually," Lucy went on, "we were both boring. We were the most boring couple in Riverbend."

Zack gave in. "In bed, too?"

"I beg your pardon," Lucy said.

"It's a legitimate question," Zack said, trying to convince himself. "After all, he may have seduced and shot a blonde."

"No, he didn't. I told you, the blonde seduced him, which was more than I was ever able to do." Lucy blushed, but plunged on anyway. "Bradley approached sex the same way he approached everything else. He did it correctly, and then he forgot about it."

"Correctly?" Zack almost spilled his beer. "There's a correct way to have sex? Where am I when these rules get passed out?"

Lucy shrugged. "All right, efficiently then. I didn't like it. I mean, he was doing all the right things, but . . ."

"He was all the wrong guy," Zack finished for her, his voice thick with disgust. "You need a keeper. How could you have married this creep?"

Lucy glared at him. "Oh, let's talk about some of your ex-girlfriends. I bet there's a million stories in your Naked City."

Zack glared back. "Didn't you notice the sex was lousy before you got married?" He took a swig of beer to hide his annoyance.

"We didn't have sex before we got married. Bradley respected me."

Zack choked on his beer.

"No, he did." Lucy frowned. "That's what I can't figure out. I mean, Bradley wasn't exciting, but I was sure he respected me. I'd still swear that he loved me. Not passionately, of course, but...well...firmly. He sort of took me for granted, but he always wanted me around. He was very upset when I moved upstairs to the attic after he tried to kidnap Heisenberg."

"I bet he was." Zack stopped, putting himself in Bradley's place, a Bradley used to having Lucy warm and loving in his bed and then suddenly losing her. "I bet he was upset. Why didn't he move upstairs, too? I'd have been up those stairs like a shot."

There was a short silence, and then Lucy said, "Bradley wasn't you."

"Guess not." Zack shifted uncomfortably. "Want some more pretzels?"

A FEW MINUTES LATER, Zack took the dogs out for their last run, made sure the doors were all locked, and then stopped by the fire to say good-night.

"I'm sorry we had to talk about Bradley," he told Lucy, his face all shadows, backlit by the fire as he stared down at her on the love seat. "I know it upsets you."

"It doesn't upset me. Thinking somebody was trying to kill me upset me. Talking about Bradley hardly qualifies."

"Good." Zack hesitated.

Lucy waited, holding her breath, and then he said, "Good night," and went upstairs.

"Good night," she said and turned her eyes back to the fire.

FIFTEEN MINUTES LATER, Zack stretched out in Lucy's old bed in the attic and stared out the little diamond-paned windows.

He could just go down there and say, "So, Lucy..."

So Lucy what?

So Lucy, you want to take off your clothes and have incorrect sex with me?

Very smooth, he jeered at himself. *Just forget it. There is nothing you can say to her that will interest her. Go to sleep.*

But when he closed his eyes, he could see her. And just as he'd feared earlier, he wasn't having any trouble at all thinking about her naked.

And she didn't look anything like Queen Elizabeth.

"Oh, hell." He sat up in bed. *Think about something else. Something depressing.*

Fast.

Okay. The Orioles. Game seven of the '79 World Series.

The game appeared before him in vivid, depressing detail. And there on third base was Lucy. Naked.

"Oh, *hell,*" he said, and fell back against the pillows.

HER FACE IN THE bathroom mirror was pale under her mass of green curls. Wrapped in her terry-cloth robe, Lucy stared at her hair in despair, and then suddenly leaned to look closer.

Her hair wasn't just plain green anymore. Part of it seemed lighter, so that her hair looked mottled in places. And part of it was a lot shorter, too. She ran her fingers through her hair and some of it broke off when she tugged.

She looked a lot like Einstein had after he'd rolled in chewing gum and she'd had to cut it out of his fur.

Except he hadn't been several shades of green.

Lucy leaned her head against the bathroom mirror. This was the absolute nadir. She would never again look this bad as long as she lived.

So, of course, tonight Zack was upstairs inspiring in her the most toe-curling fantasies of her entire life. Not that it mattered. Because she wasn't ever going to do anything about it anyway.

Was she?

Lucy stared at herself, lost for a moment.

Of course, she wasn't. Why was she thinking about it?

Because she wanted him so much she'd die if she didn't have him. She felt hot just thinking about him, the heat starting low and spreading as she thought about his hands, and his mouth, and his body rolling hard against hers, and the heat in his blue, blue eyes, and his mind-numbing, heart-stopping grin.

No.

She turned out the light and left the bathroom, depressed beyond reason. By the time she climbed into bed, she was almost in tears.

It was impossible. If she went up there to Zack right now, and crawled into bed with him like Tina had said, he'd look at her and say, "No." He'd be sweet about it, but he'd still say, "No."

But maybe he wouldn't. Maybe he'd just say, "Are you sure about this, Lucy?" and she'd say, "Yes," and he'd draw her down next to him and touch her and make love to her. . . .

Her whole body tensed at the thought of his hands and his mouth, of Zack's warmth everywhere, of Zack pressing her so close to him that she was seared by his heat. She let her mind go, feeling the way he'd touch her, remembering his kiss in the firelight, the weight of him against her in the alley, on top of her in the driveway, knowing he'd be electric and vital and safe at the same time. She began to breathe more deeply, and her fingernails dug into the sheets as she imagined him first hard against her, and then hard inside her, and she shut her eyes so tightly that she saw stars, trying to feel Zack making love to her.

And then, finally, when she couldn't stand it anymore, she gave in to it and sat up in bed, wrapping her arms around herself. She didn't care anymore about her hair or her robe, or anything. And her mind was as clear as her body was racked.

I say I want to be independent, and then I lie down here too terrified to go after what I want.

Independence means going after what I want.

And I want Zack.

She slid out of bed, crazy with need for him, and walked with a pounding heart toward the attic stairs.

8

ZACK SAT UP IN BED and turned on the light when he heard her on the stairs, so his shoulders were naked in the lamplight when Lucy saw him. He stood out in sharp relief against the yellow-flowered wallpaper, the definition of his muscles a hard contrast to the softness of the flowers behind him and the quilt rumpled over him. His dark hair was tousled and his eyes heavy-lidded, and Lucy stopped, frozen both by how beautiful he was and by how much she wanted him. Her need choked her, pressed on her so heavily that she couldn't breathe, and she leaned in the doorway and breathed him in instead of air.

"Lucy?" he said, and she found herself floating toward him, drawn by the energy he radiated, feeling at once both suffused with desire and liquid with heat.

She sank onto the bed beside him, trying to find the right words, any words, but there was so much heat in her that she couldn't speak. She pushed herself through layers of air with only Zack's warmth to guide her to him, so that she was almost surprised when her lips touched his. It was like finding him underwater or in the dark, she'd had to penetrate so much to get to him.

She moved her lips softly against his, feeling the heat there, and then tasted him cautiously with her tongue while he sat, stunned. He was nectar and ambrosia and everything she'd read about; forbidden fruit and lotus, too. She kissed him again, this time falling against him with her lips parted, her tongue slipping inside his mouth to the hot sweetness there, and now, suddenly, he was kissing her back, his hands moving to pull her hard against him, the pressure of his body filling her with such heat and need that she clawed at his shoulders and bit his lip. Then he rolled with her until she was pinned under him, straining against his weight and hardness, and he pulled her robe from her shoulders, biting kisses down her neck while his hands pulled her frantically to him again, flesh to flesh, and she cried out first at the heat in him, and then, gratefully, at the sweet roughness of his mouth on her swollen breast.

Zack touched her the way she'd fantasized, with the same intensity that he lived every minute. His mouth and hands were everywhere, hot on her skin, now light, now rough, until she writhed against him and forgot to feel anything but need and heat and touched him with a hunger that she'd never conceived possible before. He tormented her with his tongue and fingers until she moaned from the frustration and the pleasure. He devoured her with his eyes, his hands, his mouth, intense and focused on her, all laughter gone as he concentrated the entire force of everything he was on loving her.

And when he slid his fingers inside her, she cried out, opening her eyes suddenly to see him staring at her, his eyes electric with desire for her. "God, you're beautiful," he said. "I can't believe how beautiful you are. I can't believe how hot you are."

His whole body was tense, rigid with control as he moved against her, and she moved against him, too, relishing his hardness against her softness. Her tongue traced his muscles, and he shuddered under her touch and forced her mouth up to his, crushing her lips against his while he stroked inside her mouth with his tongue. Lucy writhed under the twin tortures of his hands and his mouth, needing him so much now that she finally broke away from his kiss and sobbed aloud.

"Now," she said wildly, pulling his hips to her. "Now. I want you inside me, now," and he kissed her again, swift and hard, and then moved away from her.

"No," she said, and he ran his hand up her body to caress her breast again. "Wait," he said. "Just for a minute. I promise you."

She saw him roll over to sit on the edge of the bed, and she reached for him, dragging her fingernails down his back, luxuriating in the shudder it drew from him. She'd never felt so powerful in all her life or so alive, every cell in her body swollen with desire. Then Zack turned back again and pulled her to him and kissed her, rolling so she was beneath him. Lucy arched her hips to his, and then he slid slowly inside her, and she lost her mind.

She arched up once, sharply, galvanized by the shock of him so hard inside her, bringing sweet relief and tormenting pleasure at the same time, and then she began to surge against him, over and over, again and again, out of control as he moved against her, inside her, over and over, again and again, holding her so tightly that she felt both safe and destroyed at the same time, the tormenting rhythm of him in her driving her beyond pleasure into ecstasy. She wrapped her legs around him, trying to bring him closer, to hold him forever so that the feeling would never stop, and he laced his fingers in her hair and pulled her head back to face him as he rocked inside her.

"You're amazing," he breathed and kissed her, biting her lip, licking his tongue into her mouth as he rolled over, pulling her on top of him, holding her to him as he rocked up into her, and she felt suffocated by the sweet pressure inside her, her blood screaming and hot and swelling in her veins until she exploded in his arms, locked there while her orgasm surged into her fingertips and sent her mind into oblivion.

Then she lay gasping, feeling the pounding of her blood in her temples and in her swollen fingers, and the hot hard core of her diffusing into warmth and joy. He still moved against her, and as she eased back into reality, she was caught and warmed in the ebb and flow of him in her, and then she felt him tense hard in her arms and moan into her hair, and then they were both quiet, clinging to each other.

"I didn't know," Lucy said finally, when her heart had stopped pounding, her voice muffled against his chest. "I didn't know there was this."

"That makes two of us," Zack whispered, and his arms tightened around her. "Wait." He eased himself out of her, and she made a small sound of protest. "I know," he said softly, and then he turned away again to get rid of the condom. He pulled the sheet up over her where she lay tumbled on the bed, and then slid in beside her, pulling the comforter over both of them. "Next time," he said, his voice soft with exhaustion, "we'll go slower. We got a little crazed there. I wanted you so much, but I wasn't expecting you, and then when I got you, I wasn't expecting you to be like this." He kissed her and laughed softly into her hair. "I thought you were a good girl."

"I am." Lucy fought the sex-drugged sleep she was falling into. "You corrupted me. I thought I was going to die if I didn't have you. I couldn't have waited any longer."

"Thank God, you didn't. I was so nuts I was having fantasies about making love to you on third base."

"What?" Lucy said, losing her fight to stay awake.

"Go to sleep," he said and kissed her again before he fell asleep himself, his cheek pressed against her hair.

Zack, Lucy thought as she, too, sank into sleep. *This feels so good.*

I had no idea.

WHEN ZACK WOKE UP the next morning, he was alone, bathed in the honeyed glow of the sunlight bouncing off the yellow walls. For a moment, he wondered if he'd dreamed the whole thing, but then he knew it had to be real. He could never have fantasized that calm, sensible Lucy could make love like that.

It must have been real.

Which meant he was in a lot more trouble than he'd realized. This was the first time his reality had ever been better than his fantasy. He'd found the perfect woman living in a great house with three dumb dogs. The smartest thing to do would be to run.

The smell of bacon frying wafted up to him. Breakfast. He had a sudden picture of Lucy in the kitchen, talking to the dogs. The same sunlight that was warming him would be filtering through the front windows, making shadow patterns through the lace curtains. The paper would be on the front porch, and the dogs would be ready for a morning run in the backyard.

It was all calm and quiet and regular and routine, everything he'd never wanted; and now he wanted it and Lucy, too, but most of all just Lucy, blinking at him, and telling him he wasn't logical, and rolling hot in his arms.

It was what he wanted forever.

What do you know? he thought, amazed, and, trusting his instincts as he had all his life, he surrendered without a qualm. *So this is it. I never thought it would happen, but this is it. Responsibility. Adulthood. Dogs.*

Lucy.

LUCY WAS STANDING AT the counter, blotting bacon on paper towels and trying to get her thoughts in order, when Zack walked up behind her and put his arms around her, pulling her close. She melted into him, instantly flooded with warmth and happiness, tipping her head back so that he could bend down and kiss her. Then she turned around in his arms so she could snuggle closer to him.

"No regrets?" he whispered into her hair.

"Of course not." She tilted her face up to smile at him. "You are a wonderful lover."

He smiled down at her. "I'd be a wonderful husband, too."

Her smile vanished. "What?"

"I think we should get married."

Lucy went cold with panic.

Married? After five days? She hadn't even been divorced three weeks.

Married? With her instincts for men? With her amazing ineptitude at understanding people?

Married? With all her talk about independence and freedom and . . .

Married?

"No." Lucy pulled away.

"Wait a minute." Zack pulled her back. "The 'No' was bad enough. Don't stop touching me, too."

Lucy relaxed against him again, but not with the same melting openness as earlier. "I'm sorry. You surprised me. Thank you very much for asking. That was very gentlemanly."

Zack scowled at her. "No, it wasn't. That was for me. I like it here. I want to stay."

"So stay. I like having you here. I just don't want to get married again."

Zack's scowl deepened. "What 'again'? This would be like a first time. You've never married me before. I'm not like Bradley."

Lucy smiled up at him. "That's for sure." His scowl disappeared, and then she added, "But I'm still not marrying you. It would be totally illogical. I've only known you five days."

"Five incredible days," Zack prompted. "Six, counting today. Admit it. Your life is a lot more exciting since I showed up." His eyes slid away from hers. "Is that pan supposed to be smoking?"

"I don't think you can take credit for the car blowing up." Lucy drew away from him to rescue the bacon.

"Well, there have been other exciting moments. I can think of several from last night alone. Hey, don't touch that. You'll burn yourself." He took the pan from her. "Ouch!"

"Put butter on it." Lucy took the pan back. "Cold butter is good for burns."

"How come I'm always trying to take care of you, and you end up taking care of me?" Zack spread butter over his burned hand.

Lucy began to fork the bacon out of the pan onto paper towels. "I think it's mostly mutual. I bet if we really analyzed it, it would come out about equal."

Zack stopped buttering. "You think?"

"Yep. Omelet's in the microwave."

Zack opened the door and peered inside. "We've got to get married. I love living like this." He turned to see Lucy looking at him, exasperated. "What?"

"Nothing," she said. "Sit down and eat your omelet."

THE MARRIAGE QUESTION put a damper on breakfast. They'd moved from loving warmth to polite chill in the space of five seconds, and there were no signs of a warming trend.

The rest of the morning went downhill from there.

"I'm going back in to school next Monday," Lucy said after breakfast.

"No, you're not." Zack studied the kitchen floor. "I think this gunk will come up if we keep soaking it with soap and water. You got another bucket?"

"Zack, listen to me." She waited until his eyes drifted up from the floor, and then she spoke slowly and distinctly. "I cannot stay inside this house forever. I have to go back to work."

"No."

"Listen, you," Lucy exploded. "You can say no all you want. I'm going back to work next Monday and there's nothing you can do about it. You have the rest of this week to get used to the idea, and you'd better do it because on Monday, I am out of here."

"Not a good idea," Zack said, and Lucy gave a smothered scream of exasperation and stalked out of the kitchen.

"Women are so emotional," Zack said to the dogs. "What do you think about this floor?"

AT TEN, ANTHONY dropped by, and Zack forgot the floor.

"Bradley Porter's using his credit cards," he told Zack when he answered the door. He walked into the living room and smiled when Lucy came into the room through the dining-room archway. "Hello, Luce," he said and Lucy went to him and hugged him.

"What is this?" Zack said. "Unhand that woman."

Anthony turned back to him, one arm still around Lucy. "So, you coming with me? We have to move on this. There's a patrol car out in front to watch the place while we're gone. Lucy will be fine."

"Oh, no, you don't," Lucy said, pulling away from Anthony. "I've been here since Thursday. I'm going stir-crazy. At least take me with you."

"Not a chance." Zack grabbed his jacket. "Bradley's been shooting people. I'm not taking you into that."

"Which Bradley, yours or mine?"

Zack shrugged into his jacket. "You don't have a Bradley. Remember that. Come on, Tony."

Lucy put her hands on her hips and glared at him. "Don't you think you should narrow down who you're chasing before you go charging off like this?"

"We'll argue about it when I get back." Zack started for the front door, and Anthony kissed Lucy on the cheek. Zack backtracked, grabbed his arm, and pushed him toward the door. "Why don't you cook dinner for a change?" he said to Lucy on his way out.

Lucy leaned against the back of one of her overstuffed chairs, defeated. "I'll order a pizza," she said, and Zack stopped and said, "No, you won't. I haven't gone through all of this to get you wasted by a pizza deliveryman." He followed Anthony out the front door, and Lucy felt like killing him.

"Maybe Phoebe will get him again," she told the dogs, and then the door opened again.

"I almost forgot," Zack said, and grabbed her and kissed her, bending her back over the chair in his enthusiasm. She clutched at him to keep from falling, and then relaxed into his kiss, relieved that he was kissing her again and reveling in his heat. "I will definitely be back," he said to her and kissed her again, pulled her back upright and left.

"Oh, good," she said, but he was already gone.

By noon, the silence was getting to Lucy.

She'd made a big pot of vegetable soup, and talked to the dogs, and turned on the radio, but the silence was still there, even though there was enough racket for anybody.

There was nobody talking to her.

It had never bothered her before. But now, after days of Zack's constant rambling, it made the house seem empty.

"It's not like he's not coming back," she told the dogs. "Actually, I don't think it's him at all. I think it's just that I haven't been out of this house for days. I need to get out."

She caught sight of herself in the mirror over the fireplace. Her hair was even shaggier than before. She looked awful.

"I could go out and get my hair fixed." Even as she said the words, she knew she would. It was too awful not to. And how many people got killed in beauty parlors, anyway?

The dogs looked skeptical.

"This is so ridiculous," she told them. "People blowing up my car and shooting at me. This makes no sense. I'm going out."

LUCY WAS CAREFUL. She called a cab to pick her up three houses down so that the patrol car out front and any miscellaneous killers lurking around wouldn't know she was gone. She felt guilty about the patrol car, but she was tired of arguing with policemen. Granted, Zack was probably the worst of the bunch, but she was fairly sure that the one in the patrol car wouldn't be any more understanding.

And she left a note for Zack, so if he came home early he wouldn't panic. "Dear Zack," she wrote. "I can't stand the thought of you waking up to see my hair like this anymore so I'm getting it fixed. And I'll get something for dinner, too. Don't go to bed without me. Lucy." Then she stuck it on the mantel where anyone coming into the room would see it.

She just hoped that anyone was Zack. If it was Anthony she was going to be embarrassed.

LUCY ASKED THE CABBIE to recommend a good beautician, and he dropped her at a dingy strip mall paneled in peeling redwood and rusted chrome. It had a bar, a convenience store, a drugstore, a secondhand clothing shop, and a beauty parlor. The basics.

The beauty parlor was Thelma and Lou's.

It was dim inside the pink-and-orange salon, so it took her eyes a moment to adjust to the light and to the young amazon who walked forward to meet her.

"Hiya," the girl said and cracked her gum, and Lucy's eyes swept up, startled, to her hair.

It was purple, shaved at the sides, and gelled until it stood straight up. Since the girl must have been close to six foot before the hair, the effect was riveting. So riveting that the nose ring and the skull tattoo on her chest were hardly noticeable.

"Are you Thelma or Lou?" Lucy asked, unable to take her eyes off all that purple hair.

"I'm Chantel." The girl stared at Lucy's hair, fascinated. "Thelma and Lou are in Florida. Like, permanently. What can I do for ya? As if I didn't know already. Jeez."

Her own eyes still fixed on Chantel's hair, Lucy said, "I have a hair problem."

"No kidding." Chantel cracked her gum again. "I've never seen anything like it in my life."

They had to look like Harpo Marx meets the Bride of Frankenstein on a bad color TV. Lucy started to laugh.

"Well, at least you still got your sense of humor," Chantel said. "So, you want me to fix you or not?"

"I don't know. Do you have any experience fixing this kind of mistake?" Lucy touched her hair and it crackled under her fingertips.

"I don't have any experience at all. I just got out of beauty school yesterday." Chantel cracked her gum and smiled cheerfully. "If you don't want to take a chance, it's okay. I mean, somebody obviously did a number on you once. Why take a chance again?"

Chantel's smile was as open and honest as a child's, which Lucy knew was no reason for her to put her already ravaged head into her hands.

Or maybe it was.

"Somebody did do a number on me," Lucy agreed. "I ended up with the most awful bleach job you've ever seen. And then I tried to fix it with shampoo-in color, but that didn't work."

Chantel looked at her hair again and nodded. "That explains the green."

Lucy took a deep breath. "Can you fix this?"

Chantel looked cautious. "I can try. You sure you don't want to try one of those big places downtown?"

Lucy hesitated. "Yes. Yes, I'm definitely sure. What are we going to do first?"

Chantel's eyes narrowed, and she became all business. "Condition. We're gonna megacondition that mess and hope it doesn't fall out from relief."

Lucy swallowed. "And then?"

"A cut. Real short to cover up the breakage. And some color. I suppose you want brown or something."

"Brown." Lucy looked up at Chantel's purple hair and swallowed again. "No, not brown. That's not me. I'm the spontaneous, independent type."

Chantel cracked her gum. "Oh, yeah. I could tell that right off."

THE HOTEL ROOM WAS generic: bad paintings, worn green carpeting, tan flowered bedspread, and beige curtains at the sliding-glass doors.

Unfortunately, it was also clean. One of the Bradleys had checked out four hours earlier.

"The desk clerk recognized John Bradley's picture but not Bradley Porter's. So John Bradley was here using Porter's credit cards." Anthony surveyed the spotless hotel room. "Bradley Porter was probably never here. This makes no sense. This should be such a simple case. We have Porter's credit-card numbers. We have his house. We have his ex-wife."

Zack started guiltily.

"So why don't we have him?" Anthony went on, tactfully ignoring him. "Why hasn't anyone seen him? If he's innocent, why can't the Kentucky cops find him? If he's guilty, why did he give John Bradley his credit cards? I don't get this."

"We're not going to find anything here," Zack said. "It's got to be the house. Although I'm telling you, there are no government bonds there. I even took up the kitchen floor, which is the only floor that's not plain hardwood. If something's there, it's small." He folded his arms and sat down on the chipped edge of the desk. "You know, Bradley Porter's a banker. He wouldn't keep bonds in his house. Not for more than a night, anyway. What do you think?"

"A safe-deposit box," Anthony said. "I thought of that. I asked at Gamble Hills. No dice. He doesn't have one."

"There are other banks."

"Almost a hundred. Talk about hopeless. There's no guarantee he's using his name. And we'll need some specifics to get a warrant. Any other ideas?"

"Find the key and work from there. Which means, back to Lucy's."

Anthony looked around the room again and gave up. "Fine. Let's go back and look again. This place has been wiped so clean, we'll never find anything here anyway."

"Let me call Lucy first." Zack picked up the phone on the desk beside him and dialed. "We may need groceries."

"Groceries?" Anthony looked confused. "You do groceries now?"

"Hey, I've changed. I've matured."

"What do groceries have to do with maturing?" Anthony asked and then stopped when he saw Zack's face change. "What's wrong?"

"She's not answering." Zack let it ring a few more times before he slammed the phone down. "If she's out running again, I'm going to kill her. Let's go."

"She wouldn't be that dumb," Anthony began and then stopped when he realized the alternative. "Then again, she might," he said, and they both ran for the elevator.

THREE HOURS LATER, Lucy paid off her cab and climbed the steps to her house. Just as she was fishing for her key in her purse, a young patrolman came to the door and looked her up and down, smiling in appreciation.

"Can I help you?" he said.

"Yes," Lucy said. "We've met. Your name is Matthews, but Zack calls you Junior, and this is my house. Let me in. What is this, anyway?"

Matthews stepped back immediately to let her in. "Boy, are we glad to see you. We were about ready to drag the river."

An older patrolman was on the phone, but he stopped and squinted when he saw Lucy. "Didn't you use to be blond?"

"Don't remind me," Lucy said. "Do I know you?"

"Forget it. We're done. She's here," the older man said into the phone and hung up. "I'm Falk. You sent us after Warren a couple days ago, remember?"

"Oh." Lucy winced. "I'm sorry about that. What's going on here?"

Falk grinned. "Warren couldn't find you. It upset him. So we only got most of the force looking for your body."

"Oh, no," Lucy wailed. "I left a note. Why doesn't he read notes?"

"Go get Warren," Falk said to Matthews. "Let's put him out of his misery."

ZACK WHISTLED TO BRING the dogs in and headed through the kitchen to the living room, trying not to think the worst. She could be anywhere. Except with Tina, who was making plans to have Riverbend dismantled brick by brick until she found her sister. Or at her parents, who were annoyed because he had bothered them without any concrete reason.

Or here.

He walked into the dining room with Einstein on his heels and found Junior practically drooling over a strange redhead. She was cute, Zack thought absently, her head haloed in short, bright, coppery curls, but she wasn't Lucy, and Lucy was all he wanted right now.

Then she turned, and it was Lucy.

"Where in the *hell* have you been?" He surged toward her, relief supercharging his anger.

"I left a note." Lucy glared at him. "And I told you before, you can't just put me down someplace and tell me to stay. Why did you cause all this fuss?"

"Why did *I* cause all this fuss?" Zack threw up his hands, speechless for a moment. "Well, to begin with, there wasn't any note. None. Trust me. We have been over this place inch by inch. Looking for your body, bloodstains, anything. There was no note."

"Well, I left one." Lucy folded her arms in front of her. "You know, Zack, you've got to stop overreacting like this."

"Overreacting? Overreacting?" He stepped in front of her until they were nose-to-nose. "Lucy, *somebody could be trying to kill you.*"

She stepped back. "No. That's not . . ."

"Then who blew up your car? *Heisenberg?*"

"There's no need to be insulting," Lucy said, and Anthony walked in.

"She's not . . ." Anthony began and stopped. "Lucy?" He squinted his eyes at her. "Is that you?"

"Well, of course, it's me," Lucy said.

Anthony let out a healthy sigh of relief. "Sorry, the hair threw me. You look great, by the way." He looked from her to Zack and back again and grinned. "So I guess this means we can assume you weren't kidnapped?"

"Of course, I wasn't kidnapped," Lucy said and Zack said, "There's no 'of course' about it, damn it," and they were off again.

Falk shook his head and turned to go. "I already called off the search," he said on his way out. "Come on, Junior."

Matthews scowled at him but went.

Anthony turned back to the fight. "Excuse me," he said loudly, and they both stopped and looked at him. "We're all going to go now. Glad to see you safe, Lucy. Don't ever do that again. Zack, we'll try that search tomorrow."

He kissed Lucy on the cheek and walked out the door, visibly relieved.

"We need to talk," Zack snarled, and Lucy threw her purse on the table and went into the kitchen.

I CAN'T BELIEVE THIS, Lucy thought as she banged the soup pot on the stove. *I get my hair done, and he calls out the army. Honestly.*

She flipped the burner on under the pot and turned to see Zack standing in the doorway, scowling at her.

"I was careful," she said, tossing her potholders onto the counter. "I called a cab. I made sure I wasn't followed. I didn't go anyplace I'd ever been before. I left a note. I was careful."

Zack jabbed a finger at her. "I told you not to leave. You gave the patrol car the slip on purpose. I was worried. Worried, hell. I was frantic."

"Zack, I can't spend the rest of my life in this house because you worry," Lucy said, but she felt awful. He was looking at her like she'd come back from the dead, and there was a muscle twitching along his jaw. "I know you think this is serious. But you can't keep me locked in this house forever..."

He ran his fingers through his hair in frustration. "It's not forever, Luce. Just until I figure this out."

"Well, what if you don't?" Lucy folded her arms, determined to stand her ground. "Whether you like it or not, I'm going back to school on Monday. Are you going to frisk all my seniors? Pat down the custodians?"

"I'll figure it out." Zack rubbed his hand across the back of his head. "I will figure this out. I just can't get hold of this one, for some reason. It just doesn't make sense. My instincts just aren't kicking in."

"I can't live my life waiting for permission from your instincts." Lucy turned and lifted the lid on the soup pot to stir it.

"No, but you can stop taking such dumb chances," Zack flared. "You went out today for no good reason...."

"I went out for an excellent reason." Lucy slapped the lid down hard on the pot and turned to face him. "I'm an independent woman, and I wanted to go out. And my hair was driving me crazy."

"You went out because of your hair?" Zack's voice rose again, incredulous. "That's what this is all about? Your damn hair?"

"Listen, if you'd been walking around under my hair, you'd have broken, too," Lucy snapped. "You don't know what it was like. I mean, everybody who saw me just stopped, amazed..."

"It wasn't that bad, once you got used to it," Zack said, taken aback by her fervor.

"Oh, that's a real testimonial, Zack. That makes me feel so much better...."

"Will you take it easy?"

"Take it easy?" Lucy gritted her teeth, her anger fueled by her guilt at making him worry. "Take it easy? You know how awful it was. How many times when you were in bed with me last night did you look at me and think, 'God, she has awful hair'?"

"Never," Zack said flatly. "Not once. Are you kidding?"

"No, I'm not kidding." Lucy's anger surged. "Don't you care what I look like? What is this? Once the lights are out, I'm just like any of your other women? We're all alike in the dark, is that it?"

"Lucy," Zack said through clenched teeth. "Shut up." He took a deep breath. "You are absolutely unlike any woman I have ever met, thank God, and I don't care what color your hair is, and if you ever scare me again like you did today, I will walk out of your life forever because I can't take that kind of fear." He shook his head and turned away from her to stare into the dining room. "You were right about us getting married. Dumb idea. I'm not ready for it."

"Well, that's what I thought," Lucy said, but she felt herself go empty inside.

Zack turned back to face her. "I knew it would be like this. I told Tony it would be like this. You start caring for people, and your instincts go. Hell, your brains go. I don't mind being scared for myself. I'm scared for myself all the time. That's just part of being a cop." He took a deep breath. "But the way I felt about you today...no. I was so damn scared I couldn't think. I am never...*never* going to feel like that about anybody ever again."

They both stood still for a moment, silenced by the emotion between them, and then Lucy turned back to the stove, unable to cope with the pain in his eyes.

"I'm sorry. But I think you're overreacting." She picked up the lid again and began to stir the soup. "You and Anthony both told me that this man is only trying to scare me out of the house. Nobody thinks I'm in danger anymore. Not even you."

"I'm overreacting."

"Yes."

"Fine." He turned and left the room, and fifteen minutes later he came down with his bag packed.

Lucy felt her breath go when she saw him, but she made herself sound calm. "Leaving?"

"This isn't going to work, Lucy," he said. "I'm too emotional about this to be doing you any good. And you're probably right. I probably overreacted. If you want somebody here with you for a while, I'll call Matthews."

Lucy swallowed. "Junior."

"I don't think he likes being called Junior." Zack seemed dimmed, as if a current had been switched off inside him. "You want me to call him?"

"No." Lucy drew a deep breath. "Thank you for staying with me."

"Oh, the pleasure was mine." Zack smiled tightly. "I've already called a patrol car to watch this place. A different one. The first guy is still pretty upset with you. And Tony will call you tomorrow."

"Fine," Lucy said, and he nodded and was gone.

LUCY WALKED INTO THE living room and sank down on the love seat. "What happened?" she asked Einstein when he padded over. "He wanted to marry me this morning, and now he's gone?" The ache in her chest swelled into her throat, and she bit her lip to keep from crying. "Boy, this has been a bad month. Good thing I'm independent now."

The lump in her throat grew until she thought she'd choke, and she concentrated on not crying.

After all, nobody had died.

It was just the emptiness inside her that made her feel like somebody had.

THE SQUAD ROOM WAS AS dusty and dim as Zack remembered it, but it seemed like a thousand years since he'd been there, not just a couple of days.

"What the hell are you doing here?" Anthony asked when he saw him.

Zack sank heavily into his chair. "Lucy doesn't need a bodyguard. We all know nobody's trying to kill her. There's a patrol car out in front. She's okay."

Anthony narrowed his eyes. "We knew all this yesterday. You stayed last night."

"Well, that was a mistake." Zack began to sort the mound of paperwork on his desk.

"But, Lucy—"

Zack looked up. "Forget it. You tried. It didn't work out."

Anthony looked as innocent as he possibly could. "I didn't . . ."

"Forget it."

Anthony shrugged. "All right. By the way, Mrs. Dover called again."

Zack felt himself freeze and kicked himself for it. "Maybe she's just lonely."

"I'm starting to wonder myself." Anthony leaned back in his chair, watching Zack. "She saw prowlers again last night and this afternoon. She's starting to see them everywhere."

Zack squelched the beat of fear he felt. "She's a crazy old lady with nobody to talk to except cops."

Anthony was still watching him closely. "We still haven't found what's in Lucy's house."

"Fine," Zack flared. "You go over and move in with her. I'm not going back there."

"She looked beautiful today," Anthony said. "I like her hair red."

"Shut up, Tony."

"Maybe I will drop by later, to check on her, make sure she's all right."

Zack swiveled his chair away, cranked a report form into the typewriter, and began to pound on the keys.

"Maybe I'll have dinner with her."

Zack hit the return carriage with enough force to send it across the room.

"Just a thought," Anthony said and went back to his own report.

LATE THAT EVENING, Lucy went into the bathroom and startled herself pleasurably in the mirror with her new red hair. Then she took a long, hot bath and thought about Zack.

He'd rocked her earlier with that marriage thing. Zack, of all people, planning commitment. It was like Madonna becoming a nun. Interesting but not likely to last. Especially since he seemed to be basing his decision on sex and food. He hadn't even told her he loved her. Not that she expected it. Although something along those lines usually turned up in a marriage proposal.

And then he'd walked out. Because she'd scared him.

Well, he scared her, too. He scared her because she felt so lost without him. And so lonely. It was as if the world was Technicolor with Zack and black-and-white without him. She felt colder and paler and smaller without him, shriveling without his warmth.

Well, all that was immaterial now. He was gone. It was over.

She climbed out of the tub and wrapped herself in her big terry-cloth robe and headed for the bedroom. Inside the door, she flipped on the light and walked toward the bed, only to stop about a yard from it.

It didn't look right.

She frowned at it, trying to figure out what was wrong. Nothing. Her bed, her quilt, her embroidered pillows. She put her hands on her hips and studied it again.

Maybe the problem was that Zack wasn't in it. Maybe this was an honest-to-God instinct kicking in.

Or maybe not.

She was still debating the problem when Heisenberg came trotting in and launched himself at the bed. Without thinking, Lucy swung out her arm and knocked him away before he could land on the quilt, and Heisenberg hit the floor and yipped and cowered away from her.

"I'm sorry, baby." Lucy scooped him up even as he shied away again. "I'm so sorry. I don't know..." She caressed him as she looked back over her shoulder at the bed. "No. I don't know what this is, but we're talking to Zack."

The relief she felt was so overwhelming that she almost ran for the phone.

9

ZACK'S DOUBTS HAD begun the moment he'd walked out
Lucy's door, and Anthony hadn't helped any at all with his
needling. He knew he'd had a good reason for walking. His
feelings for Lucy were screwing up his life. But she was also
the best thing that had ever happened to him, and he was
growing increasingly more miserable without her every moment. He'd been dumb. So had she. They were both dumb,
but they'd never have any dumb children now because he'd
walked out instead of staying to fight.

Or talk.

He'd been at his apartment for several hours, staring at four
empty walls and a moth-eaten couch, wondering why he'd
never fixed the place up better and kicking himself for leaving a place that was perfect, when the phone rang. If it was
Anthony trying to make him feel guilty again, he was going
to pay.

Zack picked up the phone and snarled, "What?" into it.

"There's something wrong with my bed," Lucy said.

"Lucy?"

"There's something wrong with my bed. I know it's stupid, but I'm scared."

Zack sat down on the couch, his heart hammering.
"What's wrong? What happened?"

"I don't know. I was going to bed but it just didn't seem
right. And then Heisenberg tried to jump on it, and I hit him."

Zack's hand tightened on the receiver. "You hit a dog?"

"I know. I feel terrible."

"Why?"

"I don't know. My hand just shot out. . . . I don't know."

"Instinct," Zack said. "You stay away from that bed. I'll be right over."

FIFTEEN MINUTES LATER, Lucy followed Zack up the stairs, still clutching Heisenberg. The relief she'd felt on seeing him had been overwhelming, and for the first time she really began to doubt that there was something wrong in the bedroom. Maybe she'd just done this to get back upstairs with him.

Would she hit a dog to get great sex?

Of course not.

Not if she was in her right mind.

Maybe Zack had made her insane.

If anybody could do it, he could.

Zack stopped at the bedroom door, and Lucy almost bumped into him. "Stand here in the doorway," he said. "Now what's wrong?"

She peered in through the doorway and looked around the room. "Nothing. I'm sorry. There's nothing."

Zack shook his head. "No. If you hit Heisenberg, there's something. Take your time. What is it?"

Lucy surveyed the room again. Nothing. It was exactly as she'd left it. "I'm sorry. There's nothing." Then her eyes went back to the bed, and she frowned.

"What?" Zack said. "It's the bed, isn't it?"

"I don't know." She shrugged. "It looks the same. It's just . . ." She stopped and then she shook her head. "Forget it."

Zack turned to the phone on the hall landing table. "I'm calling the bomb squad."

"No!" Lucy stepped between him and the phone. "River-bend P.D. already thinks I'm a flake. You are not calling the bomb squad because I've got a funny feeling about my bed."

Zack jabbed a finger at her. "Hey, don't knock funny feelings. They've saved my life more times than . . ."

"Yours, not mine," Lucy said.

"Yours once," Zack reminded her. "But okay. We'll compromise."

"You? Compromise? I don't believe it."

"Get a safety pin and a ball of string. And put the dogs in the kitchen." Zack stepped cautiously into the bedroom. "You sure you don't know what bothers you in here?"

"Zack, get out of there," Lucy said with an edge of panic in her voice.

He looked back, interested. "That's a good healthy instinct you've got there, lady. Go get the stuff."

TEN MINUTES LATER, the dogs were shut in the kitchen, and the end of the string was safety-pinned to a corner of Lucy's quilt.

"Everything okay downstairs?" Zack asked Lucy when he met her outside her bedroom.

"Yes. Except I hope you didn't tell Anthony to call. Einstein knocked over the phone again. That's the second time tonight."

"Forget the phone." Zack took a deep breath. "Here's the deal. Chances are, if it's a bomb, it needs some kind of pressure to set it off. Like you getting into bed, for example. So, if we pull the quilt off, we should be able to see if there's anything wrong with bedding underneath. That quilt is so lumpy they could hide damn near anything under there, but the sheets are flat. If there is something there, we call the bomb squad. You with me?"

Lucy nodded. "I'm going to feel really stupid when there's nothing under that quilt."

"You'd feel even stupider if you got into bed and there was." Zack went cold at the thought. "Thank you for calling me."

"Thank you for coming over," Lucy said. "I'm scared."

"Good. Stay scared." Zack looked at the bed again and then closed the door part way as a shield. "Stay behind me."

When she moved back, he pulled firmly on the quilt and yanked it off the bed.

The bed blew up before the quilt hit the floor.

Dust whooshed out the partly opened door, and Lucy sat down on the floor, her legs suddenly giving out from under her.

"So much for the it-won't-explode-without-pressure theory." Zack slammed the door. "Call 911. Where's your fire extinguisher?"

The phone rang.

"The closet." Lucy pointed at the next door and then ran to call the fire department.

THE PHONE RANG AGAIN as she got downstairs, and she grabbed it to tell whoever it was to get off the line so she could call for help.

"Get out of the house," a voice rasped on the other end. "There's a bomb."

"What?" she whispered.

"Get out of the house now. There's a bomb. It's going to go off. Get out."

"It already did." Lucy's voice returned with her anger. "You creep, it already did. Who are you?"

But the caller had already hung up.

Lucy yelled for Zack as she dialed 911.

THE FIRE DEPARTMENT left when all the random embers in the bed were dead. The bomb squad left after a detailed search of the house for other explosives, making several pointed remarks to Zack about amateurs messing with things they didn't understand. Most of them stopped to say goodbye to Lucy on their way out, having met her when her car had exploded. It was almost a party.

And Anthony came by to see the mess for himself.

"Well, this is interesting," he said, looking at the wreckage of Lucy's bed, and Zack said, "More than you think. Lucy got a phone call warning her about the bomb. After it went off."

Anthony leaned in the doorway, considering. "He was cutting it awfully fine. The bomb went at around eleven-thirty. A lot of people are in bed by eleven-thirty." He looked at Zack. "He could have killed her."

Zack leaned on the doorframe opposite him and shook his head. "That was Einstein's fault. He knocked the phone off the hook. The guy had probably been calling in a cold sweat for hours."

"What are you talking about?" Lucy said.

"This is the same deal as the car bomb," Zack said to her. "Nobody's trying to kill you. The bomb squad said this one was more like a big firecracker. A big firecracker with a hair trigger, but still. It wasn't meant to hurt you. There's no point in warning you if he wanted to kill you."

Lucy's jaw dropped. "But I could have died!" she said finally. "I almost got into that bed! I don't care if it was a firecracker. Firecrackers kill people. That was a real explosion in my bed!"

"Well, if there was a fake one, his plan wouldn't work," Anthony pointed out. "He's still trying to scare you out of the house, Luce. The first bomb should have been enough. Remember? We tried to get you to go to a hotel, but you wouldn't go."

"So he had to really scare you out this time," Zack said. "Only the son of a bitch almost killed you. I really hate Bradley. He's dumb and he's dangerous."

"You think Bradley's doing this?" Lucy shook her head. "No. He knows if he just calls and asks, I'll give him his stuff back. Everything he owns that he left here is in those three boxes. And he can get in any time he asks. Bradley is not doing this."

"It's not in those boxes," Anthony said. "I've been through them. Zack's been through them."

"Wait a minute," Lucy said, ignoring him. "This really makes no sense. He had to get in here to plant the bomb, right?"

"Right," Zack said. "Which door did you leave unlocked this afternoon?"

"None of them," Lucy said, outraged. "But that's not the point. If he broke in here to plant the bomb, why didn't he just take what he wanted then?"

"Because he doesn't know where it is," Zack said. "It's lost somewhere in here."

"Oh, come on," Lucy said. "We've been searching this place for days. What could we have missed?"

"I know what I'd like to find," Anthony said.

"The safe-deposit box key," Zack said, nodding, and turned back to Lucy. "If the bonds are in a box, and the key is here, John Bradley can't leave town. He's shot Bianca, the Bergmans are on their way, looking for blood . . ."

"Actually, they're here," Anthony said.

". . . and he can't get out of town until he gets those bonds."

Lucy frowned at him. "What safe-deposit box? We didn't have a safe-deposit box."

"We deduced a safe-deposit box," Zack said. "Just like in the movies."

"The only thing that John Bradley wants to do is get out of town," Anthony told her. "And the only thing that would stop him would be if he didn't have the bonds."

"And the only reason he wouldn't have them would be if somebody stole them, or he gave them to somebody for safe-keeping," Zack said.

"Bradley," Lucy said. "He'd never steal, but the safe-deposit box sounds like him. He's very careful."

"But he doesn't have a box at Gamble Hills," Anthony said. "Now if we had a key, we could find the bank, and get a warrant, and open the box. . . ."

"Bradley doesn't have a key chain," Lucy said. "He said it spoiled the line of his suit when he put a chain with a lot of keys on it in his pocket. He uses key fobs, one for each key. And then he keeps them in different pockets. He's very organized."

Anthony looked at Zack. "He lost the key. Here. Some-place here."

"Listen," Zack said. "Trust me. I've looked. I took up the couch cushions, I . . ."

"His chair," Lucy said.

"What?"

"His chair. If he sat in his chair, the key could have fallen out of his back pocket and into the chair. It slopes. The back of the seat is lower than the front. Every time I sit in it, my knees are up high and I have to lean forward."

"I remember," Zack said. "The first time I was here. You were sitting in it, all folded up." He started for the stairs. "Come on. It's in the basement."

THE CHAIR WAS EVEN MORE forlorn-looking than Lucy re-membered. Falling through the stair rail hadn't done a thing for it.

Zack started by pulling the seat cushion off and handing it to Lucy, who poked and prodded at it. "There's no seam or anything here that's open." She tossed it down. "It's just a cushion."

Zack and Anthony had the chair upside down by then.

"Nothing," Anthony said.

"The hell with this." Zack took out his pocketknife and slashed the burlap fabric covering the chair bottom. They both peered inside it.

"Nothing," Anthony said.

"Turn it right side up again." Lucy knelt down in front of it when it was upright again. "When you sit in this chair, you tilt back, so anything that falls out of a pocket would go into the crease between the back cushion and the seat cushion."

"I already checked," Zack said. "I shoved my fingers clear to the back."

Lucy shook her head. "But every time somebody sits down in this thing, it jerks forward and then flops back. Anything hat fell in the crease two weeks ago could be anywhere in this hair by now. Give me your knife. "

Zack handed it over. Lucy moved around to the back of he chair, slashed at the upholstery, and peeled it up. She pulled out the foam and the wadding and exposed the coils at the bottom of the back.

"If it's anywhere, it'll be here." She crouched until her chin was almost on the ground, peering into the coils, and then reached her hand inside.

"Lucy," Zack said. "I really did . . ."

His voice trailed off as Lucy pulled out a small key with a square black head, stamped with a number.

"How did you know?" Anthony said.

"Logic," Lucy said.

"I'll be damned," Zack said.

AFTER HE LOCKED THE DOOR behind Anthony, Zack went back upstairs to find Lucy in her bedroom doorway, staring at the wreckage.

The windows were gone, replaced temporarily with boards, and the plaster ceiling sagged, and the hole in the middle of the bed had left it only a charred frame.

Lucy bit her lip. "I don't care if it wasn't a big bomb. It did a lot of damage. There wouldn't have been much left of me."

Zack put his arm around her. "You've got great instincts, kid, but we shouldn't be here now. Close the door and come on upstairs."

"My quilt." Lucy looked down at the torn and stained mess on the floor.

Zack tried to be helpful. "It has to stay where it is for now. The lab people will be back tomorrow to look at it. But maybe after that we can fix it." He looked down at it doubt-fully. "Or something."

Lucy tilted her head to look at it. "Is that the way it was on the bed?"

"I suppose. I pulled it straight off. Why?"

"It's sideways. The square from the Confederate uniform goes at the top. I always put it at the top. Now it's over here. That's what I noticed, that the quilt wasn't right."

"Good for you." Zack tightened his arm around her and pulled her away from the door. "Come on. We're not supposed to be here."

He closed the door and put the tape back across it, and they turned toward the stairs. Then from inside the room, there came a loud cracking noise and a massive thud.

Lucy stopped cold. "Was that another bomb?"

"No." Zack opened the door to the attic stairs. "That was your ceiling. Falling. Don't go back in there, okay?"

Lucy swallowed. "I don't think I'm ever going to feel safe again."

Zack felt a surge of anger. Lucy loved this house and now some creep was making it a hell for her.

Then she turned to him, and he forced himself to grin. "Well, I can guarantee that if you go upstairs and get into bed with me, you won't be safe. I guarantee that you'll be attacked immediately. All my instincts say so."

Her eyes widened, and he held his breath.

"I thought we were finished," Lucy said. "I thought you left."

"I thought so, too." Zack stuck his hands in the back pockets of his jeans. "I can still go if you want. My instincts could be wrong, for once."

Lucy shook her head slowly. "Your instincts are never wrong."

"Good." Zack breathed deeply again and jerked his thumb at the stairs. "Get moving." She smiled at him suddenly, and he went dizzy just looking at her. "You know, I really like your hair," he said, trying to keep his voice light.

"Thank you," Lucy said, and went up the stairs.

"You didn't call Junior, did you?" Zack asked, and followed her.

ZACK WOKE UP THE NEXT morning, shifting against Lucy, feeling her warm weight as both a memory and a promise.

Thank God, he was back with her. Now all he had to do was figure out a way to stay with her. But he was going to have to be subtle. Take it slow. Think it through.

Then he looked down at Lucy, waking slowly, flushed and warm from sleep.

He'd think it through later.

Lucy yawned. He bent to kiss her, and she said, "Ouch."

"What?"

"Whisker burn." Lucy rubbed her cheek.

"I know, I know." Zack started to roll out of bed. "I'll shave."

"No!" Lucy caught at his arm and pulled him back. "Don't shave." She snuggled up next to him. "I like it."

"I thought on the porch the other day you said . . ."

"Well, I like waking up with you like this," Lucy amended. "You'll have to shave later to go to work, but I like it now. It reminds me of the first time I saw you."

Zack wrapped his arms around her and pulled her on top of him so he could see her better. "So it's all right in bed, huh?"

"Mm-hmm." Lucy balanced her chin on her folded hands and smiled sleepily into his eyes. "It helps with one of my new fantasies."

"Yeah?" Zack shifted a little to center her on top of him for maximum pleasure. "What new fantasy is that?"

Lucy grinned, the sleepiness in her smile melting into guile. "The one about the innocent schoolteacher and the vicious, uncivilized cop. Want to play?"

"Sure." Zack ran his hands up her back. "Who do you want to be?"

"I, of course, will be the innocent schoolteacher." Lucy batted her eyes at him.

"Which makes me the cop. All right, you have the right to remain naked."

Lucy laughed.

"Innocent schoolteacher, huh?" Zack watched her eyes close as he moved his hands over her. "This isn't going to work."

"Why not?" Lucy popped her eyes open.

"You're not that good an actress." Zack rolled and pinned her beneath him.

"Well, I *used* to be an innocent schoolteacher," Lucy said, and then he took her mouth, and she drowned in the heat there. *Thank goodness, I'm not anymore,* she thought, and then she thought of nothing but Zack.

THE DAY DRIFTED BY, a mix of unpleasant reminders like the forensics unit showing up to take Lucy's bedroom apart, and mindless pleasures like laughing over lunch and playing with the dogs in the backyard. Everything was back to normal between them except that they were being very careful not to discuss anything controversial, like marriage.

By the time dinner was over, Lucy still didn't know what she wanted in the future, but she knew what she wanted in the immediate present. She wanted Zack.

She leaned against the dining-room table and watched him as he sat on the floor and talked to the dogs.

And wanted him.

It was a new feeling for her, this helpless love and lust and longing that grew while she watched him. She'd never felt more out of control and had never enjoyed a feeling more.

She just wasn't sure what to do about it.

Zack looked up at her and caught her watching him, and she blinked.

"Say it," Zack said.

"What?"

"Say it." He grinned at her from the floor, Maxwell in his lap. "I've been meaning to mention that to you. You're about as transparent as window glass."

"What are you talking about?"

"Every time you start to say something you think you shouldn't say, you stop and blink."

"You're kidding," Lucy said, wide-eyed.

"Nope. Every damn time. Anthony noticed it, too."

Lucy felt herself blush. "Well, that's humiliating."

"No, it's not." Zack's smile washed over her, and she stopped blushing. "We thought it was cute. Anyway, the point is, you don't have to do that with me. There's nothing that you can't say to me. Just say it."

Lucy opened her mouth and shut it again.

"Say it." Zack tipped Maxwell off his lap and stood. He stepped toward her and put his face close to hers and his hands on each side of her on the table, trapping her there. "Nothing you can say will shock me. Just spit it out, honey."

"Make love to me here," Lucy said suddenly, as if she had to get the words out fast. "On the dining-room table. Right now."

"What?"

"Now," Lucy said. "I want you now. On the table."

"I was wrong," Zack said. "I'm shocked."

"Well," Lucy began, and then he put his hands on her waist and boosted her up onto the table.

"And delighted. Did I mention 'delighted'?" He moved himself between her knees, parting her legs as he moved closer to her, pulling her skirt up as he moved his hands up her thighs. "Don't you ever blink again. I might have missed this." Then he kissed her, and she fell into his heat, moving her hands across his shoulders to the back of his neck, tangling her fingers in his hair as he pulled her hips hard against him and licked his tongue into her mouth. She wrapped her legs around him, and he moved against her once and then stopped.

"Lucy."

"Don't stop," she said into his neck. "You feel so good."

"Oh, you do, too. Believe me, stopping is not what I want." He laced his fingers in her hair and pulled her head back to look into her eyes. "But I forgot. The condoms are upstairs. So you have a choice. You can sit down here and think hot thoughts while I set the land-speed record for a round trip on two flights of stairs, or you can set one with me and we can make it a one-way sprint. Your choice."

Lucy licked her lips. "Can we do it on the table some other time?"

"Often," Zack said fervently. "Whenever you want. I swear."

"One-way trip." Lucy slid off the table and down Zack at the same time. "Don't dawdle."

She kissed him hard and then raced into the living room, heading for the stairs while he recovered from the rush her slide had given him.

"You know, I used to think you were an old-fashioned girl," Zack called after her. "Thank God I was wrong." Then, having given her a healthy head start, he started running, too.

"OH, HI," ZACK SAID, when Anthony rang the doorbell the next day. "Be with you in a minute." He left Anthony to close the front door and went back to Lucy in the living room.

"Absolutely not," he said to her. "No way."

Lucy sat down on the arm of one of the overstuffed chairs and visibly gathered her patience.

"What is it now?" Anthony asked, keeping an eye on Heisenberg, who had rolled over onto his back. "Lucy getting stir-crazy again?"

"She wants to paint the kitchen floor." Zack ran his fingers through his hair in exasperation. "Can you imagine? A great hardwood floor, and she wants to paint it."

"It's water-stained!" Lucy wailed. "It's all blotchy! It looks ugly, and if we painted it . . ."

"No," Zack said. "It looks just like my grandma's floor. You let it be. We'll just varnish it, and it'll look great."

"I don't think so . . ." Lucy began, but Zack's mind had already leaped to another subject.

"Have we got anything to eat? I'm starving. Nachos, that's what I need. Have we got nachos?" He turned toward the kitchen.

Anthony watched him, dumbfounded, and then turned to Lucy. "What have you done with Zack's brain?"

Lucy stood to follow Zack. "What brain? I don't think he has one. I think he's just one giant exposed nerve-ending. I swear sometimes at night, I can hear his neurons snapping like popcorn."

"Why does he give a damn about your kitchen floor?"

"Well, he sort of discovered it a couple of days ago, and I think he bonded with it. And now I'm not going to be able to paint it because it would break his heart, and it's *blotchy.*"

Anthony looked at her closely for the first time since he'd walked in the room. She was wearing one of Zack's shirts with the top three buttons unbuttoned and tight jeans with the cuffs rolled up. Her hair was a halo of rumpled auburn curls, there was color in her cheeks from arguing with Zack, and she stood resolutely with her hands on her hips and her feet planted firmly apart, glaring at the kitchen and presumably at Zack inside it.

She looked positive and confident and alive and glowing. And pretty damn sexy.

Zack stuck his head out the kitchen door. "I found the nachos. Am I cooking for one, two, or three?"

"You're *cooking?*" Anthony said.

Zack looked at him in mild surprise. "Well, I have to eat."

"Three," Lucy said. "And remember, if the cheese explodes in the microwave . . ."

"I'll clean it up. Big deal." Heisenberg barked and Zack looked down. "Dead dog," he said, and went back into the kitchen, and Heisenberg rolled over, quivering with pleasure, and trotted into the kitchen, too.

"This is eerie," Anthony said. "It's like the Night of the Living Yuppies."

"Watch your mouth," Lucy said. "We never Yup."

"You know those old science-fiction movies where the mad scientist puts a steel cap on a human being and another steel cap on a chimpanzee and pulls a switch, and their brains scramble?" Anthony looked toward the kitchen. "That's what this reminds me of."

"Are you calling me a chimpanzee?" Lucy demanded.

"No, that would be Zack," Anthony said. "What's going on here?"

"What are you talking about?" Lucy blushed. "There's nothing going on here."

Anthony grinned at her. Lucy was hooked. Now all he had to do was make sure of Zack.

Zack called him into the kitchen for a beer.

"I found the bank," Anthony told him, lounging against the counter to watch him cook. "We should have the warrant by tomorrow. You coming with me?"

"Oh, yeah." Zack sprinkled cheese over a plate of nachos with a practiced hand. "I want to see inside that box."

"Patrol car out in front for Lucy again?"

"Yeah. And I think her sister's coming over, too. We met yesterday for the first time." Zack shook his head. "That wasn't pretty. Another good reason for me to leave."

Anthony snagged a nacho chip from the bag on the counter and crunched it. "You know, Zack, if we find the bonds, you'll be gone permanently. We'll spread this all over the papers. Whichever of the Bradleys is trying to break in here will give up. Lucy won't need protection anymore."

"No, but she'll need me." Zack slid the nacho plate into the microwave and punched the button. "I'm not going anywhere."

"I like Lucy—" Anthony began.

"I do, too, and I saw her first. Stay away from her."

Anthony tried again. "As I was saying, I like Lucy, and I don't want to see her get hurt."

"I don't, either," Zack said, exasperated. "That's why I moved in here, remember?"

"I'm not talking about the Bradleys." Anthony picked up another nacho, and Zack moved the bag away from him. "I'm talking about you. You worry me. I don't want you to hurt her."

"Why would I hurt Lucy?" Zack frowned at him. "What are you talking about?"

Anthony abandoned subtlety. "I'm talking about your intentions, you fool. Are you planning on living here forever?"

"Yes. And to answer your next question, I already proposed. She said no."

Anthony dropped his nacho. "You proposed?"

"But she'll give in. She just needs time." Zack leaned against the counter and folded his arms. "Hell, she just got divorced a week ago."

Anthony bent to pick up the dropped chip, but Heisnenberg was already there. He straightened. "Let me get this right. You asked Lucy to marry you?"

Zack looked unconcerned. "It may take a couple of months, but she'll say yes."

"You want to get married? You?"

"Only to Lucy." The microwave dinged and Zack took out the nachos. "We need salsa with these." He handed the plate to Anthony. "Be careful. It's hot." He began to rummage through the refrigerator, looking for salsa.

Anthony stood in disbelief as the plate seared his fingers. "This is eerie."

"No." Zack found the salsa and more beer. "This is Lucy. She has this effect on me. I like it." He slammed the refrigerator door and headed for the dining room.

"Well, I'll be damned," Anthony said and followed him.

TINA SHOWED THE NEXT morning on the dot of nine, striding into Lucy's empty kitchen as if she owned it.

"Your baby-sitter's here," she announced. "That coffee smells wonderful. I can't believe that I'm up at this ungodly hour. Only for you."

"Go upstairs and go back to bed," Lucy suggested, turning from the counter to hug her sister.

"No. Just give me some coffee. Where's the kitchen table?" Tina stepped back from Lucy as Zack came in from the dining room with the three dogs. "Oh, look, you hired a shepherd."

"You know, you remind me of somebody," Zack said.

"Spare me." Tina looked down at her feet. Maxwell had draped himself over her suede pumps. "Get off my feet, you little rat."

"Got it," Zack said. "Cruella deVil. If she doesn't scare you, no evil thing will."

"I see you're dating the cultural elite," Tina said to Lucy.

"Stop it, both of you," Lucy said. "It's too early for this."

"I'll put the boys in the backyard on my way out," Zack said as he put on his jacket. "Anthony's out front. Gotta go." He kissed Lucy on the cheek. "Don't forget the dogs. It's cold out." He passed Tina on his way out. "Great seeing you again."

When Zack and the dogs had gone, Tina said, "Don't forget the dogs? You? Who is he kidding? Exactly what is going on here?"

"Nothing."

A grin crept over Lucy's face, and Tina pounced. "Tell me everything."

"No." The coffee stopped dripping into the pot, and Lucy poured two mugs and handed Tina one. "I'm happy, and I'm being careful. You don't need to worry."

Tina leaned against the counter and sipped from her mug as she considered what Lucy had said. "What do you mean, careful?"

Lucy shrugged. "I know how bad my instincts are for men. I'm not counting on Zack sticking around. I'm staying independent." The toaster popped and she put two more slices of bread on a plate that already held four. "Strawberry or grape jam?"

"Strawberry. Where's your table?"

"We're refinishing the floor. Zack's idea. Come on, we can eat in the dining room."

Tina followed her in and sat down. "Lucy, you're not paying attention here. You don't have to worry about Zack sticking around. He's moved in. He's adopted your dogs. I think he's planning on being around for the next sixty years. In fact, I think you'd better prepare yourself to turn down a proposal."

Lucy slid into the chair across from her and reached for the jam. "He already proposed. But that was just heat-of-the-moment stuff."

"Men will say anything in bed," Tina agreed, and sipped her coffee.

"Oh, we weren't in bed. We were here. Having breakfast." She bit into her toast, enjoying the crunch.

Tina choked on her coffee. "Breakfast? He proposed in the clear light of day? In the morning?"

"Yep. Even before I fed him."

"It wouldn't have been the food, anyway. You don't cook that well." Tina sat back and marshalled her thoughts. "You're going to have to face it. He's serious."

Lucy tried to shrug it off. "Probably. But I don't know if I am."

Tina started to say something and then blinked instead.

"I don't believe it," Lucy said. "You do it, too."

"Do what?"

"You blink when you think of something you can't say. Zack says I do it all the time. And now you're doing it, too."

"I am? We do?" Tina was nonplused. "You're joking."

"Nope. What was it you were going to say?"

"Nothing."

"Something about Zack."

"No." Tina stopped and blinked again. "I don't believe it. I could feel it coming, and I couldn't stop it. That is one habit I am definitely breaking."

"What were you going to say?"

"Just that if you think you're not serious about Zack, you're deluding yourself." She looked again into Lucy's glowing face. "I give up. He's not the guy I would have picked for you, but he's obviously the guy you've picked for you."

Lucy looked prim. "Don't be ridiculous. I just got divorced. It would be foolish to talk about getting married again so soon. Really foolish."

"Illogical." Tina buttered a piece of toast and bit into it.

"Right."

Tina licked the butter off her fingers. "Don't put me in pink for the wedding. I hate pink."

ZACK AND ANTHONY stood in the dry metal-lined basement of the Third National Bank of Riverbend and stared into a dry, metal-lined safe-deposit box, the contents of which they had just inventoried. It did not have one hundred and fifty ten-thousand-dollar government bonds in it.

It had one hundred and thirty-two.

"He spent a hundred and eighty thousand dollars in less than a year?" Zack shook his head. "This guy needs a budget."

"Running from the police and homicidal in-laws is not cheap," Anthony said. "I think it's time to alert the media and get this guy off Lucy's tail."

"Hell, yes."

But when they got back to the station, there was a new report.

Bradley Porter—or somebody—was using his credit cards again.

In an Overlook motel.

OVERLOOK WAS A MISERABLE part of town, bleak and gray. As Zack got out of the car, an old hamburger wrapper blew down the street in front of the motel, startling a dirty mongrel who skipped away, limping, and a metal sign creaked and banged over a derelict gas station. The only signs that humanity had ever been there were the two cars parked in front of the motel, and the overflowing trash cans outside the burger place next to it.

There were no people.

"You take me to the best places," Zack said to Anthony, as they went into the motel lobby.

Anthony ignored him.

Fifteen minutes later, they were back on the street again. John Bradley had stayed there and then checked out. There were other people in his room now. In fact, there had been several other people in the room since.

Bradley Porter had never been there.

"This is nuts. This makes no sense," Zack said. "What is he, the Invisible Man?"

"Zack..."

"We know he's in this with John Bradley. So why doesn't anybody ever see him?"

"Zack..."

"If this guy really is in Kentucky all this time..."

"*Zack!*"

"What?"

"You've got to stop obsessing about Bradley Porter," Anthony said. "Get back to the case. It is entirely possible that he's not really that involved, that he was just doing a few favors for an old friend and got in over his head."

Zack set his jaw. "Porter's involved. Let's ask the people in that burger joint. They had to eat. Maybe they went there."

Anthony stared at the cracked plastic restaurant sign with distaste. "If they did, they were desperate."

"Exactly," Zack said.

Five minutes later, Zack was back outside with a greasy burger and a great feeling of annoyance. The counter girl had never seen Bradley Porter, but she'd recognized the picture of John Bradley immediately.

"Are you sure you haven't seen this man?" Zack had pressed her, showing her Bradley Porter's picture again.

"Positive. He's hot. Him, I'd remember."

Great. He was hot. Great.

Zack had picked up his burger and stalked out, leaving Anthony to question her about John Bradley. Now out on the street, he unwrapped the burger. It didn't look like food. It didn't smell like food. And he didn't want to know what it tasted like. He went to put it in the trash and noticed the mongrel he'd seen earlier, sitting by the can. It was a middle-size dog, dirty gray-brown and mangy, but it had huge eyes that looked up at him.

And at his burger.

"This is your lucky day, mutt." He broke the sandwich in half and then in fourths so it wouldn't choke trying to swallow the whole thing at once.

He put a quarter of the sandwich down, expecting the dog to lunge for it. The dog looked at the sandwich and then at him with huge, pleading eyes.

"Go on." Zack nodded. "Go on. Eat it."

The dog moved cautiously toward the sandwich and then grabbed it and wolfed it down.

"Easy." Zack put the second quarter down. "Easy. You're going to choke, and I don't do the Heimlich maneuver on dogs."

The dog wolfed that section down, too.

When Zack reached down with the third quarter, the dog took it directly from his hand. Gently.

"You were somebody's dog once, weren't you?" Zack crouched down across from him, watching the third section disappear. He held out the last section and the dog took it, as gently as before. Zack wadded up the paper while the dog chewed and tossed it in the trash can. It immediately blew out again and tumbled down the street, startling the dog into skipping back a few paces.

The dog limped.

"Rough life, huh?" Zack said, and the dog came back, cautiously, to stand only an arm's reach away.

Zack reached out and scratched him carefully behind the ears.

The dog closed its eyes in ecstasy.

"Don't get used to this," Zack said, and then he heard Anthony behind him say, "You talk to dogs?"

"Of course, I talk to dogs." Zack straightened quickly and scared the dog back another couple of steps with his movement. "It's not like I talk to plants or anything non-sentient."

Anthony cocked an eyebrow at him. "Non-sentient?"

Zack winced. "Sorry. Lucy's rubbing off on me."

"Well, if your conversation's finished, we've got things to do."

"Right." Zack got in the car, deliberately not looking at the dog. It was just a dog. Big deal.

Anthony started the engine, and Zack turned to the door to get his seat belt.

And there was the dog, sitting exactly where he'd left him. Staring at him.

Oh, hell.

"Wait a minute," he said, and Anthony stopped.

"What?"

Zack opened the car door: "You coming?" he said to the dog.

"You're kidding," Anthony said.

The dog just sat there, looking at him.

"Well, come on," Zack said, and the dog stood and walked slowly toward the car.

"Get in," Zack said. "We don't have all day." And the dog climbed in carefully, favoring its back leg, and curled up at Zack's feet.

"I don't believe this," Anthony said.

"Just drive to Lucy's." When Anthony didn't move, Zack glared at him. "Listen, I have no choice. If I left this dog, she'd never speak to me again."

"She'd never know."

"You don't know Lucy." Zack suddenly grinned down at the dog, and it thumped its tail. "Besides, this is a great dog."

Anthony stared at the mangy mutt and Zack with equal incredulity. Then he started the car and drove to Lucy's.

10

WHEN ZACK AND Anthony came in the back door, Lucy was startled. She dropped a spoon back into the cake batter she was stirring and wiped her hands on a dish towel. "You're back early. What happened? What's wrong?"

Tina appeared in the doorway from the dining room and made a face when she saw Zack.

"Nothing," Zack said, his hands in his pockets. "We found the money. But we found something else, too." He steped to one side.

Behind him was the most pathetic-looking dog Lucy had ever seen.

"You poor baby." She sank to her knees on the bare wood floor and held out her hand.

The dog limped over to her instantly, and Lucy began to scratch it gently behind the ears, trying not to cry.

Zack had brought her a dog. Nobody in her life had ever brought her a dog. They rolled their eyes when they found out she had three, and they acted as if she were crazy, and they made jokes about her zoo. But Zack had brought her a dog. A wonderful dog that obviously needed her. And him.

She looked up at him, her eyes shining with tears and love. "Where did you find him? He must be starving. Tina, get me the biscuits. The poor baby. Where did he come from?"

Zack snagged the biscuit box off the counter and crouched down beside her. "Actually, he's full of hamburger. He was in Overlook, but he's a nice dog."

"He's a beautiful dog," Lucy crooned as Zack fed him a biscuit.

"That's the ugliest dog I've ever seen," Tina said from the doorway.

Anthony met her eyes. "Thank God. I was starting to feel guilty, because I wouldn't have touched it with a cattle prod."

Zack and Lucy ignored them.

"All he needs is a bath and some food," Zack said. "I'll give him a bath tonight."

"He's precious," Lucy said, and the dog sighed and lay down beside her with his head on her knee.

"And he's not that much bigger than Heisenberg and Maxwell," Zack said. "He won't be much trouble."

"He won't be any trouble," Lucy said. "But he's going to be a lot bigger than Heisenburg and Maxwell. Look at his feet."

The dog had feet as big as saucers.

"He's only half-grown," Lucy said. "That's probably why whoever had him dumped him in Overlook. He wasn't a puppy anymore, so they didn't want him." She scratched the dog behind the ears again. "I think people like that should be shot."

"Well, he's ours now," Zack said, trying not to sound pleased. "Just what we needed, another dog."

"We have room," Lucy said.

Tina and Anthony exchanged glances.

"We'll have to think of a name," Zack said, and Lucy said, "You get to name this one."

"Okay," Zack said, and patted the dog's hip. "Pete."

"Pete?" Lucy stopped scratching. "Pete?"

"I had a dog named Pete when I was a kid," Zack said defensively. "It's a real dog's name. Not like...well, some I could mention."

"I didn't know you'd had a dog." Lucy smiled at him suddenly. "Okay, Pete it is." She scratched the dog behind the ears again. "Hey, Pete."

Pete drifted off to sleep, his head on Lucy's knee.

"I COULD HAVE FIXED YOU up with somebody rich who'd bring you diamonds," Tina said. Zack and Anthony were gone again, the dogs had been introduced to their new brother with a minimum of snarling, and Lucy was stirring her cake batter again. "But you want a guy who's never going to make six figures and who brings you flea-bitten dogs."

"Yes," Lucy said.

"You're hopeless," Tina said.

WHEN ZACK CAME HOME at six, he walked Tina out to her car.

"There's something I've been wanting to ask you from the beginning," Zack said as she got in her sleek red two-seater.

Tina looked at him impatiently.

"Why did you put those locks on Lucy's house?"

Tina shrugged and started the car. "I didn't want Bradley taking anything out. It was her house."

"Bull," Zack said. "I don't believe it."

Tina started to say something nasty and then stopped and cut the engine. "Get in the car."

Zack went around to the passenger side and got in, sinking down into the butter-soft black leather seat.

"Give," he said.

Tina took a deep breath and turned to face him. "I'm afraid of Bradley."

"What?" Whatever Zack had been expecting, it wasn't this. "I didn't think you were afraid of anything."

"I'm not afraid for me." Tina drew back, annoyed. "I'm afraid for Lucy."

"What did he do?" Zack said, murder in his voice.

"Nothing," Tina snapped back. "If he'd ever done anything, I'd have had him arrested and executed. This is why I didn't want to say anything. He never did anything. Get out of the car."

"No," Zack slouched lower in the seat from stubbornness. "You don't have to prove anything to me. If all you've got is a feeling about him, that's fine. Just tell me. I need to know."

Tina frowned at him.

"I need everything I can get on this," Zack said. "I'm afraid for her, too."

"It's hard to explain." Tina stared across the steering wheel at the empty street. "It was the way he looked at her. Like she was the most precious woman in the world and he owned her. It used to scare the hell out of me." She turned to face Zack. "He hated me. But it wasn't because of what I said or did. It was because Lucy loved me. He hated that. He wanted her all to himself. And he hated the dogs, too. Anything that Lucy loved, he was jealous of. He scared the hell out of me."

Zack tried to stay calm. "Did he ever lose his temper? Hit her?"

Tina flushed, and Zack remembered too late that she'd been married to a man who had. Before he could apologize and get himself in deeper, Tina went on.

"No. He treated her like . . . a queen. He didn't know her, not the real Lucy." She stopped and then tried again. "When you first meet Lucy, she's very quiet and polite because she's shy."

"The first time I met her, she beat me up in an alley."

Tina smiled suddenly and Zack was amazed. It was Lucy's smile, and Tina was an entirely different person with it. "Well, then you know the real Lucy," Tina's smile faded. "Bradley didn't. He thought he was marrying this . . . I don't know, this quiet, proper, wife kind of person. I think she tried to tell him that she wasn't, but he didn't want to see anything that wasn't what he wanted. And he was awful when she wasn't what he wanted. She told me that he wouldn't speak to her when she was wearing jeans. He just pretended that she wasn't there if she wasn't wearing what he wanted."

Zack clenched his jaw. "I really hate Bradley."

Tina nodded. "I know. It's the only thing you and I have in common."

"Why did she stay with him?"

"She's not a quitter. And he wasn't beating her or cheating on her or even yelling at her. He never yelled. So she just moved upstairs and they lived this very polite fiction. I honestly think Bradley may have preferred it that way. Making love to Lucy was probably too emotional for him."

"Bradley is an idiot."

"No," Tina said. "Bradley is scary as hell, but he's not an idiot. That's another reason why I hated him so much. I didn't think he would ever be dumb enough to do something that would make Lucy divorce him."

"Ah," Zack said. "I begin to see the light."

Tina clenched the steering wheel as she remembered. "When Lucy called me, crying, that day, I wanted to kill Bradley, but I was also really grateful. Because he'd finally done something wrong. I bribed a locksmith to get there in minutes because I knew he'd be back, and I was afraid she'd let him in and listen to him." She turned to look Zack in the eye. "Lucy is very fair. I'm not."

"Good for you," Zack said, looking at Tina with unqualified approval. "You know, I like you."

"It won't last," Tina said. "I'm a bitch. Ask Bradley. You should have heard the things I threatened that man with when he showed up at the door. I think I seriously told him I'd have him killed. Not just as a figure of speech. The real thing. I threw everything I had at him, shrieking."

Zack's smile broadened. "I really like you. Thank God you were there."

"He's not going to just go away, you know." Tina looked very sober. "He's not going to give up. He's almost . . . obsessed with her. This government bond thing may be keeping him busy right now, but he'll be back for her."

Zack spread his hands. "Hey, I'm here. I'm not leaving her."

"Well, that's another thing." Tina darted a glance at him. "He's going to be furious about you. I'd watch your back very carefully if I were you. Bradley's too proper to ever do anything actually illegal in the normal course of things. But if he lost his temper for once, I think he could be homicidal. And the person he'd kill would not be Lucy."

"I'll remember that." Zack grinned at her. "I didn't know you cared."

Tina shook her head. "I'm not joking."

"Listen, people try to kill me all the time. It never happens. I'm Superman."

Tina rolled her eyes to the heavens. "Oh, terrific. Listen, I don't give a damn who you are. Right now, you're the only thing standing between my sister and that . . . that . . ."

"Rat," Zack supplied.

"No," Tina said. "That homicidal loon who wants her back. You be careful. We need you."

"Relax. I'll be careful." Zack hesitated, and then plunged on. "Listen, as long as we're being honest here, I should probably warn you. You're not going to like this, but I'm going to marry your sister. She hasn't said yes, but she will."

Tina sighed. "I know. I'm past that. You're not my choice, but you're Lucy's. She won't admit it yet, but you are."

Zack relaxed. "Well, that's a load off my mind. I want you on my side. You'd make one bitch of an enemy."

"And don't you forget it," Tina said, narrowing her eyes. "If you ever hurt my sister, I'll cut your liver out. Now get out of my car. I've got things to do."

Zack opened his car door and then, on an impulse, leaned over and kissed her on the cheek. "You're not that tough," he said and then slid out of the car before she could retaliate.

"WHAT IN THE WORLD were you talking to Tina about?" Lucy asked when he found her in the kitchen, pulling cupcakes out of the oven.

"I was asking for your hand in marriage." Zack opened the refrigerator. "She said sure. What's for dinner?"

Lucy froze, the cupcake pan in one gloved hand. "She said sure?"

"She knows quality when she sees it. We've got steak? When did we get steak?"

Lucy put the pan down and slid another unbaked one in the oven. "Tina brought it," she said, easing the oven door shut. "And her cook made stuffed potatoes, too."

"You know, I like your sister a lot." Zack took the steaks out and started opening cupboards, looking for a pan.

Lucy's mouth dropped open. "You do? You really like Tina?"

"Oh, yeah. She's great."

Lucy looked at him closely to see if he was being sarcastic. He wasn't.

"What kind of pan do you cook steaks in?" he asked, his head in one of the bottom cupboards.

Lucy gave up and went to find the broiler.

ON FRIDAY MORNING, Anthony came by with bad news. He stood in the living room and watched Zack mediate a truce among the dogs, and then he dropped his bomb.

"We've made the paper, but we're not on the front page. Another plant closing, more graft at city hall, and storm warnings for a major snowfall headed this way, but not us. We're on page two. The guy at the paper said he could have done better it we'd actually caught somebody, but just the ponds alone weren't very interesting."

Zack stood and left the dogs to stare suspiciously at each other. "Oh, come on, we've had two bombs here."

Anthony shook his head. "I tried that. Both already reported. Yesterday's news."

"Hell, *they* made the front page."

"Yes, well, if there'd been a bomb in the box, this would have, too."

Zack sank down onto a chair arm. "So all we can hope for is that John Bradley will read the paper all the way through. Great." He looked up at Anthony. "We're screwed."

"Possibly," Anthony said. "Maybe John Bradley reads his papers cover to cover. But just in case he doesn't, do not take your eyes off Lucy."

"I never do," Zack said.

ON SUNDAY EVENING, they put the dogs out for a long run and sanded the kitchen floor. Zack had sent Anthony out for varnish, and he'd brought back three gallons and a spray can.

"What do we need spray varnish for?" Lucy asked.

"For the hard-to-reach places," Zack said.

"There are no hard-to-reach places on a floor."

"Wait," Zack said. "Whatever can go wrong, will go wrong. Be prepared."

Lucy looked over at him and felt her breath catch, the way it always did lately when she looked at him. He was on his knees, scraping at the last stubborn spot of glue before they began to varnish, giving it the considerable force of all his attention. His shirttail was out of his jeans, and his hair was rumpled, and his eyebrows were drawn together as he concentrated. He looked solid and electric and safe and exciting and like everything she'd ever wanted, and she felt her breath go again, just watching him.

She slumped back against the cabinets and tried to breathe normally as she looked at him. Even now, semirelaxed, he looked like a coiled spring. She ached to touch him, to feel all that electricity under her fingertips. There was so much energy in Zack, it flowed into her, too. And some of her calm went into him. Maybe he was right. Maybe they should get married. Because she knew for sure that after only two weeks, she never wanted to be with anyone else. Ever.

How could she ever want anybody else but him?

She thought of all the times in the past few days that they'd laughed and argued and talked to the dogs, and even just sat side by side together in front of the fire, warm and happy from just being together. And then she thought of how they'd made love together in the past week, how hard his body was under her hands, how sweet his skin tasted under her tongue, and her heart began to beat faster. She closed her eyes and thought about loving him there on the floor, pulling his shirt from his shoulders and running her tongue down his body, tasting him everywhere. *I can't believe I want him this much,* she thought. *I want all of him, all the time, everywhere.*

I was never like this before.

It must be Zack.

He looked up then and caught her staring at him. "What?"

Lucy blinked.

"I told you to cut that out." Zack pointed the scraper at her. "What?"

Lucy hesitated, torn between her usual reserve and surging lust. Zack opened his mouth again and she cut him off. "Wait a minute. I'm trying to think how to say this."

Zack frowned and rolled off his knees to sit with his back against the stove. "Don't think. This is me. This is us. Just say it."

"Okay." Lucy swallowed. "Okay. Well. Okay. It's like this." She opened her mouth to speak and then shut it again. It was such an inappropriate thought. Saying it out loud was out of the question.

She blinked again.

"What?" Zack said, exasperated.

"I want you," Lucy said. "I want you...in my mouth." She blushed. "I want you hard in my mouth."

Zack closed his eyes for a second. When he opened them, he said, "You know, you've got to quit taking me from zero to eighty in two seconds without a warning, or I'm going to have a stroke." He tossed the scraper over his shoulder and rolled back onto his knees to crawl across the floor to her. "Come here."

Lucy met him halfway, and he pulled her to him. She arched up into him to feel the pressure of his chest on her breasts as he pushed her down onto the stripped wood floor and she ran her hands up his sides under his shirt to feel the hardness of his body. And when he kissed her, his mouth warm and open against hers, she wrapped her legs around him and pulled him tightly to her.

And the phone rang.

"Oh, hell." Zack pulled back from her, breathing deeply from her kiss. "I have to pick it up for the phone tap."

"No. Ignore it," Lucy said breathlessly and pulled him back down to her, licking her tongue in his ear as she unbuttoned his shirt.

Zack said, "Right," and kissed her again, stroking his tongue into her mouth as he moved his hands over her. He ripped open the snap on her jeans and slid the zipper down, sliding his hand down into her jeans as he kissed her harder. Lucy rocked with the charge that surged through her, arching her hips up to meet his hand and biting him on the lip.

And the phone rang again.

"I want you so much," she said, her eyes locked on his. "All the time."

"Lucy," he said and fell into her to kiss her again, pulling her up hard against him.

She pushed up at him, tilting her hips so that he rolled onto his back and she was balanced above him. He ran his hands up her sides under her big work-shirt and then back down to pull her hips tighter against his.

And the phone rang again.

She leaned forward onto him to shove her jeans off, laughing as her fingers tangled with his on the waistband as he helped her strip them down over her hips, stopping to kiss him again.

And the phone rang again.

"Oh, *hell*." Zack stopped as his hands gripped her hips. He glared in the direction of the living room. "If that's Anthony, he's not going to quit." He rolled and tipped her off him gently and kissed her.

And the phone rang again.

Zack sat up. "I'm going to kill him. Then I'm going to leave the phone off the hook."

"Hurry," Lucy whispered, and Zack kissed her again, hotly, once quickly and then again, slowly.

"Count on it," he said when he came up for air.

The phone rang again.

Zack snarled in the direction of the phone and then stood, stopping to look at Lucy for a moment as she lay sprawled half out of her jeans on the floor. "You stay here, just like that," he said finally. "You stay hot, too. I don't want to find those jeans back on when I get back here."

And the phone rang again.

"*Damn* it!" Zack said and went to answer it.

Lucy pushed her jeans all the way off and walked through the dining room to stand in the archway to the living room in her shirt and underpants. Zack turned as he got to the phone, and she held up her jeans and dropped them on the floor. "Ta-da."

"More," Zack said. "Take it all off." He picked up the phone in the middle of the next ring and said, "*What?*" and then he swore and hung up as she walked toward him. "I don't know who that is who keeps hanging up . . ." he began as he turned back toward her. "But . . ."

And then one of the front windows behind them suddenly exploded, and Zack yanked Lucy off her feet and onto the floor with him.

"Stay down!" he yelled, and another window shattered, and he rolled with her to a corner near the windows but away from the shattered glass.

"What is this?" Lucy screamed back, clutching him. "What's going on?"

And then there was silence.

"Are you okay?" Zack was holding her so tightly that she couldn't breathe. "Are you all right? Tell me you're all right. Say something."

"Yes," Lucy whispered, and his grasp on her loosened. "Those were gunshots, weren't they? Somebody's shooting at us."

Zack let her go. "Just stay down and stay *here*. Don't move." He spoke quietly as he drew away from her, but Lucy could hear the excitement in his voice. She reached out and hooked her fingers in the waistband of his jeans and yanked on it hard. His knees slid out from under him sideways on the hardwood floor and he fell, half on his hip, in front of her.

"Hey, cut it out," he whispered, annoyed. "There's glass all over..."

"What do you think you're doing?" Lucy whispered back. "Where do you think you're going? Somebody out there has a *gun*. Somebody out there is *shooting* at us."

"I know." Zack flashed his grin at her as he tried to pull her fingers off his jeans. "Isn't it great? Let go of my pants."

"What do you mean, isn't it great? Are you *crazy*?"

"Listen," he whispered, as he peeled her fingers one by one from his jeans. "I'd almost given up hope of ever finding this guy. Now that he's here, I think I should say, 'Hi.' Or something. Now shut up and stay down and *stay put*. There's glass all over the place and you're half naked."

"No," Lucy's voice rose with fear for him. "He's *shooting* at you, for heaven's sake. You stay put. I'm calling 911."

She leaned forward to crawl across the floor to the phone table, and Zack blocked her. "No!"

"Why not?" Lucy snapped, and the third window exploded, showering the phone table with glass.

"That's why," Zack said, pushing her back against the wall. "And also because by now your neighbors will have made the call for you. Mrs. Dover alone has probably called the Army, the Navy and the Marines." He let her go and started to move away again. "Now stay put. I've got things to do."

"Like getting shot at?" Lucy hung onto his arm. "No. Just wait for the police."

Zack yanked his arm away from her. "Lucy, I *am* the police. It's my job to get shot at. Get used to it."

"Get used to it?" Lucy sat stunned while Zack began to inch his way toward the dining room again.

"Can we talk about this later?" he said, as he crawled toward the kitchen. "While you're yapping at me, Bradley is getting away. Stay there."

"You're a Property Crimes cop, for heaven's sake," Lucy hissed after him. "You're supposed to be chasing burglars and embezzlers. How many crooked embezzlers shoot people?"

Zack had pulled his jacket from the dining-room table. While she watched, he took his gun from the inside pocket and checked the clip. "More than you'd think." He snapped the clip back in, and then, before she could reach him again, he was gone into the kitchen, and she heard the back door open and close softly. It was then that she suddenly felt the cold, not only on the outside from the February wind that blew the lace curtains away from her shattered windows, but deep inside, too, and it was the cold inside that made her shudder while she waited for him to come back.

IT WAS VERY QUIET FOR a while—quiet enough that Lucy could hear sirens in the distance. Gunshots anyplace would bring the police, but gunshots at her place would bring everybody in southern Ohio. It was getting to be like the O.K. Corral. With bombs.

Then she heard the shots.

There were three of them, one right after the other, and then silence.

The silence was worse.

Zack wouldn't shoot first, she knew. Which meant that Bradley had. And once he had fired at Zack, Zack would shoot back. Except he hadn't.

It was really cold now where she was sitting. The February air was icy, but she hardly felt the wind on her body. The cold that was eating at her would have been the same in August, if she'd been the same place, hearing those shots, and wondering if Zack was bleeding someplace.

Or dead.

She was very calm, she realized. That was good. Amazing, but good. It was amazing how calm you could be when you didn't know whether or not you'd lost everything that mattered to you.

She heard cars pull up, sirens screaming, and their red lights swung through her living room, and she still sat frozen in the corner of her living room, shivering in the dim light from kitchen, waiting for Zack. She heard voices, but not his, and slamming car doors and running feet.

But not Zack.

And I was afraid of commitment, she thought. *I was afraid of getting married and getting hurt again.*

What could hurt more than this?

Well, there's one thing for sure. If there was ever a litmus test for love, this has got to be it. If he comes back, I'll tell him....

If he comes back ...

She heard the shouts outside, and then more car doors slamming, and then, after about fifteen frozen, tortured minutes, somebody cautiously kicked the rest of the glass out of the bottom of the middle window and climbed through.

He was too tall to be Zack.

"Lucy?" Anthony peered into the dimness. "Are you all right?"

"He's dead, isn't he?" Lucy's voice came out funny, strained and scratchy.

"Zack? No, he's fine. He's mad, but he's fine. Are you all right?" He came over to her and crouched down beside her.

"Don't lie to me," she whispered.

"I'm not," Anthony said gently. "I wouldn't. He got shot at but not hit. He's got nine lives, didn't he tell you? He's Superman." He put his arm around her and urged her up. "Come on. Let's get you out of this glass. It's cold in here."

She stood, shivering from fear and cold, and he looked down at her long pale legs in gloom.

"Barefoot all the way up, huh?" he said, and picked her up.

She buried her head in the hollow of his neck and he carried her into the kitchen, kicking the door shut behind him to get her some kind of warmth. Then he put her down and took his coat off and wrapped her in it while she clung to him.

"I don't know what I'd do if anything happened to him," Lucy whispered. "I just didn't realize it until now."

Anthony held her until she stopped shaking. "I can't tell you nothing's ever going to happen to him," he said into her hair. "Zack tends to attract trouble. But he's not stupid, regardless of what he looks like, and he's not reckless, and he likes life a lot." He tilted her head up with his finger so she could look in his eyes. "He likes it a lot more, now that you're around. He'll be more careful because of you now."

Lucy swallowed, and the back door opened, and Zack came in and stopped. "Very nice. My best friend and my babe. Unhand that woman, you rat. I'm out there getting my butt shot off...."

"Shut up, Zack," Anthony said, letting go of her. "Getting-shot jokes are not funny right now."

Zack took one look at Lucy's pale face and shut up, moving toward her so fast that Anthony stepped back to get out of his way. "I'm fine," he said as he wrapped his arms around her. "The guy has no aim at all. Never even got close." He hugged her so tightly she couldn't breathe. "I am fine."

"I know," Lucy said, muffled against his chest. "But it was bad there for minute. Does this happen to you a lot?"

"Hardly ever." Zack put his cheek against her hair. "And even then, crooked accountants are lousy shots. Most of them are pretty nearsighted, too. And of course, I move with superhuman speed."

"Of course," Lucy said, finally looking up at him. Her color was coming back slowly and both Anthony and Zack relaxed. She tried to glare at Zack, but it was weak because she was still so worn-out from the cold and the fear, and he held her close while she buried her face in his coat again. "Listen, you big dummy," she said finally, pulling back from him a little. "If you ever do that again, *I'm* going to shoot you."

Zack tried to look annoyed. "Hey. It's my *job*. It's what puts nachos on the table. Not to mention into your dogs."

"My dogs don't need nachos that much," Lucy began, and Anthony interrupted them.

"Well, since things are back to normal here, I'll just take my coat and go back out front. You should probably go on upstairs and take the dogs with you, Luce. We'll be downstairs for quite a while digging bullets out of your wallpaper. We've got people coming to board up your windows for the night, too, although if I were you, I'd call your sister and have her put in bulletproof glass for you."

"My windows!" Lucy pulled away from Zack. "That glass was almost a hundred years old. It was *beveled!*"

"Sorry about that. My coat?" Anthony held out his hand, and Lucy took it off and gave it to him, still fuming about her glass.

"Nice legs," Anthony said, grinning at Zack, who moved in front of her.

"You can go now," Zack said. "Some friend."

The back door opened again and Matthews came in, followed by the four dogs.

"Don't let them into the living room, there's glass all over." Lucy moved around Zack to stop them, while Matthews watched her with great appreciation.

"Okay, that's it," Zack said. "Excuse us." He pushed Lucy into the dining room and picked up her jeans. "Get dressed. And you, sit," he said to the dogs who obediently sat down in a row, Pete a beat behind the rest. Then he picked Lucy up and carried her through the living room to the bottom of the stairs, crunching glass as he went. "Go," he said, putting her on the bottom step. "And don't come down again until you're wearing shoes."

"The dogs," she said, but there were more people coming through the front windows, so she turned and ran upstairs while Zack watched, scowling.

Then he went back to the dining room and carried the dogs to the stairs, one by one, while Lucy stood at the top and called to them, shutting them in the attic so they wouldn't go back down. Maxwell, Heisenburg, and Pete enjoyed the trip, but Einstein weighed about eighty pounds and was not happy about being carried. Several people in the forensics unit applauded when Zack finally got him to the stairs.

Lucy called to Einstein and then grinned down at Zack, and he forgot to be mad. "It's a good thing you're cute," he told her, still scowling for effect.

Then he turned back to the mess in the living room.

"Somebody doesn't like you much," one of the technicians said. "Three .38s, right through the front windows."

"I don't like him much, either," Zack said. "The difference is, I'm the good guy and I'm going to win."

ANTHONY STOOD WITH Zack in the wreckage of the living room when everyone else had left.

"This doesn't make sense," Zack said. "We could have been killed. This wasn't a scare thing. This guy wanted us dead. Or at least me dead. He may not have seen Lucy stripping in the dining room. It was dark in there and he was looking through lace curtains. He was shooting at me."

Anthony turned to him, interested. "Lucy was stripping?"

"Yeah. This guy is one hell of a chaperon." Zack scowled. "This was not John Bradley. This was Bradley Porter. Whether John Bradley read about the bonds or not, this was Bradley Porter."

Anthony shook his head. "You've got Bradley Porter on the brain. This is our same guy, trying to scare Lucy out. I'm going to lean on the paper on this one. The bonds, two bombs, and all Lucy's windows gone should be newsworthy enough for the front page."

"It won't matter. It was Bradley Porter," Zack said. "I'll make sure Lucy doesn't go to work tomorrow, just in case. But it was Bradley Porter."

IT WAS ALMOST TWO before Zack crawled into bed beside Lucy, shoving Maxwell and Heisenburg aside and waking her from an uneasy sleep.

"Move," he said. "I'm freezing."

Lucy, still foggy with sleep, rolled against him, wrapping her warmth around him, and the three smaller dogs settled against his back and across his feet. When he put his arm around her, he could feel Einstein radiating heat against her back.

"You okay?" Lucy asked groggily.

"As long as I don't try to move. It's a little crowded in here." He put his cheek against her hair and held her close. "I'm sorry I scared you, honey."

"Me, too," Lucy said sleepily. "Don't do it again. Although I guess it makes us even."

"How's that?"

"I scared you last Saturday, you scared me today. We're even."

"No, we're not. You took ten years off my life to have your hair done. I went after a dangerous criminal. We'll never be even."

"Oh, have it your own way." Lucy shifted a little against him. "Have you got enough room?"

Maxwell put his cold nose against Zack's neck and made him shudder. "We've got to get a bigger bed." Zack shoved the dog down away from his neck. "Or maybe we could get the kids their own room. What do you think?"

Lucy put her cheek against his chest and held him tightly. "You know, for a while, I thought I'd never have you like this again. And I decided then, if I got you back, I'd make every minute with you count."

Zack lost his breath, both because of her warmth and because of the ache in her voice. "Every minute, huh? You planning on a lot of these minutes?"

"Every one I can get." Lucy began to kiss her way down his neck.

The dogs spent the rest of the night on the floor.

THEIR FIRST MONDAY argument started at six-thirty in the bathroom when Zack realized Lucy was still planning on going to work.

"Somebody just shot out your windows," he said, his mouth full of toothpaste while he watched her towel her hair dry. "You could have been killed."

"Well, in that case, it makes sense that I go to work." Lucy spread the towel neatly over the shower rod to dry. "Why stick around someplace where somebody shoots at you?"

She tried to move past him, but he caught at the back of her robe, stopping her.

"Luce, it's too dangerous—"

She shook her head. "I'm going to school. That's final. Whoever wants in here doesn't want me, he wants the key, and the paper's going to print the story on the safe-deposit box today now that the windows have been shot out. It's over."

"But the shots last night—"

Lucy got away from him by slipping out of her robe and walking out of the bathroom naked.

"Hey," he called after her. "I was saying something important." He dropped the robe, rinsed the toothpaste out of his mouth, and hung up his toothbrush next to Lucy's. *Remember to propose again today*, he thought. *Find a new approach.* Then he followed her into her bedroom.

She was wearing pink cotton underwear, and as he walked in, she pulled a fuzzy pink sweater over her head.

"If you think you're going to win all the arguments from now on just by being naked," Zack told her, "you're probably right."

Lucy pulled her sweater the rest of the way down and laughed, her face lit from inside with love for him.

"At least let me meet you here after school," he said.

"Thank you. I'd like that." She turned and bent to pick up her skirt from the bed.

"How long do you have for lunch?" Zack asked, enjoying the view. "We could . . ."

"Half an hour and no, we couldn't." Lucy turned back to him. "I get off at three-thirty. Can you wait that long?" She bent over again to step into her skirt.

"Just exactly that long. I'll have to speed coming home." He reached for her as she zipped up her skirt, and she came into his arms, soft and warm and laughing again, and he held her close and thought, *We can't let go of this. Whatever happens, we've got to keep this.*

"I'm running late," Zack said half an hour later as he let the dogs out for their morning run. He was wearing a tailored shirt and a tie, and Lucy marvelled again at what an adult he looked like when he was well dressed.

"What?" Zack said. "You're staring at me. What?"

She leaned back against the sink and surveyed him carefully. "I was admiring you. You look very . . . adult. Sophisticated. Mature. It's a good look for you."

Zack scowled. "Don't say 'mature.'"

"I like the tie. It turns me on."

"A tie turns you on?" Zack shook his head. "You are sick."

"Well, I'll try to control myself." Lucy turned back to the sink.

Zack turned her around and bent her back in his arms. "Never control yourself." He kissed her long and hard, and Lucy leaned into him, drowning in the heat from his mouth on hers. When he finally let her go, he grabbed his keys and his jacket and then pulled her to him again. "We have a date at three-thirty, babe," he said. "Don't dress." Then he kissed her quickly and went out the door.

Maybe I'll propose this afternoon, Lucy thought. *At about four-thirty.*

The doorbell chimed while she was spreading jam on her toast.

Zack wouldn't ring the front door chime, so it had to be Anthony. She went to let him in.

The man on the porch was tall, dark, and well dressed, and she'd never seen him before in her life. Lucy watched him for a moment through the stained glass in the front door and then turned away. It was rude to leave him standing there, but it was the smart thing to do.

She went back into the kitchen and listened tensely as the doorbell chimed again. *Go away,* she thought, and tried to figure how she was going to get to her car with that man on the porch. He was probably only selling magazines or religion, but still . . . she wished that damn chime would stop . . .

The door chime stopped, and Lucy sighed in relief. She shoved her toast away, her appetite gone, and began to clean up the kitchen counter, picking up Zack's spray can of varnish last.

And then a black-gloved fist smashed through the glass on her back door and threw the dead bolt.

11

LUCY SCREAMED, AND THEN he was in the kitchen, pointing a gun at her and kicking at the barking dogs that surrounded him.

"Don't move," he said, and she froze, the can of varnish in her hand.

"The key," he said. "All I want is the damn key." He was tall and tense and terrifying, and his eyes burned into hers, angry and desperate.

"It's too late," Lucy said, and her voice came out in a terrified whisper. "They found it. It was in the chair. They already opened the box."

"You're lying," he said through his teeth, and Lucy shook her head frantically.

"No, it's true. I can prove it. They counted what was in the box. There was $180,000 missing. The police have it all."

His jaw clenched, and she saw him clutch the gun tighter. "Then the police can give it back."

Lucy took a deep, deliberate breath, trying to stay calm. *Somebody help me*, she thought, and then she shoved the thought away and concentrated on saving herself. "You're better off just getting away."

"No." He kept the gun on her. "I can get the bonds. I've got you as a hostage. Where's the phone?"

Lucy tried to think around the terror that lapped at her brain. "That hostage stuff never works. Haven't you seen the movies? They surround the place and bring in negotiators. You'll never get out of here. Really, you're better off just getting away."

"We're not going to call all the police," he said and smiled at her. It was a chilling smile that never went near his eyes, and it made the next breath she drew sound like a sob. "We're going to call just one. Just the cop you've been screwing."

Lucy swallowed hard, too scared to be outraged. "What?"

"The dark-haired one. Call him and tell him to bring the bonds."

For just a second, the bottom dropped out of Lucy's mind, plunging her back to the night before, the darkness, and the shots, and the terror of losing Zack. "*No*," she said. "There is no way I will call him here so you can shoot him. *No*."

"You don't have any choice," he said.

"No." Lucy brought the spray can in front of her and hugged it to her chest, popping the lid off as she clutched it. "No. I won't."

"You don't have any choice," he said again. "Because I will shoot your dogs, one at a time, until you do."

He aimed the gun at Heisenberg, and Lucy screamed, "*No!*" and hurled herself at him, and the dogs screamed and leaped in response, so that when he fired the gun, the bullet missed Heisenberg and went harmlessly into the floor.

By then, Lucy was on top of him with the only weapon she had. And when he jerked his head up to her, raising the gun at the same time, she sprayed him full in the face with the varnish.

He stumbled backward, screaming and clawing at his eyes with his free hand, tripping backward over Einstein who had leaped behind him at the sound of the shot, propelled by Pete who didn't have the upbringing of the other three dogs and who went for his throat.

Lucy shoved past him in her scramble to get to the back door. She grabbed the baseball bat as she landed against the wall, and then, without thinking, while he tried to fight Pete off and clear his eyes, she swung the bat as hard as she could and connected solidly with the side of his head.

His head made a sound like a melon dropped from a great height, and he toppled over.

Lucy yelled for the dogs and flung open the back door, and when they were safely over him and out, she ran out after them and stumbled next door to Mrs. Dover's.

The old woman opened the door before Lucy could knock and stood there, scowling at her.

"I have to call the police," Lucy said, breathing hard, trying not to tremble. "A man just broke into my house and tried to kill me."

But Mrs. Dover had already swung the door open wider. "Get in here. I already called them. Gunshots. What's the world coming to?" She was saying all the words she always said, but there was no venom this time. She patted Lucy's arm awkwardly, frowning at her. "Is he still looking for you? Should we hide?"

Lucy's mouth dropped open. "I don't think so. I sprayed him with varnish and hit him with a baseball bat."

"Good for you," Mrs. Dover said, still scowling. "Want some tea?"

ZACK HAD JUST REACHED the door to the squad room when Matthews grabbed him. "Shots and screams at your place. It's Bradley. Falk's already there. I just waited to tell you. Go."

And Zack had gone, his heart frozen and his breath stolen.

Shots and screams.

His place.

And then he was there, and there was an ambulance, and he parked the car crazily against the curb and ran to find out how badly she was hurt.

That was when he saw her standing on Mrs. Dover's cement porch.

"I'm okay," she called to him, but he went to her anyway, holding her carefully to reassure himself that he hadn't lost her.

TWO HOURS LATER, THINGS were calmer, but Zack wasn't.

"What does he say?" Zack said, pacing back and forth through Lucy's living room.

"He doesn't say anything," Anthony said. He was stretched out in one of the overstuffed chairs, collapsed more from relief than from tiredness. "He's in surgery for a cracked skull. God knows what the varnish did to his eyes. Lucy really did a job on him. And more power to her. He's John Bradley, all right."

Zack stopped pacing. "We've got that for sure?"

Anthony nodded. "We've got it for sure. The Bergmans identified him. With great pleasure. I'll tell you, between Lucy and his in-laws, anything we do to him in court is going to be superfluous."

"We're still going to do it to him. What about the gun?"

"A .38. It's a match."

"So that's it," Zack said. "It's over." He didn't sound relieved.

"Well, we still need to talk to Bradley Porter," Anthony pointed out. "He has some explaining to do. But he didn't steal the bonds, and he didn't shoot Bianca. He's important, but not like this guy. The worst is over."

"Great," Zack said.

Anthony sighed and pushed himself out of the chair to stand in front of Zack. "I know what's bothering you. You weren't here for Lucy. But you couldn't have been here. He was waiting for you to leave so he could get her. You protected her as well as you could. And she's fine."

Zack hunched his shoulders. "Yeah, I know she's fine." He turned and walked away to drum his fingers on the mantel. "Tony, this whole thing *stinks*. Every instinct I've got says we screwed up."

"How?" Anthony demanded. "We've got John Bradley. We've got a bullet match, we've got him attacking Lucy, we've got him tied to the plastic explosive.... Hell, we've got everything but videotapes. He was trying to get Lucy to get the key. She got him first, thank God. It's over."

"No," Zack said stubbornly.

"Fine." Anthony shook his head. "I give up. You and your instincts stew. I'm leaving. I haven't had a full day off since I met Lucy, and I need one. I'm going back to do the report on this, and then I'm going home. If you need me, call." He turned to the door.

Lucy came in from the kitchen with two beers. "I know you're on duty—"

"Right." Zack took one of the cans.

"Thank you, Rambette, but no," Anthony said. "I'm just leaving, and regardless, I want all my reflexes sharp in case you attack."

"Don't laugh," Lucy said. "It was awful."

"I should have been here," Zack said and his voice cracked.

Lucy shook her head as she went to him. "It was awful, but I'm glad I did it. He tried to destroy my house. He tried to hurt my dogs. I'm glad I took care of it." She put her arms around him and looked up at him while he stared down at her miserably. "I wanted to be the one to handle it. That was important. I didn't know it until it was over, but it was."

"It's bad for my ego." Zack cradled her face with one hand while he pulled her closer with the other. He brushed her cheek gently with his thumb and tried to grin, but he was tense still.

Anthony broke in. "Fortunately, as we all know, your ego has miraculous powers of recovery. And by the way, Lucy, I almost forgot. We got you something."

"We?" Lucy said, turning to him, and Zack said, "We who?"

"We everybody. Wait here." Anthony went out to the hall and brought back a long thin package. "It's from all of us— Falk, Matthews, Forensics. We all signed it."

Lucy stepped away from Zack and took the package. She opened one end and tipped out a brand-new baseball bat covered with scribbled signatures. "You're kidding! You all got this for me?"

Anthony grinned at her. "Actually, Forensics felt guilty about taking your bat as evidence, so I went out and got one about an hour ago. Everybody's signed it except Zack, and I'm sure he'll get to it later."

"Sure," Zack said.

Anthony studied him carefully. "You coming back to the station today?"

Zack nodded without looking at him. "In a minute."

"Well, I'm going now." Anthony put his arm around Lucy and kissed her on the cheek. "We're all very proud of you, kid. The only bad part is that we're not going to get anymore 911's from here. The boys are going to miss those trips."

"I'm not." Lucy leaned into him a little. "I just want my house fixed, and my life back to normal."

When Anthony was gone and Lucy had stashed the new bat in a place of honor by the back door, Zack leaned against the kitchen counter and said, "We need to talk."

"All right," Lucy said, her voice wary.

Zack folded his arms and tried to look calm. "Am I part of the 'back to normal'?"

Lucy started to blink and stopped herself. "Of course, you are," she said. "What are you talking about?"

"Well, look. I know you don't want to get married," Zack said, "but . . ."

"Well, actually," Lucy broke in, "I . . ."

They both stopped to let the other finish, and the door chime went.

"Wait a minute," she said. "It's probably one of your guys. Somebody probably forgot something."

He followed her to see, almost bumping into her in the vestibule when she stopped suddenly as she looked through the colored glass on the outside door.

She turned, and Zack, looking past her through the jeweled window, knew what she was going to say before the words were out.

"It's Bradley."

THE NEXT MOMENTS WERE jumbled for Lucy, trying to reassure Zack while not shutting out Bradley—a Bradley who looked so white and shaken and angry and so grateful to see her, all at the same time, that she felt sorry for him after all.

"Are you all right?" Bradley grabbed her by the upper arms and looked her over frantically. "I saw the police cars. Are you all right?"

"She's fine." Zack held out his hand to Bradley. "I'm Detective Zachary Warren, Riverbend P.D. We'd like to ask you a few questions about John Bradley. Where have you been?"

"Detective Warren." Bradley looked at Zack's hand for a moment, and then he released Lucy so he could shake it. "I've been in Kentucky. I left a forwarding address with the bank." He put his arm around Lucy. "Thank you very much for helping my wife."

"Ex-wife," Zack said, his teeth clenched.

Bradley looked down at Lucy. "Thank God, you're safe." He gave her shoulders a squeeze. "I think it's time we talked."

"I do, too." Lucy stood rigid inside his arm, keeping an inch of space between them by sheer force. "I think we should have talked about this a long time ago. Why didn't you call?"

"Tina told me not to," Bradley said. His arm dropped away, and Lucy relaxed a little. "And you were being unreasonable. You threw my clothes out on the lawn. You threw my chair down to the basement." He stopped as if he realized he was sounding petulant and then smiled down at her, tightly, forgiving. "But I understand. You were upset. I think we should talk now."

"I don't," Zack said, almost spitting the words out. "I think *we* should talk now."

"Zack," Lucy said to him, willing him to understand. "I need to know what happened. Then I can pick up and go on."

Zack glared at her. "Lucy, I'm a cop. He has information about a crime. I need to take him in for questioning."

"I know," Lucy said. "But I'm his ex-wife. I need a few answers myself. Give us just a little time. Please."

Zack clenched his jaw. "Swell. Let's all go in and talk."

Bradley's grip tightened on Lucy's shoulder. "There's no need for you to stay. This is between Lucy and me."

"Just half an hour alone." Lucy pleaded with him with her eyes.

Zack hesitated and then said, "All right."

Lucy stepped back so that he wouldn't kiss her. She didn't want Bradley putting up any more walls. She wanted to know what had happened, and how that blonde had come into her life and blown it into pieces just like the other Bradley's bomb had blown up her house.

And when she knew that, she'd have a new life, one with Zack this time, full of laughter and promise.

But first she needed to know what had happened.

Zack looked back at Bradley one more time. "All right. I'll wait outside. You have half an hour."

And then he was gone, out the front door.

Lucy took a deep breath. "Come on," she said to Bradley. "I'll make you a cup of tea. Two sugars."

ZACK SAT IN HIS CAR in front of Lucy's house and seethed.

Something was wrong. It wasn't jealousy. Okay, he was jealous as hell, but that wasn't it. He knew Lucy wasn't going back to Bradley. He knew she'd stay with him. At least, he was pretty sure she would. Hell, they'd adopted a dog together.

Think, he told himself. What was wrong with Bradley? He'd felt uneasy before he'd met Bradley, but afterward, he'd been crazy with suspicion. So it was something Bradley had said. Or done. And all he had to do was go through everything word by word, movement by movement, until he figured it out.

Fast.

LUCY WAS UNEASY.

There was something really wrong with Bradley. He kept looking at her like she was some precious treasure he'd lost and found, and, worse, he kept talking that way, too, in spite of everything she'd said.

"It's good to be home." Bradley surveyed the kitchen. "Where's the table? What happened to the floor?"

"It . . . came up." Lucy took a mug from the shelf and filled it with water, trying to think of how to get the answers she needed. Two weeks with Zack had taught her the futility of subtlety, so she put the mug of water in the microwave for his tea, punched the button, and then turned to face him. "Bradley, what's been going on?"

He frowned at her, annoyed by her directness. "It's very simple, really. An old friend of mine from high school came into town and asked for help."

"John Bradley."

"We called him J.B. in high school."

"He was an embezzler," Lucy said.

Bradley suddenly grew remote. "Unfortunately, I didn't know he'd broken the law. All I did was help an old friend."

"How?"

He frowned at her. "I arranged a hotel room for him."

"In Overlook?"

Bradley's frown deepened. "He didn't have much money. I offered to lend him some, but he refused. J.B. was always very proud."

"He had money," Lucy said, folding her arms. "He had almost a million and a half in government bonds."

"He didn't tell me that." Bradley was visibly angry with her now, annoyed that his statement had been questioned, and

Lucy fought the coldness that his anger always drenched her in.

He couldn't do that anymore. Zack was going to keep her warm forever.

"You knew," she said calmly. "You put them in a safe deposit box."

"Once he told me he had them, of course, I did." Bradley was rigid with anger now. "It was the only prudent thing to do. I can't understand how you could even question that."

"I'm not questioning it," Lucy said. "I'm amazed by it. Where did you think he'd gotten that many bonds? K mart?"

"Really, Lucy—" Bradley began, and she interrupted him, fueled as much by his anger as by hers.

"So how does the blonde figure into this?" Lucy said, glaring at him. "You know, his wife. The one you . . ."

"So that's it." Bradley's anger disappeared. "You're still upset about that."

"Well, *of course*, I'm still upset about that. I—"

"She lied."

Lucy stopped, dumbfounded. "What?"

"She lied," Bradley said. "She wanted to force me to tell her where J.B. was, so she said if I didn't, she'd tell you that ridiculous story, that we'd been . . . together. I told her not to bother. I told her you'd never believe her." Bradley's eyes were suddenly hurt and accusing. "And you believed her."

"Bradley, she described my bedroom," Lucy said, trying to keep her temper. "And you didn't say one word. Not one."

"I told you I could explain. You wouldn't listen."

"I listened," Lucy said. "You didn't explain. You said you would, and then you just stood there."

The microwave beeped, and Lucy took the mug out and plopped a tea bag in it before she shoved it at Bradley. Water slopped over the edge.

Bradley took the cup and watched the water drip off it. "A wife who loves and trusts her husband believes him without an explanation," he said, not looking at her at all.

"Not in this century," Lucy said, and when he didn't say anything, she went on. "So you never had an affair at all. And I've gone through all this pain and all this soul-searching for nothing."

"You should have trusted me. You know how much I love you." He looked up at her. "I was going to tell you the day of the divorce. Bianca said she'd meet me at the diner if I brought J.B. and then she'd explain it all to you. But she didn't come. We watched from across the street, but she didn't come. It seemed like no matter how hard I tried, things just got worse. I thought for sure if she'd come..." He stopped, and Lucy felt almost sorry for him, he sounded so trapped and frustrated. Then his voice changed. "And then we saw you with that man. J.B. said he was from the police." He frowned at her, cold and remote again. "You were with another man."

"He was asking me questions about your friend," Lucy said. "About J.B. Bianca had telephoned him that J.B. would be there."

"She was a terrible woman," Bradley said. "She wanted the bonds, and she thought she could get them if J.B. was arrested." He put his tea down on the counter untouched and leaned forward to take her hand, speaking to her earnestly but without warmth, as if she were an important depositor at the bank. "But it doesn't matter now. What matters is that we're back together again. From now on, you'll trust me. We'll be fine."

"No," Lucy said gently. "We're divorced."

Bradley tightened his grip on her hand. "We'll get married again."

"No," Lucy said, not gently, and tried to pull her hand away. "We won't."

Bradley gripped her hand even harder, and she winced. "I know you've been upset with me. But it's over now. It's just us. They're both gone, J.B. and the policeman. I'm back, Lucy. And I've missed you so much."

Lucy heard the determination in his voice and opened her mouth to tell him firmly to get lost. Then she looked in his eyes and saw something she hadn't expected to see.

Passion. Not sexual passion, but a blinding, possessive, obsessive passion for her, all the same.

She closed her mouth and blinked instead.

ZACK WENT OVER THE conversation for the millionth time. "Thank you very much for helping my wife." Zack glowered at that memory. Claiming her as his wife and then bitching at her for throwing his stuff on the lawn and in the basement. He was lucky she hadn't thrown it in the river. Zack pictured Bradley's face when he'd seen his clothes all over the lawn. It was petty, but it helped.

It couldn't have been pretty seeing his chair smashed at the bottom of the basement stairs, either....

Zack froze.

When had Bradley seen his chair at the bottom of the basement stairs? Lucy had done that after the locks were on.

He hadn't been in Kentucky.

He'd been in the house.

He'd helped John Bradley set the bomb.

And now he was in there alone with Lucy.

Zack started to get out of the car so he could kick down Lucy's front door, but then he stopped.

"He was crazy about her," Deborah had said. "He could be very jealous," Lucy had said. "He wasn't really sane when it came to Lucy," Tina had said.

Zack closed the car door quietly and walked around to the back of the house.

"I CAN'T, BRADLEY," Lucy said, trying to sound calm. "I'm sorry. I can't go back to you. It's over." She tried again to disentangle her hand from his, but he held on tight.

"This is because of that detective, isn't it?" Bradley clenched his lips until there was a white line around his mouth. "You even dyed your hair for him—"

"I really dyed my hair for me," Lucy temporized while she tried to think of something soothing to say, but Bradley plunged on, not listening.

"—so he wouldn't have to wake up in the morning and see you with brown hair."

"Green," Lucy said automatically and then raised her eyes to his face, startled.

"I loved you with brown hair," Bradley said.

"You read my note," Lucy said around the icy lump that suddenly filled her throat. "You read it, and you took it."

Bradley stepped closer, and she took a step back, bumping into the counter. "You don't need to change for me."

"You were here," Lucy said. "You helped that man put a bomb in my bed."

Bradley shook his head. "It wasn't supposed to hurt you. J.B. was going to call you and warn you about the bomb so you'd be scared and leave. But the phone was busy."

"That bomb had a hair-trigger fuse," Lucy said, her voice shaky with fear and anger. "Anything would have set it off. It could have killed me."

"I wouldn't have let him hurt you." Bradley blocked her against the counter. "I love you."

"No," Lucy said, trying to push him away. "No, you don't. You don't even know who I am."

"I know who you are." Bradley's jaw clenched so that he could hardly speak. "You're my wife." He shoved her arms away from him and pulled her to him before she could protest, and then he kissed her with as much passion as he could.

It was horrible.

BRADLEY HAD TO HAVE gotten in somehow.

Zack prowled around the outside of the house, trying to think how Bradley could have breached the security of Tina's locks. They were all fine. He'd tried every one, and now he was back at the basement doors. He yanked on the locks again, but they held.

"This makes no sense," he said aloud, and then out of the corner of his eye he saw a flash of yellow fur.

He spun on his heel, startling Phoebe, who stopped practically in mid-leap. "Back off, you furry little bitch," Zack snarled. "I'm not in the mood."

Phoebe snarled back at him and leaped away.

Oh, good. He was up against insane house cats now. Lucy took care of armed men, and he repelled flea-bitten unhinged . . .

He stopped in mid-thought.

Unhinged.

He reached down for the door and, this time, instead of tugging at the center of the bars, he tugged on the hinges to the left.

Nothing.

But when he pulled on the hinges to the right, they lifted away, the double doors fused together with Tina's locks, swinging up smoothly on the left-hand hinges.

Bingo. Zack started down the stairs.

And, although he didn't see her, so did Phoebe.

LUCY DUCKED AWAY, shoving hard to break Bradley's hold. "No. *Stop it.*"

"It's that policeman, isn't it?" Bradley's face was wooden, but he let go of her.

Lucy backed into the corner of the kitchen nearest the door, giving herself an escape route. "No, Bradley, it's you. You let that man in here to bomb this house and try to kill me. You knew he was dangerous. He shot his wife. You knew that."

Bradley stepped forward to reach for her again, and Lucy stepped back, grabbing the back-door knob, and then they both froze, trapped by the scream of a cat in the basement.

"That's Phoebe." Lucy moved toward the basement door. "How did she get in the basement?"

"I know," Bradley said, and when she turned he was holding a gun.

"Bradley?" Her voice came in a squeak.

"Get away from the door," he said calmly. "There's a prowler down there."

Lucy edged away from the door, praying Bradley wasn't the type to hold a grudge. How rude had she been?

How out of touch was he?

He moved slowly toward the basement door, like an avalanche gathering speed. Just before he opened the door, he stopped and looked at her. "You stay here. We still need to talk."

"Right," Lucy said, bobbing her head frantically. "You bet."

STIFLING HIS SCREAM WHEN Phoebe went for his leg had been one of the hardest things Zack had ever done, but he'd managed it, smacking her away with his fist and provoking a scream from her that could have peeled paint. She ran back up the stairs to the outside, and he froze for a moment until he was sure no one had heard.

He was on the first step up the stairs to the kitchen when Bradley opened the door and pointed the gun at him.

"Back." Bradley let the basement door swing closed behind him, and then he walked carefully down the stairs until he was halfway to the bottom.

"Where's Lucy?" Zack asked, backing away. "Is she . . ."

"Forget Lucy," Bradley said coldly. "Lucy is my wife. She's staying with me."

Zack tried to think. Present tense was a good sign. Maybe he'd sent her out for milk. Maybe she wasn't bleeding to death on the kitchen floor.

He hadn't heard any shots.

"I'm going to have to kill you." Bradley sounded as if he wasn't positive that killing Zack was a good idea, but he was willing to chance it.

"Hey," Zack said, wishing Anthony was there. "I think we should talk about this. You're not a bad guy. I'm not a bad guy. We've got a lot in common. How about you put down the gun, and we discuss the situation?"

If possible, Bradley grew colder. "Evidently we do have a lot in common. You've been sleeping with my wife." He pointed the gun at Zack's midsection.

This was not good. "Your wife? Lucy? Not at all." Zack shook his head. "Nope. Just protecting her. Trust me."

"I'm not a fool. I read the note she left for you that day. And I can tell from the way she looked at you in the hall." Bradley raised the gun higher. "I'm going to kill you."

"Bad idea," Zack said quickly. "Murder is always a bad idea, but killing a cop? No." He shook his head. "Don't do it. The hassle is enormous."

"It's not murder," Bradley said after a moment. "It's self-defense. I heard an intruder in the basement and shot him. It's self-defense."

"Well, actually, Brad, it's not," Zack said, trying to sound calm and friendly. "Self-defense only works if the intruder is actually approaching you in a threatening manner. Just offing somebody in your basement doesn't count." Bradley appeared to hesitate, and Zack took heart and moved on. "Now, obviously you were duped by John Bradley, so there's no need . . ."

"No." Bradley looked into Zack's eyes. "You're not stupid. You know about the windows."

"The ones John Bradley shot out," Zack said helpfully.

"You know it was me."

Terrific. Shut up, Bradley.

"You knew it was me all along. That part of this was always between us." Bradley smiled as he said it. "You knew. I kept calling to see if you were here, and you always were. So

I told J.B. to call you for me, and I stood in the front yard, and when you picked up the phone, I shot at you."

"You almost shot Lucy that night," Zack said, and Bradley's smile disappeared.

"I would *never* hurt Lucy. When I shot at you on the street that day and almost hit her, I was terrified. I was trying to hit you, not her. I won't miss this time."

This was bad. Bradley raised the gun another inch and Zack stared down its barrel. A .45. Again, a .45. They'd be scraping him off the house next door. He had to get out of Property Crimes. It was too damn dangerous. Then he looked past the gun into Bradley's angry eyes and made a discovery that scared the hell out of him.

Bradley wasn't nuts. He was just mad as hell. At him. Because he'd slept with Lucy. And Zack knew exactly how that anger felt because it was one of the reasons Zack didn't like Bradley much, either.

If I thought he'd slept with her while she was seeing me, Zack thought, *I'd be furious, too. Imagine if I'd been married to her. Imagine if she obviously wanted him more than me.*

I'd want to kill him.

Which meant that unless he came up with something fast, he was going to die.

"You know, Bradley," Zack said suddenly, "if you shoot me, you'll never get Lucy back. If we sit down and work this out, you could get off with probation, a suspended sentence. Once Lucy finds out the blonde was lying, she'll understand why you did it. Unless you shoot me. I'm a cop, Bradley. They'll throw away the key. And you'll never get to explain to Lucy."

"I already explained it." Bradley dropped the gun slightly. "She doesn't care. She wants you. As long as you're alive..."

He began to sight down the barrel again, and Zack gave up.

"Put the gun down, Bradley."

Lucy's voice cut through the silence, and they both froze. Zack stared past Bradley to the stairs where she'd appeared, a few steps above him, her brand-new autographed baseball bat balanced above her shoulder.

"Lucy?" Bradley turned slightly, just enough to see her from the corner of his eye. Not enough to give Zack room to move.

"Put it down, Bradley," she said. "This won't help things. If you shoot him, you'll only be in more trouble. Put it down."

"Lucy, you don't understand. Go back upstairs." Bradley turned back to Zack.

"Go, honey," Zack said, and Bradley's face went red with anger.

"No, Bradley," Lucy said. "Listen to me. I have a baseball bat here, and I will hit you with it if you don't drop your gun." She said it very calmly, as if it were the most sensible thing in the world instead of the most ridiculous, but Zack could see the bat tremble in her hands, and he felt a chill of fear for her like nothing he had ever felt for himself.

Bradley turned back to her, and Zack had a nightmare vision of him suddenly swinging the gun around to her.

"Go away, Lucy," Zack said, and Bradley turned back to him, furious.

"Drop it, Bradley," Lucy said, and Bradley twitched his eyes back to her and then back to Zack.

"Don't be ridiculous, Lucy." Bradley's voice began to shake with impatience. "You won't hit me with a baseball bat. The whole idea is ludicrous. You are not a violent person."

"Oh, I can be." Lucy swallowed hard. "I cracked your friend's skull with a bat this morning. It made the most awful sound, Bradley. Like a bad melon. I don't want to hit you, Bradley, and I know you don't want to shoot Zack. Just put the gun down. Please."

"Oh, I want to shoot Zack." Bradley took careful aim at Zack. "I really do. And you won't hit me, not even to save him. You can't. You're not capable of violence. I know you. You're my wife, and I know you better than you know yourself." He began to squint his eyes, ready to pull the trigger.

Zack gave up hope and looked at Lucy because he wanted her to be the last thing he saw before he died.

"Well, the thing is, Bradley, I've changed," Lucy said.

And then she swung the bat solidly into the back of his head.

His head jerked forward, and he flung his arms wide as he fell through the broken rail to the floor, jerking on the trigger of the .45 in reflex action, narrowly missing Zack, who had gone in low the moment that Lucy had moved. Bradley fell hard and then staggered to his feet, and Zack was there, putting him down with one punch that had a lot of pent-up frustration behind it.

Lucy sat down hard on the stairs, clutching her bat and staring at them both in amazement.

Zack picked up the gun and held it on a dazed Bradley. "I enjoyed that," he said as he nursed his left hand. "Call 911."

"I already did," Lucy said. "Before I came down here. I opened the front door so they'd come in when they got here." Even as she spoke, she heard cautious footsteps above. "Are you all right?"

"Yes," Zack said. "I think I broke my hand, but it was worth it. I've been wanting to punch him out for two weeks. By the way, thanks for saving my life."

"If I saved it, does that mean I get to keep it?" Lucy asked, but there were people coming down the steps, and he didn't hear her. She sat on the stairs and watched it all, sad for Bradley and relieved at the same time.

WHEN EVERYONE HAD GONE, Zack went to find her to tell her that Tina was coming to stay with her while he went downtown, to tell her that she really was safe now, to tell her . . .

He found her still on the steps, and sat beside her, trying to figure out how to tell her the most important part.

"He really thought he loved me," Lucy said. "Before this John Bradley mess, I mean. I still feel terrible about that. He thought he loved me, but I only loved the house and then you. It's almost my fault that this happened."

Zack scowled at her. "No, it isn't. That's dumb. Obviously..." Then he stopped, his scowl vanishing. "Back up a minute. You said you loved me."

"I know. Do you think I could talk Tina into getting Bradley a lawyer?"

"Not in a million years. Forget them for a minute." He took a deep breath. "I think we should get married. I know you think it's too soon, but you're wrong."

Lucy started to say something but he stopped her. "Now just listen for a minute. There are a lot of good reasons why we should get married. For example, the dogs need a father."

"Zack—" Lucy began.

"Hell, they're *boys*. They need a male around."

"Zack—" Lucy began again.

"Okay, okay. Here's a good one." Zack put his arm around her because it felt so good to have her close. For a moment, looking down into her big brown eyes disoriented him, and then he remembered what he was doing. "Where was I? Oh, right. We're bound to make a go of it because people always work harder on their second marriages, so you'll give it everything you've got. And not only that, but you'll be comparing me to Bradley, and Lord knows I'm a step up, so you'll think I'm terrific, which will make me happy. There's no way we can fail."

Lucy tried again. "I think—"

"Okay, how about this. We're great in bed together. There's a sure-fire guarantee for marriage—great sex."

Lucy frowned at him. "That's a terrible reason to get married. I think—"

Zack gave up. "Okay, forget the reasons. I love you. I'm crazy about you. I even understood why Bradley wanted to kill me, because if I'd been him, I'd have wanted to kill me, too. I want to spend the rest of my days plotting with the dogs to kill that damn cat next door, and the rest of my nights making love to you. Actually, I wouldn't mind spending a fair part of the days making love to you, too, but that's not logical."

"I don't believe in logic," Lucy said. "I believe in love. Especially with someone who is spontaneous, irresponsible, and inappropriate." She surveyed him critically. "That's you."

The relief that flooded through Zack was as intense as his amazement.

"What? When did all this happen?"

"Last night when Bradley shot out the windows and almost killed you," Lucy said. "I thought you were dead, and it was the worst thing I could imagine." She stopped, chilled at the thought and at how close he'd come again that afternoon, and then she went on. "And then you were all right, and that's when I decided to marry you."

"You did? Last night?" Zack glared at her. "Why didn't you mention it before now? I've been tying myself in knots trying to figure out a way to get you to say yes."

"Evidently," Lucy said. "'The dogs need a father'? That's pathetic."

"I was desperate," Zack said. "I can't believe this. You really are going to marry me? Not that you have any choice. I'm moving in anyway."

"Yes, I will marry you," Lucy said, and Zack said, "Damn right, you will," and kissed her, holding her tight, until she broke the kiss, laughing and gasping for air, and then he buried his face in her coppery curls, almost paralyzed with gratitude that everything was finally all right.

"SO YOU'RE GOING TO marry a cop," Tina said later, when Zack was gone with Anthony, and they were alone. "They have the highest divorce rate next to dentists, you know."

"Don't be so logical," Lucy said.

Tina blinked.

Lucy laughed.

Earth, Wind, Fire, Water
The four elements—but nothing is
more elemental than passion

Join us for Passion's Quest, four sizzling, action-packed romances in the tradition of *Romancing the Stone* and *The African Queen*. Starting in January 1994, one book each month is a sexy, romantic adventure focusing on the quest for passion, set against the essential elements of earth, wind, fire and water.

On sale in March

March comes in with a roar with Lynn Michaels's *Aftershock*. The earth moved under her feet...and not only because Rockie Wexler's father had accidentally created a device that would cause earthquakes. Rockie's whole world quaked when she met Dr. Leslie Sheridan. The hard-edged, self-described pain in the butt was the one man who could help find her kidnapped father. But Sheridan had his own reasons for hating anyone with the last name of Wexler....

The quest continues...

Coming in April—*Undercurrent* by Lisa Harris.

Passion's Quest—four fantastic adventures,
four fantastic love stories

HTPQ2

**Relive the romance...
Harlequin and Silhouette
are proud to present**

by Request™

A program of collections of three complete novels by the most requested authors with the most requested themes. Be sure to look for one volume each month with three complete novels by top name authors.

In January: **WESTERN LOVING**   Susan Fox
                                       JoAnn Ross
                                       Barbara Kaye

Loving a cowboy is easy—taming him isn't!

In February: **LOVER, COME BACK!**   Diana Palmer
                                          Lisa Jackson
                                          Patricia Gardner Evans

It was over so long ago—yet now they're calling, "Lover, Come Back!"

In March: **TEMPERATURE RISING**   JoAnn Ross
                                           Tess Gerritsen
                                           Jacqueline Diamond

Falling in love—just what the doctor ordered!

Available at your favorite retail outlet.

REQ-G3

 HARLEQUIN® 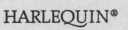 Silhouette®

My Valentine 1994

Celebrate the most romantic day of the year with
MY VALENTINE 1994
a collection of original stories, written by
four of Harlequin's most popular authors...

**MARGOT DALTON
MURIEL JENSEN
MARISA CARROLL
KAREN YOUNG**

*Available in February, wherever
Harlequin Books are sold.*

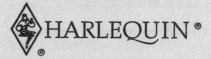

HARLEQUIN ®

HARLEQUIN®

COMING SOON TO
A STORE NEAR YOU...

THE MAIN
ATTRACTION

By *New York Times* Bestselling Author

This March, look for THE MAIN ATTRACTION by popular
author Jayne Ann Krentz.

Ten years ago, Filomena Cromwell had left her small town
in shame. Now she is back determined to get her sweet,
sweet revenge....

Soon she has her ex-fiancé, who cheated on her with
another woman, chasing her all over town. And he isn't
the only one. Filomena lets Trent Ravinder catch her.

Can she control the fireworks she's set into motion?

HARLEQUIN®

Don't miss these Harlequin favorites by some of our most distin-
guished authors!
And now, you can receive a discount by ordering two or more titles!

HT#25409	THE NIGHT IN SHINING ARMOR by JoAnn Ross	$2.99 ☐
HT#25471	LOVESTORM by JoAnn Ross	$2.99 ☐
HP#11463	THE WEDDING by Emma Darcy	$2.89 ☐
HP#11592	THE LAST GRAND PASSION by Emma Darcy	$2.99 ☐
HR#03188	DOUBLY DELICIOUS by Emma Goldrick	$2.89 ☐
HR#03248	SAFE IN MY HEART by Leigh Michaels	$2.89 ☐
HS#70464	CHILDREN OF THE HEART by Sally Garrett	$3.25 ☐
HS#70524	STRING OF MIRACLES by Sally Garrett	$3.39 ☐
HS#70500	THE SILENCE OF MIDNIGHT by Karen Young	$3.39 ☐
HI#22178	SCHOOL FOR SPIES by Vickie York	$2.79 ☐
HI#22212	DANGEROUS VINTAGE by Laura Pender	$2.89 ☐
HI#22219	TORCH JOB by Patricia Rosemoor	$2.89 ☐
HAR#16459	MACKENZIE'S BABY by Anne McAllister	$3.39 ☐
HAR#16466	A COWBOY FOR CHRISTMAS by Anne McAllister	$3.39 ☐
HAR#16462	THE PIRATE AND HIS LADY by Margaret St. George	$3.39 ☐
HAR#16477	THE LAST REAL MAN by Rebecca Flanders	$3.39 ☐
HH#28704	A CORNER OF HEAVEN by Theresa Michaels	$3.99 ☐
HH#28707	LIGHT ON THE MOUNTAIN by Maura Seger	$3.99 ☐

Harlequin Promotional Titles

#83247	YESTERDAY COMES TOMORROW by Rebecca Flanders	$4.99 ☐
#83257	MY VALENTINE 1993	$4.99 ☐
	(short-story collection featuring Anne Stuart, Judith Arnold, Anne McAllister, Linda Randall Wisdom)	

(limited quantities available on certain titles)

	AMOUNT	$
DEDUCT:	10% DISCOUNT FOR 2+ BOOKS	$
ADD:	POSTAGE & HANDLING	$
	($1.00 for one book, 50¢ for each additional)	
	APPLICABLE TAXES*	$ _____
	TOTAL PAYABLE	$ _____
	(check or money order—please do not send cash)	

To order, complete this form and send it, along with a check or money order for the
total above, payable to Harlequin Books, to: **In the U.S.:** 3010 Walden Avenue,
P.O. Box 9047, Buffalo, NY 14269-9047; **In Canada:** P.O. Box 613, Fort Erie, Ontario,
L2A 5X3.

Name: _____

Address: _____ City: _____

State/Prov.: _____ Zip/Postal Code: _____

*New York residents remit applicable sales taxes.
Canadian residents remit applicable GST and provincial taxes.   HBACK-JM